THE SUMMER OF LOVE

(AND SOME BACK-ULLAGING TOO)

BY RICHARD HERNAMAN ALLEN

 **New Generation Publishing**

INTRODUCTION

After I completed "the Waterguard", I was curious as to how the lives of Nick and Rosemary Storey might develop after they got married. I wanted to continue to write about HM Customs and Excise and place the story in a historical context. 1967 seemed to be a suitable year, with plenty of suitable themes to draw on.

As with the previous story, I have tried to maintain a sufficient plausibility of Customs procedures and Cabinet Office arrangements, without attempting to achieve total accuracy or, probably, complete historical correctness either. To those for whom various inconsistencies grate, I apologise. I have also used several locations chosen from street maps and peered at through the Google World cameras, where I could. These choices were pretty well random and no suggestion is made that anything of the sort that appears in this story ever occurred there. Similarly, I have given my characters names, some of which must occur in real life. I wish to make it absolutely clear that no name mentioned in this story is intended to refer to any person live or dead. I admit to having borrowed bits of the characters of people I have met during my life in several of the characters, but I hope I have done this in such a way that no individual, living or dead, can be recognised from it. I have certainly not intended to identify any single individual. The same goes for any companies or organisations whose names I have invented.

HM Customs & Excise, like the rest of the Civil Service, made copious use of initials to describe offices, ranks and procedures. It would make the book seem extremely stilted and unreal to avoid them. In most instances I have provided the full words the first time any set of initials appears – and have also provided a glossary at the end. For anyone who finds Civil Service grades obscure (& Customs & Excise at that time was more complicated than most), I've also included an organisation chart, which I hopes clarifies as much as is necessary.

I would like to dedicate this book to those friends I have made throughout my career in the Civil Service. I have drawn a historical picture of it, one that I would recognise from when I started my career in HM Customs and Excise in 1970. It - and the sort of people in it – has changed significantly over the ensuing 40 years. By and large, it is friendlier, more open, less rank-conscious, formal and hierarchical than it was then. Many of my friends helped to make that change.

Finally, I make a special dedication of this book to Vanessa - my "Rosemary" and to my daughters Jo and Kat, who have helped with the tedious task of proof-reading.

Richard Hernaman Allen
June 2013

ONE
A NEW JOB

Rosemary and I had just moved into a brand new, two-bedroom, first floor flat in Beckenham. Two years of scrimping and saving had enabled us to scrape together a deposit and I had finally reached the head of the queue of those waiting for mortgages from a venerable institution known as the Customs Fund. We waved goodbye to commuting by bus and said hello to British Rail. Once we had settled in – by the summer, we told ourselves - we would try to start a family.

Our working lives had changed little. Rosemary continued to work in a building close to the new tower block just off Victoria Street which was destined to become the latest "New Scotland Yard" and would shortly be moving there. She was currently involved in assessing how pieces of information about criminals, addresses, cars, etc might be organised in preparation for being fed into a computer, which was supposed to be able to disgorge relevant information within minutes. Her ability to come up with ideas and solutions had recently earned her temporary promotion to Sergeant. I was immensely proud of her.

Meanwhile, I had been working in a part of the Secretaries Office known as "Section 24B", on a series of ideas for using Customs charges or procedures to make imports more expensive or rebates to make exports cheaper. As the Government continued to face balance of payments difficulties, which led to periodic crises of pressure against the value of the Pound, the need for such measures seemed to come rather than go. Quite a few ideas appeared to be scuppered by various international agreements which Britain had signed, but that didn't prevent the bright young Principals and

5

Assistant Principals from "Division" from coming up with a seemingly endless stream of clever wheezes, most of which were either contrary to our international commitments or impractical to operate or both. I suppose I was there to remind people in the Secretaries Office that there were thousands of people in what they called "the Outfield", who actually had to make their ideas work. So a fair amount of my time had been spent in explaining why such-and-such a proposal wouldn't actually work and in some cases how, if it were done in a different way, it might. When I was reasonably content, the idea would wing its way to the Chief Inspector's Office (CI's Office) and, as necessary, the Inspector-General of the Waterguard's Office (IGW). Both appeared to be filled with people whose sole purpose in life was to find difficulties and reasons for not doing something. This attitude caused the new, brainy and remarkably youthful Assistant Secretary (i.e. the Head) of "International Customs Division C" such intense irritation that he had recently complained to the Board Member who supervised this area of work. Commissioner Florence Davidson, the only woman in a senior position in HM Customs & Excise, was not someone to get on the wrong side of and had reportedly torn a strip off the Chief Inspector that could be heard from the Board Room up and down all nine floors of King's Beam House. I had rarely met this redoubtable lady – a lack which gave me no cause for regret.

I was beginning to get itchy feet and had started looking at OWOs ("Omnibus Weekly Orders" – an information circular) and listening to the grapevine over coffee and tea in the rather gloomy staff canteen on the 9th floor to see where there might be a suitable vacancy. I was also trying to cultivate the rare human being among those who worked in Estabs, so that I might understand how the system of filling vacancies worked within the Secretaries Office("Secs Office"). While relative seniority among those who applied for a vacancy ruled universally in "the Outfield", it seemed more complicated – inevitably – in the Secs Office. But as I seemed destined to spend a fair number of years in London, probably many in this rather gloomy building, it was sensible to know how to make the best of it.

I had just been to a lengthy and unproductive meeting – the bane of working in the Secretaries Office – when the phone rang. It was Iain Cogbill, whom I hadn't seen or spoken to for at least two years.

"Good morning, Storey. Have you got anything on at lunchtime today?" he enquired, in that curious tone – a mixture of a Leith accent and a wish not to be overheard, on grounds of security.

"No," I replied. "Rosemary and I have just got a mortgage, so it's home-made sandwiches and an apple for me."

"Well, perhaps you could save them for your tea. Would you be amenable to having lunch with me? Do you recall the place, the 'Lamb and Flag' in Cursitor Street?"

"Yes."

"Twelve-thirty?"

"I'll be there."

I wondered what this could be about. The last time I'd had dealings with Iain was in connection with a large diamond-smuggling operation by the Russians that left at least four people dead, several in prison, several Russian hoods from the embassy variously maimed or outfoxed, a Counsellor from the Embassy in the Grand Union canal, a major Hatton Garden jewellers destroyed and me with a wife I adored.

I went into the bar of the pub and found Iain already standing by the bar.

"Do you want to order something to drink?"

"That's kind of you. I'll have a pint, please."

In Section 24B, the majority of staff appeared to down at least three pints most lunch-times, so I reckoned if I had one it would scarcely be noticed when I got back.

We went downstairs to the room which appeared to be specially arranged for the IB (Investigation Branch). In one of the "offices" there were three men having a fairly animated discussion. Iain led me to the opposite side of the room.

"Are you well? How's your wife?" he asked.

"Fine and so is Rosemary. She's recently been promoted to Sergeant, although only temporarily at the moment. But we're planning to start a family soon anyway ... And you?"

"Can't complain. I'm no longer working for Williamson, but for Richard Sawyer, who's a much more reasonable boss ... I'm also about to change my job and that's why I wanted to speak to you. You know something about computers, I assume?"

"Yes. Quite a bit of Rosemary's work involves analysing different types of information required for a new police computer."

"They're definitely the way things are going. Of course, they were mainly developed by the military, but they're beginning to be developed by businesses like LCL and BCC here in the UK and IBM in the USA. So I've learnt recently, they give the West a significant military advantage over the Soviets. Naturally, the Soviets want to steal the latest technology that goes into computers. Inevitably, there are some people who're prepared to sell it to them if the price is high enough."

"But aren't we struggling to keep up with the Americans?"

"They've got vastly more resources, so they do better overall. But there are still areas where British scientists lead the way. I've been told that there are a few, absolutely vital pieces that will improve the speed of computers and their ability to store vastly more pieces of information. The Government wants to do a deal with the Americans to share this technology with them in exchange for stuff we know they've got. However, they are absolutely paranoid about their stuff getting out to the Soviets. So a small team has been set up across Government to provide them with assurance that we have controls and systems that will absolutely prevent any of this information getting into Russian hands. The Chief or Richard Sawyer represents the IB on this team alongside Mr Watling, the Commissioner. Several other Departments and Box 500 (the Secret Service) are also involved. The Department has been required to provide an assurance that our export control systems and physical controls are such that we can give a guarantee of that sort."

"When you say absolutely, you mean 100 per cent?"

"Yes."

"I'd've said that was a guarantee we could never give. We don't check anything like 100 per cent of export consignments and as for light aircraft....."

"I don't think we need to get into that yet. The first thing is to identify exactly how exports leave the country and where the risks are. We can then decide whether any gaps that are identified can be filled and how much assurance we can give that they are watertight."

"The devil is always in the detail, as the blokes in Division keep muttering at me when I tell them their latest wheeze won't work."

"Anyway, that's why I got in touch with you. There's going to be a new section set up within the Secs Office, Temporary Section 29, I believe it'll be called. It'll report to Mr Watling, supervised by me, but not reporting to me, if you understand. At present Mr Watling is identifying a suitable Principal who the Section will report to directly. The Section will be headed by an SEO (Senior Executive Officer) and I'd like to recommend you for the post."

"That's very kind of you, but why?"

"You've got sufficient Customs and Waterguard knowledge. You should know by now how the Secs Office works. But more important, as I recall only too well from a couple of years ago, you've got an enquiring mind, you're persistent and think for yourself. You're prepared to ask the awkward questions and not take no for an answer – and you prefer to ground your ideas in facts rather than airy-fairy theorising. You also have the advantage of knowing some Russian, which might come in handy."

"So what exactly would I be doing?"

"Examining our export procedures and controls on paper and then going out and seeing how they actually work on the ground. Essentially we need to know where the weaknesses are, what they are, how and whether they can be overcome and, I suppose, a broad view on the nature of any guarantee we might give to the Americans."

"And how long do I have to complete this work?"

"Two months. Three at most."

"And how many people will there be in this Section?"

"No-one will complain if you go up to six or so."

"When would I have to start?"

"From next Monday. I'd like you to start tomorrow, but the machinery doesn't seem to work that fast......So will you do it? Or do you need some time to think?"

"No. I'll do it......I assume it won't involve me in lots of travelling around the country, will it?"

"I see newly-wedded bliss hasn't worn off yet....No, I think you should be able to manage it without overnight stays."

Rosemary was delighted when I told her – especially when she realised it meant that I got a temporary promotion out of it.

"Perhaps we'll be able to afford to go somewhere warm for our holidays this year."

Our holiday the previous year had been in North Wales, travelling by train and then mountain- and hill-walking between pubs and B&Bs, occasionally using buses. The fortnight had largely been cool and rainy and our ambition of making love in a secluded spot *al fresco* had been thwarted except for one fondly-remembered occasion. However, even then we realised we had failed to anticipate the number of insects who might wish to share our space and had been glad we carried waterproof capes to lie on. Still, lying naked in each other's arms in the middle of the Welsh hills, with a glorious warm sun warming our skin was a wonderful memory during the cold and wet days of a London winter.

We also had an ambition to swim naked together in the sea. For both of us, that required warmer climes. Though my father often – and always via my mother - recommended the coast of Roumania and Bulgaria as places where one could enjoy a cheap foreign holiday, we doubted whether our ambition was either compatible with, or, indeed, feasible, on, straight sandy beaches, packed with holidaymakers from the workers' paradises in East Germany, Czechoslovakia and Poland, etc. The coast of Brittany appeared to offer more promising opportunities and the French seemed to have a more relaxed attitude about that sort of thing as well.

I doubted whether our seniors would have approved of our ambitions. But, as we told each other, if you can't achieve this sort of ambition before you have a family, you're unlikely ever to do so.

That evening our main ambition was to beat the other at squash. Wanting to keep fit, yet not at the cost of having to spend half our weekends away from each other playing rugby or hockey, we'd started playing squash together in a sports centre near Stoke Newington for over a year. There was a sports club in the same road as our block of flats, with a couple of squash courts, so we played for an hour or two three times a week at least. Rosemary's speed and agility was generally a match for my greater reach and power – at least until she tired. Afterwards, much as we would have liked to shower together, club rules forbade it, so we had to make do with sharing the bath in our flat.

By the Friday before I was due to start my new job, I still had received no official notice. In normal circumstances, a letter from someone in Estabs would arrive in my 'in' tray, informing me of my move, where to go, who to report to. But by Friday lunchtime, not a dicky bird had appeared. So I rang the number of the person the telephone book suggested might be responsible for posting people in my area of work and grade. Needless to say, it wasn't him. Three phone calls later, I eventually got a lady who suggested that I should present myself in Room 206 in Custom House on Monday morning. Apparently there was no spare accommodation in King's Beam House. In Custom House moves were afoot at this very moment to provide me with my SEO cubby-hole and my new Section with their section room. Unfortunately, she didn't know whether I had any people to sit in the chairs at the desks that were being so hastily provided for them. She could, however, suggest a colleague, who might be able to enlighten me. After two more calls, I ascertained that I had been allocated a Clerical Assistant (CA) by the name of Bernard Cox.

"You may need to do a bit of trawling around," the man from Estabs advised. "Your jobs won't be in the OWO until the week after next....."

"The week after next?" I expostulated.

"There are printing deadlines, you know," he replied firmly.

"So what posts are being offered," I enquired. "After all, I'm only the bloody SEO!"

"One or two HEOs (Higher Executive Officers) and two or three EOs (Executive Officers). It's vaguer than we'd like."

As many as that? I said to myself. What on earth will they all be doing? Unless the Principal came along with some clear ideas or Iain Cogbill had identified tasks at a greater level of detail than he'd mentioned to me, I suspected that, as SEO, I was going to have to work it out myself. It might also start to give me an idea as to who I might want to encourage to join me.

It being Friday lunchtime, my colleagues had, to a man, headed off to "the Crutched Friars", probably intending to give me a send off. But as my first experience of such occasions had taught me, five pints of even the most excellent beer at lunchtime would ruin my Friday night. And, as well as I got on with my soon-to-be-former colleagues, I valued my Friday evenings with Rosemary a whole lot more.

So I decided I would do a recce of my new accommodation in Custom House and, at the same time, make use of an empty room, uninterrupted by jovial returnees from the pub, to do some thinking and planning. Custom House - technically the London Customs House – was little more than a hundred yards away, so it took no time to get there. I was sufficiently well versed in the ways of the Secs Office to know how to get the Revenue Constable on the door to let me into the building, to my new accommodation. It was on the top floor, in the furthest western corner, with a view along the river towards London Bridge and the decaying warehouses between London Bridge and Tower Bridge. It seemed that we had squeezed some of the Training Branch from accommodation previously occupied by them, as I received a few cold looks as I made my way into the rooms.

The SEO room, my room, certainly was a cubby-hole. With a desk, small table, four chairs, a four drawer metal filing cabinet and five-by-three combination cupboard already taking up most of the space, there was barely any space for me to squeeze past them. The desks, chairs and cupboards for the rest of my Section seemed much more spacious.

It felt strange being in my own room. Even though it had a large window looking on to the Section room, as was traditional in SEO rooms, so that the SEO could keep a watch on his Section, it felt rather isolated. Still, it would feel even more isolated on Monday, with me in my room and Bernard Cox the sole occupant of the room outside.

I spent the rest of the afternoon thinking about the tasks which Iain Cogbill had mentioned and how I might best use the people at my disposal to tackle them. On one matter, I made a firm decision. Among my Section, I wanted at least one person who had recent and good knowledge of the Waterguard and an OCX (Officer of Customs & Excise) with similar knowledge of export clearance procedures. If the phones had been installed yet, I would've attempted to contact Wally French, now a Waterguard Superintendant at Tilbury, to see whether he had anyone suitable he might be prepared to lend me for a couple of months. That would have to wait until Monday morning. I realised that a phone call to Jim Round, now AC Gatwick Airport, would also have to await Monday, assuming the phones had been installed by then. As there were no phones already installed, I assumed that these rooms had been used as training rooms or as storage previously.

As I made my way to London Bridge station, I looked back towards the Custom House. Though I wasn't sure I could make out my room, I was pleased that I was again in a building that seemed in keeping with the Department's traditions, rather than King's Beam House, that anonymous office block in Mark Lane in the heart of the City. In the Custom House, there remained a huge and historic Long Room, where shipping and forwarding agents and even the occasional importer and exporter still came to get their entries and other documents checked and cleared. It might also be a convenient place to start my examination of export procedures.

But I wasn't in the habit of letting work spoil my evenings and certainly not my weekends. Though I doubt either of us had truly learnt our lesson from our previous experiences, neither Rosemary nor I were looking for opportunities to do what she always called "amateur sleuthing". We were uncomfortably aware that on several occasions we had escaped death or serious injury more by luck than by the use of common sense. Besides, feeling as we still did, that days working kept us apart, we enjoyed just being in each other's company, even if we didn't do much. In any case, on Saturday we would wheel a large shopping trolley round various shops in Beckenham High Street, ending up at a little café which provided a decent lunch at reasonable prices. In the evening, we would cook our own food. Guided more or less by several cookbooks provided by our respective mothers, we had taught ourselves the basics of cookery, so far without poisoning ourselves.

Weekends were always over far too soon and early on Monday morning, we kissed and headed our separate ways, Rosemary to Beckenham Junction, me to New Beckenham. Within less than an hour I was in my new office, greatly relieved to find a telephone on my desk, and that it worked.

I rang Jim first and got a promise that he would cast his eye around for a likely chap.

I was about to ring Wally when my CA, Bernard Cox, arrived. He was seventeen or eighteen, dressed in Mod gear with a Mod hairstyle, all I guessed modelled on the Small Faces. He seemed keen enough, however, and I set him the job of getting the Central Registry in King's Beam House to allocate us file numbers and to get our identity placed in the correct part of the HQ Telephone Directory. I decided I had better wait until a Principal arrived before making any announcement in an OWO, but Cox could, at least, ensure there was some space available for us. I also encouraged him to indent for a copy of Estabs Instructions and to get Stores Branch to send us pronto a copy of the latest Export Instructions - and at slightly slower speed, a copy of the Customs and Excise Act 1952 and any and all Statutory Instruments and Regulations pertaining to exports. If nothing else, that would keep him busy enough to stop humming "Sha-la-la-la-lee", which was beginning to get to me, not least because I had always hated songs that had jingles rather than proper lyrics.

Then I rang Wally, who immediately suggested that if I wanted someone, I should contact a Waterguard Superintendant called Fred Perceval at Heathrow. Morry Gold had been belatedly promoted to PO and had transferred there.

16

"If you want someone who knows how the Waterguard works and who'll ask difficult questions and find the loopholes and chinks in the armour, Morry's your man," Wally observed sagely.

Fred Perceval did not appear overwhelmed with regret at the prospect of losing Morry on secondment for two or three months. But Morry wasn't an easy customer, as I had observed on at least one notable occasion – and incidents like that tended to travel around with people during their careers. Of course, he couldn't guarantee that Morry would be willing to take the job – not least because I couldn't guarantee any seizure rewards, and Morry was practically top of the class already for seizures in the Oceanic Terminal. But within half an hour, I got a call back informing me that Morry was content to come, provided he could return by the end of June. That seemed to be no problem, so I agreed that he would start on Wednesday morning and we would get our respective Estabs to sort out the necessary paperwork.

I rang Estabs in King's Beam House and told them what I had agreed and then sent Bernard off to get hold of the necessary forms. The fourth person I contacted there was also able to confirm that as far as she was aware, no Principal had been allocated to Temporary Section 29.

So, leaving Bernard to carry out his various tasks, I went down to the Long Room to observe how export procedures worked in the ancient, but rapidly decaying, Port of London.

TWO

YOU HAVE TO START SOMEWHERE

I had never met the AC (Assistant Collector) in charge of the London Port Long Room before, but when I had sought permission to look at the export procedures, he appeared to offer no objection. So I made my way downstairs to the ground floor and into the Long Room. It was a magnificent sight. For a start it was huge, built in a sort of Victorian classical style, though I had been told that this incarnation was rather more recent; an earlier version having been hit by a bomb during the war. For a port that was reportedly in decline, it certainly seemed busy, with a dozen agents at the counter and what seemed like a hundred or more Customs staff busily clearing entries, checking documents and dealing with the agents.

I went to the counter and, on production of my Commission, was let through and taken to meet the Surveyor, Stan Webb, in his office. It was, I noted, somewhat larger than mine – but then I was only temporary.

"You're Storey? They said you wanted to see how we handle exports? For some kind of review?"

"Yes. I'm in charge of a new Temporary Section in the Secs Office to examine export regs and procedures and where the risks lie."

"That's easy enough. Not enough bloody staff! And everyone wanting to get exports through as fast and easily as possible!"

"Well, I suppose you can see why?"

"That's the trouble with you people from the Secs Office. It's all about keeping the politicians sweet, rather than stopping crooks from abusing the system."

"I'm not sure that's entirely fair....And before that confirms your view of people from the Secs Office, I should point out that I've only been there for two years. Before that I was an OCX (Officer of Customs & Excise) at Harwich."

"Harwich....You were around at the time of the Imrie business?"

"Yes. It was few months after I started there."

"What did you think of him?"

"I didn't see a lot of him, but from what I did see, he struck me as rather unpleasant and not to be trusted. I know you shouldn't speak ill of the dead, but...."

"Quite so. He was my Surveyor in Hull. If anything, you're too kind to him. He was a shit and a bastard."

Having agreed on our mutual dislike of the late and unlamented Jock Imrie, Webb appeared to find no difficulties in me wandering on my own, observing export procedures in operation, asking questions as necessary.

There appeared to be five staff working on exports – an OCX with two DCOs (Departmental Clerical Officers) and two DCAs (Departmental Clerical Assistants). They cleared all the export forms rapidly and with rarely more than a face vet – i.e. little more than a glance at the front page of the export entry. Some of the documents covered quite a large number of goods – for instance, 400 cars from Fords at Dagenham being exported to Rotterdam – which were itemised in the attached documents. In some cases the entry appeared to have arrived after the goods had left the country.

"Do you get many cases where you see the entry only after the goods have left the country?" I asked Norman Purcell, the OCX – a short, burly man with a greying beard and the look of someone who was permanently grumpy.

19

"A fair few. Of course, we know about them before they're allowed to leave. They have to give us invoices or the manifest at least 48 hours in advance, so we could pull them if we wanted to. But this easement is only for reputable traders who we've deemed are trustworthy."

"What do you think?"

"Well, trustworthy or not, who's to say whether someone has tampered with the consignment before it leaves? Either put something subject to P&Rs (Prohibitions and Restrictions) in or taken something out for sale on the home market to avoid excise or PT (Purchase Tax)."

"Do you pull much for physical exams?"

"Practically nothing. The AC would have our guts for garters unless we had a pretty cast-iron suspicion. And the only thing people are really bothered about is high duty excise goods being diverted to home use. Anything else – well it helps with the balance of payments and if it's dodgy – well, it's going abroad, isn't it?"

"What about P&Rs?"

"We do a face vet for goods subject to licensing. Usually you can tell by the name of the exporter. Then we check for a copy of the licence. The prohibitions are mainly currency, arms and nuclear stuff – and, frankly, this system gives us practically no chance of catching them. If they're prohibited, they're not going to be declared. So we try to spot the occasional exporter or the ones we know are dodgy. But really we rely on the IB tipping us off or an examining officer at the docks with a nose for dodgy loads. There's a couple of Waterguard at Tilbury that take a particular interest in exports and they've picked up a few things. We got some guns we think were destined for Rhodesia a month or so back and a biggish consignment of LSD going to Amsterdam. For nuclear stuff, we really rely on MoD (Ministry of Defence) informing the IB that some stuff has gone missing. But a lot of the technical stuff is virtually impossible to identify."

"And documents containing nuclear plans and designs, for instance?"

"Virtually impossible to spot. Besides, why take 'em out through freight? You could just fly out as a passenger. Unless you're actually flying direct to Moscow or Prague, say, the chances of your bags being searched when you leave the country are pretty well zero."

"Do you get much small scale technical stuff – like computer parts, for instance?"

"A bit. They tend to put them under a generic tariff heading. Then you find the accompanying documents have hundreds of different components and if you dig around, you realise they're actually covered under dozens of different Tariff sub-headings and ought to be declared as such. But most of them mean bugger all to us. Can you tell a Zener diode from a Rosenbaum converter transistor? Well, we bloody well can't! So unless you're prepared to pay an electrical expert to examine the entries and then the goods, you'll never know really what's there."

"And if they were going anywhere they shouldn't?"

"If you thought they were going anywhere they shouldn't, your best bet is either a tip-off from the IB, a dodgy exporter or consignee or a dodgy-looking route. But even then, you'd still need your expert to tell you what was what."

"Any other types of exports here?"

"We get some goods returning on TPR (Temporary Processing Relief) and other TI (Temporary Importation) arrangements. Generally, they've got a good documentary chain and tend to be reliable traders.

We sometimes ask the local OCX to have a look at them when he's in the area, or doing a PT visit if they're registered for PT."

"Do you do any checks of other exporters?"

"Unless they're registered for PT or under excise controls, not really. All the resources go into tackling importers."

"How can you tell which exporters are fishy?"

"Mainly experience. Some of them have form on PT. For others, we rely on what the paperwork looks like and tip-offs from the IB….and bar room gossip, of course!"

"I was going to ask you were the risks were, but I think we've already covered that."

"The whole bloody system is shot through with risks! If you want to get anything out quick, without questions asked, stuff it in a coffin with a corpse that's going overseas! That's my tip for the day!"

"Thank you. I'll bear it in mind."

As I returned to my office, I felt that this was probably not the start that some of those who had commissioned this work would have wanted. But I was determined that they would get the unvarnished truth from me. If others wished to decorate it, that was their business.

"You 'ad a phone call from a Mr Seymour," volunteered Bernard on my return. "King's Beam 2933."

I phoned the number. A rather sharp voice announced that he was in the middle of a meeting, but could I come over after lunch. I discovered his room number from the telephone book and, unsure when "lunchtime" officially ended in "Division", I went over to King's Beam House at two o'clock. Evidently, "Division" worked later hours, as he didn't return until after 2.30. "Sorry to have kept you," he remarked. He was nearly as tall as me, thin, ascetic and, as I already knew, had a reputation for a rather pernickety intelligence.

"I should explain that I'm your Principal as far as this export report is concerned," he continued, sitting behind his desk and indicating a chair in front of it for me to sit in. "But I've been allocated it in addition to my day job. We've got a lot happening on the betting and gaming front, so I doubt I'll be able to give this work much of my time. I don't know yet whether there's going to be any Asst Sec involved. Mine certainly won't take it on! So it's possible we'll just work direct to Wilf Watling. So basically, you're going to have to consume your own smoke."

"What aspects do you wish to know about? Are there particular papers you wish to see?"

"Why don't you tell me how you plan to go about it and I'll let you know."

"OK. I'm getting all the relevant law and regs together, so we can be sure what powers we can and can't use...perhaps even powers that we aren't currently using, but could. Ideally, I'd like to get someone in the Sols Office to look at that. Then I want to look at the Export Instructions to see what we are supposed to be doing. And I also want to see for myself how we actually operate on the ground. My previous experience tells me that what's written in Instructions and what actually happens is rarely the same thing. Then I'll write that up into a report, noting particularly where the risky areas are and what, if anything, we might be able to do about them."

"I've a contact in the Sols Office. If you can send me a draft letter to send to him, I'll see whether he can oblige.....As for the rest, it all seems fine. I suggest you write it up as a plan of activity and send it over to me. Also I suggest you prepare a skeleton for your final report now – and let me have that too. You may find you can start slotting bits into it as you go along. But a word of advice, most people I've come across with Outfield backgrounds like yours tend to brevity when it comes to words on a page. At this stage, don't worry about length. Include as much substance and detail that you come across. We can more easily prune back later."

He was evidently in a hurry and with that I was dismissed.

When I got back to Custom House, I decided to try and contact Morry Gold, to see whether I could visit Heathrow the following day, as I reckoned it might be easier to find out how the Waterguard tackled exports of freight and outward passengers while he was one of their number. Unfortunately he appeared impossible to locate, so I spent the rest of the afternoon writing out a draft plan of how this report would be written. I got Bernard to find where the messengers were. And encourage them to visit us at reasonably regular intervals. When one arrived, I had a transit envelope ready to go to the nearest typing pool – which was in King's Beam House, as I knew from experience that though there were typists in Custom House, they belonged to London Port Collection and wouldn't touch a draft from anyone in the Secs Office.

Then I phoned Estabs to find out whether there were any supernumeraries, recent recruits awaiting posting or anyone free who might be persuadable to work in my Section. Bernard confirmed that all the Instructions and other material we wanted were available in Stores Branch and we could either collect – at our convenience – or they would send – at theirs. I decided that the Department could stand the cost of a return ticket for Bernard to Woolwich and told him to collect the stuff the following morning.

At home, Rosemary was dancing around the flat

"I got a letter at work today. Apparently my temporary promotion is backdated to the first of January, so this month I'll get three month's back pay."

"How much is it?"

"The letter didn't say. I suppose I could work it out – but it can't be much short of fifty pounds!"

"Have you decided how to spend it yet?"

"I had an idea….Well, I had lots of ideas, but one in particular…"

"Go on."

"You know we're coming up for our second anniversary. I thought it might be nice to celebrate it with a weekend away. I know it's not the exact day, but it's as near as we can get."

"This weekend? Where had you in mind?"

"Paris. I picked up a copy of the "Standard" in the train and they were advertising Skyways all-in weekend breaks for £22. You get a coach from Victoria Coach station to Lympne Airport in Kent, fly to Beauvais and then coach to Paris. Then you stay in a hotel close to the centre of Paris, it says. Do you think we could manage that?"

"It's your money…. If you want to spend on a frivolity like a naughty weekend in gay Paree, who am I to complain?"

"It's our money, not just mine. Don't you want to go?"

"Of course I do, you silly Police Sergeant! Who could resist the charms of Paris in the Spring and you?"

"Can you book it then tomorrow please? I expect there'll be a rush to get tickets at those prices. I'm not allowed private calls at work except in an emergency."

"Provided I tell the switchboard it's private, it's no problem for me. Have you still got the paper for the phone number?"

So our first foreign holiday as a married couple was arranged. Though a 5pm departure would mean a very late supper in Paris, it meant we would have the whole of Saturday and Sunday until 3pm to explore.

I spent the following day writing out the "skeleton" for my report and, having got it typed, sent it to Nigel Seymour, to await his comments. Estabs notified me that a CO called Paul Barton-Jones would be joining me on the following Monday and Jim Round phoned to let me know that he had persuaded an OCX called Ken Gray to join me for a couple of months. He described Ken as, "so silent and observant that I keep thinking he's practising to be a secret agent....but then you're used to them." Ken, also, would start on Monday. I also managed to track Morry Gold down and got him to agree that his first day with me would be in his present workplace. I also decided that as I had nothing else for him to do, Bernard could accompany me to Heathrow and take notes, as best he could. Whether it would be "All or Nothing" remained to be seen.

I agreed to meet Bernard at the arrivals point at the Oceanic Terminal, as he had a relatively easy journey from West Ealing, whereas I had the delights of a coach journey from Victoria. Unsurprisingly, he was already there when I arrived and we went round to the Customs examination just the far side of the arrivals gate. After overcoming the slight problem that Bernard had no Departmental identification – the Secs Office not requiring anything apparently – we were taken through to Morry, who introduced me to Fred Perceval, his Surveyor.

"You're young for a Surveyor, even in the Secs Office," was pretty well all he said.

Morry took us round to the Departure gate and we watched the outward controls on passengers and their hand luggage, before going to see how hold luggage

26

was checked. Finally we went to a different shed, where consignments of freight were moved through.

It was clear that the only significant check on outward passengers – or "pax" as the Waterguard at Heathrow called them – was in relation to taking excess currency with them. The checks were almost invariably by face to face questioning. Only if the APO's (Assistant Preventive Officer) or PO's (Preventive Officer)'revenue nose' twitched, were their bags examined. Virtually no hold luggage was ever checked, unless it linked up to a passenger regarded as fishy.

"If you want to check more pax," said the CPO (Chief Preventive Officer) overseeing the morning's outward passenger movements, "you'll need more staff. Or you'll need a much better system of identifying people to check. At the moment it rests on the ability of the POs and APOs to sniff a wrong 'un. Some do it well. Some have never made a seizure in their lives – and that's even on inbound holiday jaunts where practically everyone brings in more than the booze limits."

"Do you ever get anything like the outward equivalent of MIB (merchandise in baggage)? Passengers taking documents or low volume/high value items out?" I asked.

"Only if they declare it as freight and put in some sort of entry. Otherwise we wouldn't have a clue unless we had a reason to challenge them."

"Do you ever get any tip-offs from the IB or anyone else?"

"On outward pax? Once in a blue moon."

"What do you think the risk is?"

"I reckon one in ten pax probably takes out more currency than they should. For any valuable documents or high-tech stuff, the risk of being stopped or even challenged is one in fifty, at best, I'd say. Unless we get

27

dozens more people and were prepared to delay flights if necessary, the only way you'll ever pick someone up is if you've been forewarned in advance."

The freight clearance shed looked like a converted hangar. The PO we met, Bert Jameson, told us that the airport were building a purpose-built freight building, as they believed that air freight was starting to increase significantly. He appeared an extremely ordinary man, apart from a pair of very pale blue eyes, that were constantly darting glances here, there and everywhere.

"At present, it tends to be high value/low volume stuff – like diamonds, for example. Or things that need to get somewhere abroad rapidly. We had a couple of boxes of legal documents for an oil exploration company the other day. They've also sent out technical drawings as well. Occasionally we get bits of computers – but usually those are government or military or one of the defence contractors."

"What do you check?"

"The Long Room face vet all the paperwork and we check anything that doesn't seem quite kosher, begging your pardon, Morry. But there's not much point checking documents, especially technical ones. I mean, we could spot whether a document looks like some sort of legal contract, but whether technical specs were for the latest car engine or for the inside of a nuclear missile, we wouldn't have a clue."

"So how would you be able to spot something like a spec for a missile or high tech electrical components that shouldn't be leaving the country?"

"It'd be down to whether the paperwork looked fishy, whether we thought the exporter or consignee looked fishy or, best of all, if we had names to look out for. We also need experts we could get hold of quickly to identify stuff for us. No-one wants to delay either pax or exports these days."

"Do you get any entries for stuff after it's already gone?"

"Quite often. But we always get manifests and some sort of documentation in advance. If we ever need to pull something we have enough warning. But airports aren't like your traditional port. Everything moves a hell of a lot faster and people expect that. Once the ports start getting loads of lorries rolling through at places like Dover, they'll begin to see what it's like here."

"And if you wanted to get something small and subject to P&Rs out without being caught, what would my chances be?"

"99.9%, I'd say."

Morry advised us that we'd learn nothing new from a visit to the Europa Building, so we agreed to let him guide us to somewhere to have some lunch.

As we ate in a BOAC canteen which was both heavily subsidised and available for Customs staff who worked in the Oceanic Terminal, Morry added his pearls of wisdom.

"Of course, the one thing no-one here will say out loud – especially to someone they don't know from London HQ – is corruption. No-one is convinced that the staff employed by the airport people in all areas, notably the baggage handlers, aren't wide open to being bribed or just engaged in pure thievery. Of course, Customs think they're above such things. But I doubt that. If the bribe was big enough, I don't believe some of my shortly-to-be former colleagues have the moral fibre to resist. Why is it that some people who have been here ten years – ever since the place opened up pretty well – have never made a single seizure? Ten percent of the POs and APOs make ninety percent of the seizures. You'd think the lure of seizure rewards would encourage more. But it certainly doesn't happen here."

"From what I've seen, it'd be simple," remarked Bernard. "You'd scarcely have to do anything to earn your wedge."

"The skill is to make sure you're on duty when the big thing is going through and also to make it look as though you haven't done anything to help it on its way. That isn't always as easy as you might think. You don't want finding out later that something big has gone through and someone does some back-ullaging and comes up with you standing there?"

"Back-ullaging?"

"It's a term in Customs folklore," I explained. "It comes from the Excise. Basically it's a way of testing how much spirits or wine was in a barrel at a particular time, based on knowing the volume of the barrel, its structure and the rate of evaporation of the liquid concerned."

"I fear I used it rather loosely. In the Waterguard, it basically means checking back after something has already happened," added Morry.

Much of the rest of lunch was taken up with Bernard grilling Morry about the work of the Waterguard at Heathrow and what the pay was like. I could see if you lived as close as he did and the money was right, the work of an APO would be a lot more interesting than his current job. Not knowing him at all, I just hoped he hadn't seen a way of enriching himself through judicious acceptance of backhanders.

Morry walked us back through the security controls through which airport staff, like baggage handlers, were checked in and out. It didn't look particularly thorough.

"Are there any checks on who can become a baggage handler or is otherwise allowed through the security controls?" I asked Morry.

"I don't know, but I could do some checking."

By the time we had finished looking around it was almost three o'clock, so I decided to finish for the day. By the time we got back to Custom House it would be virtually time to leave anyway. So we went our separate ways and I had the pleasure of arriving home a little early, in good time to have a spaghetti bolognese awaiting Rosemary's return.

The following morning I received something that was depressingly familiar in my dealings with "Division". My draft plan and skeleton report were sitting in transit envelopes, scrawled over in blue ink with a large number of amendments. By and large these weren't expected to be optional. Considerably more than half were purely stylistic and while I was prepared to accept that my written style could undoubtedly be improved, I wondered whether this was really the best way those intelligent people in "Division" could spend their time. Some of the amendments to the skeleton were helpful and sensible, but I decided that I would probably ignore the changes to my plan of getting the material for the report. Nigel Seymour had suggested cutting down the number of visits to see how exports were managed on the ground by two-thirds, but if I was going to get a practical understanding of how exports actually left the country and what the real risks were, I needed to see for myself. Principals might be able to envisage such things and theorise about them. But to my mind what was needed for this report were some hard facts, backed up with as much evidence as possible. I would at least wish to discuss this with Iain Cogbill, when he next showed an interest in the work he had got me into.

Before the skeleton of the report was re-typed, I included some of the information which I had gained from my visit to the Long Room in Custom House and from our day at Heathrow Airport. Meanwhile, I got Morry to consider which places we could visit most conveniently and Bernard to organise a programme of visits for us, finding the local Surveyor, Waterguard Superintendant or CPO, and arranging convenient times.

All this was halted when I received a phone call from Nigel Seymour.

"I've been getting complaints about this report already, even before it's barely started," he said. "Could you possibly drop by later?

"What do you mean by later?" I asked.

"Around 6 o'clock."

"I'm afraid I finish at 5. Could we perhaps discuss on the phone?"

"Perhaps you'd better come over now."

So I made my way to the fifth floor of King's Beam House and, as I had suspected, was kept waiting for nearly quarter of an hour. A couple of young men and an older man departed as I was ushered in.

"I'm sorry to drag you over......It is really inconvenient having your Section over in Custom House. I've been on to Estabs, but they say there's no alternative......"

"These complaints?"

"Oh yes. From London Port and London Airports Collections. They complain that there's been a review of their operations by the Secs Office without proper notification or agreement."

"What? I fixed both visits up with local staff – with the Long Room AC in Custom House and with the Waterguard Superintendent at LAP."

"That may be so, but the Outfield at Collector level expect to be informed whenever someone from the Secs Office is on the premises, especially when work is being reviewed."

"I'm not clear why the people I contacted couldn't've informed their Collector. Besides, I'm not reviewing their work."

"I'm afraid that protocol demands that you inform the Collector's office whenever you intend to visit his Collection. And you may well be right that you aren't reviewing what they're doing. But they don't see it that way. If someone from the Secs Office comes out to their patch and examines what is going on, including asking staff questions about it, they regard that as being reviewed, even if we don't."

"I'll ensure I inform them in future.....But may I ask what the position is if anyone refuses to allow me to go to his Collection?"

"You'd better refer them back to me."

I went back to Custom House feeling a little like a schoolboy who'd been caught out by his teacher for ignorance rather than naughtiness. Being in "Division" seemed to inculcate in people a sense of superiority that bordered on the supercilious. Given that almost everything that had passed between Mr Seymour and me had increased the distance between us, so it seemed to me at any rate, my expectations that the report I was engaged on would turn out well decreased by the day. Unfortunately, I'd never come across any visitors from the Secs Office when I'd been in Harwich so I was completely ignorant about this fine point of protocol.

However, I did not express any of this to Morry or Bernard – merely passed on the good tidings that for every proposed visit, we would need to seek the agreement from the local Collector's office.

For the rest of that day and Friday, we worked together to try and produce some simple charts that set out in a form that was easy to follow, how exports went through Customs systems and controls on their way out of the country – in all the different ways that we had encountered so far. The only thing that I had found useful from "Division" came in handy on Friday afternoon. "Friday is POETS Day" a Principal called Mervyn Jordan had remarked, to a meeting I was attending in about the third week of my previous job. "Push off early, tomorrow's Saturday." So I encouraged my Section to celebrate the occasion by leaving at 4 pm. That would give me time to change into my weekend clothes, grab my bag and head for Victoria Coach Station and the delights of Paris in the Spring.

THREE

PARIS IN THE SPRING

Rosemary and I met in good time at Victoria Coach station and boarded the Skyways coach to Lympne Airport, not far from Ashford in Kent. We made quite slow progress along the Old Kent Road and then through the suburbs, passing within a few miles of our flat. But eventually we got on to the A20 and the traffic thinned out a bit. Once we reached the Downs above Sevenoaks, Rosemary fell asleep on my shoulder. I had forgotten just how tiring she was finding her job. As a young and attractive woman in charge of a dozen men – both Police Constables and 'civilian' workers – she had to earn her senior rank through hard work and showing that she had the brains and good judgement which they lacked. That still didn't stop some of them – especially the older PCs - regarding her as 'a chit of a girl' and one of the gnarled Chief Inspectors from having remarked as she left for our holiday that she looked as though she was about to go under cover in Soho. I wished I could go in there sometime and tell them about Rosemary's incredible courage, but I knew she would never let me. I kissed her head. Her short, black hair felt warm and smelt good. How precious she was to me! I wondered whether perhaps we might make similar journeys, when our hair was grey and we were growing old together. I was sure we would still be just as deeply in love when we celebrated our golden wedding anniversary.

She woke up shortly before we arrived at the airport. It was a small place. I wasn't even sure whether anyone used it other than Skyways and private flying clubs. The buildings were small and primitive compared to Heathrow. There was still a Customs and an

Immigration presence, however. The Immigration Officer examined our passports and asked how long we were going to Paris for, no doubt being certain of the answer in advance. The PO asked us whether we had more than £500 in Sterling and when we assured him we hadn't, waved us on our way. So much for export controls over passengers!

We had to sit around briefly in the departure lounge while the incoming Skyways flight disembarked its passengers. Were they like us, a mixture of tourists and people returning home for the weekend? I guessed probably yes. Then we were ushered on to the aircraft, a sixty-seater turbo-prop, which made me feel glad that we were only flying some 60 miles to Beauvais. Rosemary sat next to me, by the small window.

"Do you realise I've never flown in an aircraft before!" she confessed. "How do you feel when you take off?"

"It feels pretty fast. I've usually found it quite exhilarating, unless the plane rattles around too much."

"I don't think I'd like that too much."

"When we flew out to Nairobi, the RAF told us that there were always bits falling off their planes. It was only when we took off I realised they weren't just pulling our legs."

"Do you realise I haven't even been abroad, either?" she said, ignoring my previous comment.

"Neither had I until I did National Service. You may think this aircraft isn't much to write home about, but compared to military transport planes it's the height of luxury."

"I wouldn't like being cooped up in something like this – not all the way to Kenya. How long did it take?"

"I can't remember, It seemed like hours and hours. I do remember we stopped for a couple of hours in

Cyprus. It was in the middle of the night, so we couldn't see anything. But it was still bloody hot."

"As an experienced flyer, I think you should put your arm round me."

"I fear the air stewardess will deny me that pleasure. They have strict rules about seat belts and how you sit for take-off and landing."

"Well, hold my hand then. If this plane starts to rattle, I may need some reassurance."

As it took off, it bumped and rattled a fair amount, but Rosemary didn't need my reassurance. She was peering out of the window all the time, watching the lights flash by as we gathered speed and lifted off into the sky.

"Now that was fun!" she exclaimed. "It's a pity we couldn't do it in daylight."

"A treat in store when we return."

"Do you think we'll bump about much when we're in the air?"

"Probably. We're only going about sixty miles, so we won't climb very high. From what I've been told, it's generally rather bumpier at lower levels."

But it turned out not to be too bad. At least, though neither of us found the experience enjoyable, we didn't require recourse to a sick bag as several people evidently did, judging by the noises around us and the smell. Fortunately, the air stewardesses had perfumed sprays which masked the odour. And we were descending into Beauvais airport in what seemed practically no time.

French Customs and Immigration were non-existent. Perhaps they closed down and went home for the weekend at 5 o'clock on Fridays? But at least it meant we were quickly on to the coach to take us to Paris.

At this point I was glad it was dark, as I could only surmise that the French coach-driver believed he was a

Grand Prix driver and, from what I glimpsed occasionally in the street - and house-lights of the villages through which we roared, it seemed he was determined to get us to Paris faster than a mile a minute or leave us all dead in a ditch. As Rosemary and I agreed, presumably he had done this often enough to know what he was doing. Or so we hoped.

Anyway, we arrived safe and sound in the Place de la Concorde. We collected our bags and were told of the address of our hotel and given a map of Paris by our Skyways courier, who also reminded us that if we failed to be at the place where we had been delivered by 3 pm on Sunday, we would have to make our own way back to London.

Under the deal that Skyways had presumably negotiated with various Parisian hotels, we were allocated to one of several hotels. I heard a couple about our age complaining that they were being sent to a hotel in Montparnasse, miles from the centre. Our hotel, the Hotel Roch, in the Rue St Roch meant absolutely nothing to me and it took some time, peering at the map by the light coming from a nearby hotel, that I discovered it was quite close, just a short walk along the Rue de Rivoli by the Tuileries. To our joy, we were right in the historic centre of Paris.

The hotel was small and quite welcoming, even though our little used O level French turned out to be even rustier than we had thought. Our room was small and looked out into the Rue St Roch, but it had a separate room with a washbasin and shower.

The concierge informed us that at this late hour, we would be unable to find a restaurant that would give us a full dinner, but suggested a couple of bistros nearby that would be serving snacks all night long. But if we were likely to return after midnight, she would give us a key as the hotel doors were closed from then.

Wishing to enjoy a full day's sightseeing the next day, we declined her offer.

A couple of streets away we found a bistro, the Bar Moliere – doubtless one of many bearing that name. Rosemary had a glass of red wine and I had the surprise of asking for what I thought was beer and getting a bitter concoction, I later learnt was called 'byrrh'. So much for my French accent! Rosemary laughed like a drain. We were on safer ground with the food and each had a slightly tired 'croque monsieur'. They also had something which was called a 'croque madame', which I encouraged Rosemary to try. But she said that on her first night in Paris, she would stick to eating something she knew. Afterwards we had a coffee – small, black and bitter – and I had a brandy and Rosemary a green chartreuse. At the existing exchange rate for Sterling, it seemed quite cheap.

We were back in our room a little after eleven. The shower was quite small, which made showering together all the more enjoyable and reminded us of our flat in Stoke Newington. Then we lay naked on the bed, with the lights out and just the street lights shining gently into the room, with the sounds of the late night Paris traffic in the distance and made love, slowly and lovingly. The shower had been fierce and passionate. Now we were reflective and tender.

We hadn't settled on any plan for the following day, other than seeing the Eiffel Tower, the Arc de Triomphe and Notre Dame. The hotel provided an excellent breakfast, with freshly baked rolls and rich, but not harsh, coffee. Discovering that the Louvre opened on Sunday from 11 am and that it was practically on our doorstep, we decided to leave the cultural part of our visit until the following day. Then we walked all the way up the Champs Elysees to the Arc de Triomphe. That exertion required some refreshment and we found a small café in the Avenue Kleber where we had another coffee and a croissant. This fortified us sufficiently to walk down the Avenue Kleber, which took us to the Palais de Chaillot, on the north side of the Seine, immediately opposite to the Eiffel Tower. And there was no way either of us was going to leave Paris without going to the top of the Eiffel Tower! As the prices in the cafes round there looked rather steep, we decided to take the metro, reversing much of our morning's journey, back to Chatelet, close to Notre Dame.

A dim memory suggested to me that we might find a cheaper lunch on the Left Bank, so we crossed the Seine over the Pont Neuf and found what looked like a traditional French café and ate onion soup and cassoulet for lunch, washed down by a glass of red wine. It was very tasty.

"If we don't spend too much time at Notre Dame," observed Rosemary. "We might be able to see a couple of the shops on the Boulevard Haussmann. According to the adverts with the map, there are several Department stores there. I'd love to see what chic French ladies are wearing this spring."

"OK. Just as long as you don't expect me to buy a beret."

As it was, we probably spent less time in the magnificent, but slightly gloomy surroundings of Notre Dame and more time in the exquisite Sainte Chapelle. We had never seen anything like it! The architecture was so graceful, the decoration unlike anything we'd ever seen before and the stained glass windows were out of this world! We stood, holding hands, enraptured, gazing around for ages. Then we descended to the beautiful lower chapel, before returning to feast our eyes on the wondrous sights of the main chapel again.

It was hard to tear ourselves away, but Rosemary was not entirely devoid of a feminine interest in fashion. We made our way – a somewhat circuitous way – by Metro to the Boulevard Haussmann and found ourselves within easy distance of the Galleries Haussman. Touring this store was amazing and educational. I had no idea that women required such an immense choice of underwear, notably bras, or nightdresses and nightgowns. And as for dresses, skirts, blouses and coats – all I could say was that the variety was only matched by the prices.

"Some of this stuff is really smart and quite different to what women are wearing at home," remarked Rosemary. "Some of it's lovely, but I can't imagine who has the sort of money to pay these prices."

Nevertheless, we came away with several pairs of trendy tights, that I knew would suit Rosemary's legs brilliantly, and an unusual tie, which she demanded she bought for me. It was distinctively not English. However, compared to what it could have been, the damage to our bank balance was small.

At a store somewhat further from the centre, we did manage to find a couple of dresses which combined French chic and affordability – and Rosemary looked absolutely stunning in them. I insisted that we bought them. If our Paris weekend was her anniversary present to me, the dresses were my present to her, I argued.

We walked slowly back to our hotel, enjoying the late afternoon atmosphere of the Parisian streets, the different noises, police cars, with their strange sirens, the chuntering of 2CVs and the vans that looked as though they had been made from several dustbins, snatches of the sharp, explosive language, the smell of coffee, garlic and Gauloises. Oddly, however, what seemed to me to be lacking was exactly what you'd expect of Paris in the Spring – joie de vivre. Generally, people seemed dissatisfied, grumpy – even the young. While you might regard the outlandish fashions of clothes and hairstyles in London as weird, outrageous and silly, young people appeared to be enjoying themselves, having a good time. In Paris, they were going about their business, without smiling, without laughter, without enthusiasm, without happiness, it seemed to me. Of course, Rosemary and I were visibly not French, not Parisians – tourists. But as we wandered around, hand in hand or our arms round each other, people – even younger people – stared. It almost felt as if traditions had been reversed – romantic English lovers in a staid, businesslike, stern old city. The air didn't just smell of Gaulloises, coffee and garlic, there was a pervasive odour of resentment, even anger, an intangible tension. Though this feeling didn't last long, it made quite an impression on me.

When we got back to our hotel, Rosemary decided that she would wear one of her new dresses when we went out that evening - our aim being to have a meal somewhere where we could dance afterwards, as, we had been told, that was what Parisians did on a Saturday night. Of course, putting on fresh clothes indicated a shower and, as our access to showers together was non-existent at home, it seemed a pity to waste the opportunity. A freshly-made bed, with starched white sheets was also too tempting as well.

"I think that's what the French call a cinq a six," I said afterwards, showing off one of the few phrases of French I could remember, but not with any great rendition of the French accent.

"I think you've mispronounced the last word," Rosemary replied with a smirk.

We dressed and went out to find a restaurant where we could eat and dance at not too much expense. Assuming that the area round Montmartre might meet our requirements, we set off on foot, mainly because we couldn't work out where there was a convenient Metro station that didn't involve changing trains at least once. We made our way north along the Rue de Richelieu and the Rue Drouot. Passing by Notre Dame de Lorette, we finally reached the Boulevard de Clichy and within a few minutes found a restaurant with a dancing floor, but, as far as we could tell, no floor show.

A waiter led us to a table for two and we ordered a Dubonnet, on the basis that it was French, we had heard of it and we'd try most things once.

"That's not as strange as that byrrh stuff, " I remarked, "but I'm not sure I'd want to drink it again."

"Did you realise that we're being followed?" said Rosemary quietly. "Don't – repeat don't – look round, but I'm sure that all the time we've walked from the hotel a man has been following us. He's just sat down at a table on his own by the door. When you get a moment, have a glance at him, but don't make it obvious."

"Are you sure? I didn't notice anything."

"I wouldn't say I'm 100% certain. Perhaps 95%. You really didn't notice?"

"I was thinking more about where we were going. It's probably your police training. They don't train Customs people to spot when they're being followed."

"What I don't understand is why? We're just here for a holiday. Why would anyone want to follow us?"

"I dunno. We've not been doing anything married couples aren't allowed to do. Perhaps we've been mistaken for someone else?"

"You don't think it's the Russians, after that business two years ago?"

"Does the man who's been following us look like a Russian?"

43

"Not that I can see. But I haven't been looking too closely, for obvious reasons."

"Well, I need to go to the toilet. I'll go past him and glance as unobtrusively as I can."

I completed my little journey. When I came back, there was a woman sitting next to the man. Judging by the way they were sitting, they weren't there for amorous purposes. It looked more as though they were about to start a business meeting.

"Neither the man, nor the woman who's just joined him look like Russians to me," I confirmed. "But they don't look particularly French either. But if the woman has arrived, do you think it was just coincidental that he happened to be going the same way as us?"

"Just after he arrived, he used the phone by the bar, I think. I believe he just summoned a colleague so he wasn't too conspicuous. But why us?"

"The only thing I can think of is the work I'm doing is linked to the possibility of the Americans letting the British have access to some seriously important computer technology. I've no idea what it is, of course. My review is just to determine whether the UK Government could give a guarantee – or what sort of guarantee – that if we were given access to this stuff how effectively could we prevent it getting into the hands of the Soviets. But why would anybody be interested in my bit? There's nothing secret in what I'm doing. I don't have any access to the actual stuff – and never will."

"And we certainly don't look as though we're loaded with money. Otherwise we wouldn't be flying Skyways or staying at one of their Paris hotels."

"Perhaps I should just go over and ask him?"

"I imagine he'd just deny it…….But anyway, let's not let him spoil our last evening here."

We ordered our food – a pavé, frites and salad for me and a plate called 'choucroute' for Rosemary. The waiter claimed that it was cabbage with a pork chop and bacon, which persuaded her to try it, as a 'pavé' sounded rather large. But what came up was a mound of sauerkraut with half a dozen bits of pork, including bacon, a chop, two sausages and a large lump of barely-fried fat.

"I don't think I could manage all that," she said, looking rather overwhelmed.

"I'll help you with some of it, if you like and if you don't like the sauerkraut, you can have my salad," I replied. "I haven't had any since I was in West Berlin."

Between us, we consumed about half of it, washed down with a glass of red wine. Just as we were finishing, the loudspeakers in the restaurant increased in volume and couples began to dance on the dance-floor area. We allowed our food to settle down for a bit and listened to the music, which seemed to be entirely French pop. Though the Beatles had plainly influenced French pop music, it appeared unpatriotic to play their music here. I fear I found the French versions or imitations by people like Johnny Hallyday and Richard Anthony not as good as the originals.

We got up to dance. They began to play some slow Francoise Hardy songs. I had heard some of them at home and they had struck me as pretty, but a bit twee. But dancing with our arms round each other, our bodies pressed together, they seemed altogether sexier. Rosemary's new dress was very short and made of some silky man-made fibre that clung to her body, so I could feel her breasts, her stomach, her thighs pressing against me. We kissed as we danced, our hearts beating against each other, oblivious of where we were, whether we were being followed – or watched. We danced slowly, as one person, inseparable, totally wrapt

45

up in each other. We stroked each other's hair and I let my hand rest on her small, firm buttocks and stroke the back of her thighs. It felt as though we could not get enough of each other.

Then someone put on French version of "Hippy Hippy Shake" and the moment was over. While Rosemary liked the twist, the shake and other similar dances, I did them reluctantly and self-consciously. In any case, after a quarter of an hour dancing as we had, it would have been an anti-climax. We went back to our table.

"Do you think they'll put that music back on again later?" asked Rosemary. "It was just right for us."

"I don't know. They had quite a lot of stuff like this. I suppose they may just put it on for people to smooch to much later on. You realise it's only just ten and I expect somewhere like this doesn't close until the early hours."

"You did get a hotel key, didn't you?"

"Of course ... I see our friends are still here. I wonder if they had a dance?"

"They don't look as though they did. They don't look as though they're here for fun."

"Do you want to wait for the smoochy music again? I think we'll probably have to order some more drinks if we do. It looked as though there were some people hanging around outside and we might get booted out if we aren't spending any more money."

"In that case, let's go back to the hotel. After all, we can always dance together in our room."

So we paid and left, setting off with our arms round each other's waist, kissing each other every few steps. Though enjoyable, it also had a further purpose. It confirmed that the man continued to follow us – all the way back to the hotel. When we got into our room and peered out of the window with the lights still off to see

46

whether he was watching in the street, we could see no-one. But several cars were parked in the street and he – and his partner – could easily have been sitting in one of them.

Anyway, we soon forgot about them. Keeping the lights out, we danced by the light of the streetlamps, in our clothes, without out clothes. Only when our passion had exhausted itself did we fall asleep in each other's arms, feeling that Paris had fulfilled its promise as the most romantic city in the world.

The following morning, we enjoyed a time of slow, cozy, tender love-making before we rose. Late as we were, the hotel still offered us a tasty continental breakfast. We made the short journey to the Louvre, but the queues seemed rather daunting, so we decided to walk all the way up to Montmartre and climbed the hill to Sacre Coeur. Though we couldn't enter, as there was a service going on, we were able to look across the whole of the centre of Paris on a gloriously sunny spring day.

If nothing else, the two people – the man and the woman - who seemed to be taking it in turns to follow us, would have got some sort of a reward for all their walking.

Realising that we needed to be nearer the Place de la Concorde, we caught the Metro back into the centre of the city and found a small bar where we ate 'salade paysanne', consisting of lettuce in a wonderfully sharp mayonnaise with cold potatoes, and pieces of sausage, bacon and cheese. Absolutely delicious and complemented by a glass of Alsatian Gewurztraminer wine, which the waiter recommended. It was much spicier than any white wine I had ever tasted before – and much better. We were sitting outside enjoying the early afternoon sun, watching the world go past – conscious that our watchers were inside, presumably having to devour their food at speed, in case we decided to make a hasty exit.

I would have loved to have asked them what they were up to. But, of course, they would have undoubtedly denied having anything to do with us.

"I don't remember them travelling with us," observed Rosemary. "Do you think they started following us when we arrived? I didn't really notice anything until yesterday evening when we walked to that restaurant."

"I suppose they probably were following us. But I'm afraid I only had eyes for Paris and you – and not necessarily in that order."

"Well, we'll see whether they follow us on to the coach back, I suppose."

The time had gone too fast and we had to collect our bags from the concierge at the hotel and make our way to the collection point for our coach. Even with the strangeness of being followed, we agreed that it had been a fantastic weekend.

"We must do this sort of thing more often," said Rosemary. "But not in Paris for a while. I don't want the memories of our first time here to be blurred too soon."

"Perhaps I could take you to West Berlin sometime, if we could get there reasonably cheaply. Unfortunately Skyways and firms like that don't do cheap flights to many places – and Berlin isn't one of them…..and it'd take too long by train - at least to do it in a weekend."

As we got on the coach, I noticed that the woman who had been following us got into a car and waited in it. As our coach drew away, the car started, but it didn't follow us for long, turning off and out of sight within a hundred yards. I supposed that they considered it unlikely that we would leap off the coach – not least because, whenever untroubled by traffic lights or other traffic, this coach driver attempted to emulate his colleague of Friday evening, and drive as if he was trying to win the Monte Carlo Rally.

Despite the way the coach lurched and swung round the bends of the road out to Beauvais, we got a fair view of the countryside, Rosemary's nose practically pressed against the coach window. To be honest, it didn't look immensely different from English countryside. Only the villages differed much, mainly because of the style of their buildings and, in the larger ones, a little Mairie standing proudly in the centre, with a tricolor flapping in the breeze from a flagpole in front.

But what we were really looking forward to was seeing the countryside and the Channel from the air. Yet again there were no French officials visible before we embarked on the Skyways plane and set off. Unfortunately, almost as soon as we took off, we entered a low bank of cloud which obscured everything until shortly before we landed at Lympne. The journey back to London resembled our journey going out, with Rosemary sleeping peacefully and innocently on my shoulder as I watched the Kentish countryside and the London suburbs roll past us.

We arrived home and realised that we had remarkably few provisions in the house. Fortunately, there was enough to make cheese on toast – or "Mr Croc", as Rosemary called it. Not long afterwards, exhausted, we went to bed, without even thinking again about the oddity of having been followed all the time we were in Paris.

FOUR

THE IMPORTANCE OF MEETINGS

Inevitably, going to work on Monday morning, under grey, dripping skies was a considerable anti-climax. But we had to work to pay for our pleasures. I also remembered that I had two new recruits starting in my Section – Ken Gray the OCX from Gatwick Airport and Paul Barton-Jones a CO from somewhere in the Secs Office. Ken turned out to be in his early 40s, a small, saturnine man with thinning reddish hair and rimless spectacles. Paul was in his late 50s, a former bank manager who had suffered a nervous breakdown and joined the Civil Service about five years earlier, to work in a less stressful environment. A note in his Estabs file informed me that it was imperative that he was not put into positions that might cause him stress. I must not, therefore, "chuck him in at the deep end". For my part, I wasn't at all sure there was a deep end to be chucked into. Ken had been at Gatwick virtually since the airport opened and was, for all his reputation for taciturnity, vehement that if we had visited Heathrow, we should certainly also see how exports were controlled at Gatwick.

I had already thought it would be a useful thing for the Section as a whole to work out a programme of visits that we could undertake over the next three weeks or so, to get a representative picture of the routes through which goods and people left the country. It seemed to me that we would need to make a couple of visits later that week. The only real constraint was that we should avoid overnight stays and, unless there was a very good reason, no more than two members of the team would carry out a visit. It was also essential that someone remained in the office, as I didn't want to be caught out by Nigel Seymour trying to contact me and being unable to do so.

Leaving them to this task, I phoned Iain Cogbill to ask if we could meet for a word.

"That shouldn't be a problem, Storey," he replied. "I understand that Commissioner Watling has summoned us to a meeting tomorrow. We can speak then."

I received my invitation via Nigel Seymour later in the morning. The meeting would take place at 11 am in the Commissioner's room in the Board's corridor in King's Beam House. He informed me that it was in the nature of a progress meeting, but also what he called a 'pre-meeting' for a meeting at the Cabinet Office in Whitehall, to which Commissioner Watling was bidden on Friday morning.

I duly attended the meeting at the appointed time, with an updated plan of visits and a fuller skeleton report, fleshed out with information from the visits to London Port Long Room and Heathrow Airport. I had also added some very preliminary thoughts on what this meant for the conclusions of the report.

Commissioner Watling's room was beyond the Board Room on the Great Tower Street side of the Board's corridor. It was a big room, with dark wooden panels, a huge mahogany desk, with wall to ceiling bookcases behind it, also made of mahogany. The room boasted a table large enough to seat eight people around in comfort. As we were invited in by the Commissioner's SPS (Senior Personal Secretary), an attractive dark-haired woman in her early twenties, Commissioner Watling rose from behind his desk to greet us.

"Stan – I'm glad you could come," he said to the CIO, Stanley Woodruffe. "Nigel – good to see you, too," he added to Seymour.

He then stared at Iain Cogbill and me. He was a couple of inches shorter than me, balding, with a pallid skin and eyes that darted around, to my mind with the inhuman unpleasantness of a large snake or other venomous or carnivorous reptile.

"This is Cogbill, one of my SIOs," explained Woodruffe. "He covers the IB aspects of this."

"And may I present Storey, T/SEO, who's compiling the report on our behalf."

"Can I expect anyone from the CI's Office?"

"No, Sir," said the SPS in a pleasant Irish accent.

"So that's it? Then let's begin."

We sat down.

"Right," began Watling. "As you'll be aware, the Cabinet Office have decided to give this exercise the dignity of official committee status – official, not Ministerial, fortunately. We shall be working to MISC 38 of 1967, with a secretary called Richard Lewis from the Cabinet Office. I understand he's a Prin?"

"Asst Sec, I believe," said Seymour. " From the Foreign Office. We attended a training course together a few years back. His deputy is a Prin called Osbaldistone, who I've never met"

"Apparently he's asked the Foreign Office, MoD, MinTech, the Board of Trade and ourselves to put in short explanatory papers for Friday's meeting. In theory they should've been in by now, but they've given us all until tomorrow lunchtime. In view of the time, you'd better draft it, Nigel, with Storey in support. You know the sort of thing we'll need – the Customs role and powers, the basic processes and our plan to analyse…"

"Fine. We can do that," replied Seymour with apparent confidence.

"Who's chairing the meeting?" asked Woodruffe.

"Sir Rodney Walmesley," replied Watling. "Foreign Office seconded to Cabinet Office, ex-Ambassador to Moscow, if I remember. Self-serving little twerp, as I recall."

No-one felt moved to challenge this sourly-pronounced judgement.

"Friday is basically just firing the official starting gun. Nothing serious will happen," he continued. "So I don't really need to know – but where have we got to so far?" He stared round at us, his ice-cold eyes flickering with barely veiled hostility.

"I believe Storey is best placed to report," replied Seymour.

"With Mr Seymour's help, we've drawn up a plan of how we'll look at our export controls and procedures and how we'll analyse the risks. We've also prepared a skeleton of the report and are fitting into it information we've picked up from our visits to see the procedures on the ground. So far we've been to London Port – the Long Room in the Custom House – and Heathrow."

"Is that all?" demanded Watling severely but without raising his voice.

"Until last Wednesday, it's been just me and a CA and having to start from scratch."

"Why is it that it's always excuses?"

"However," I added, determined that this unpleasant man wouldn't bully me. I hadn't thrown off my father's bullying ways to put up with it from anyone else. "Our two visits have been very useful. Also, I travelled to Paris by air last weekend, so I can add that experience to our knowledge. Putting it simply, we barely control exports. Our resources are largely directed at imports. Anyone who wanted to export some piece of valuable technical information in a document or a highly valuable and restricted high-tech component could do so with a minimal chance of being detected, especially if it was small."

"What about currency controls? Exports of arms to Rhodesia and the Soviet Bloc? We've told Ministers we've put additional people on to these. We've told them we can prevent illegal exports. What are you telling me?"

"I'm just telling you what I've seen and what I've been told. Everyone is so pushed to increase exports, there's enormous pressure on staff not to hold consignments up. Quite a lot of the information is collected post-export. Arms are reasonably easy to spot. But generally we rely on knowing that certain exporters are fishy or we get tip-offs from the IB. Passengers get asked about how much currency they're taking out, but again – we can't stop and search everyone. There has to be something that makes the PO suspicious. So passengers like me going to Paris could take documents or small components out in their bags. They wouldn't be checked on the French side. And from Paris, they could fly on anywhere."

"But the staff have detailed instructions....."

"If they carried out all the import and export instructions to the letter, the trade of this country would grind to a halt within a day or two. Or you'd need to increase staffing perhaps four or five times. People do the best they can – but they aren't experts in computer technology."

"What have you got to say about this Stan?"

"I've been saying for a long time, with nobody taking a blind bit of notice – that we haven't got enough staff. And they aren't adequately trained. Politicians think they can get all these embargos on the cheap, while still pushing us to facilitate exports as fast as we bloody well can at the same time."

"Nigel?"

"I'm sure we could nuance this if we need to."

"Well, it's a good job we aren't being asked for the final report this week. Somebody's going to have to put their thinking cap on. The Foreign Office, MoD and MinTech are desperate for Britain to get our hands on this American stuff and the last thing they want is a report that basically says the British can't be trusted to hang on to it because we can't stop it being funnelled out to the Russians…or the French, for that matter."

"I hope that when we use the word 'nuance'," interrupted Woodruffe, "what we don't mean is we're going to tell Whitehall to tell the Yanks that black is white. You know what'll happen if we do that. If anything goes wrong, all the shit'll land fairly and squarely on us – and we'll bloody well deserve it!"

"Besides," I added, "I'm not signing my name to any report that isn't accurate and truthful."

Watling raised his eyes to the heavens. I wondered what icy thunderbolt would come next.

"I'm sure we can draft our way round this at the appropriate time," said Nigel Seymour hastily. "Once we've got a fuller picture and we can analyse the risks, we can surely come up with proposals as to how to mitigate those risks. That may require a few more people in a different team, but I'm sure it can be managed. Friday's meeting will be useful if for no other reason than being able to assess the positions of the OGDs."

"I sincerely hope so," said Watling, glaring round the table. "Who's supposed to be accompanying me?"

"The CIO next to you at the table – and I suggest Storey and myself behind in case you need any detailed stuff, even though it's unlikely. It'll give Storey a better idea of the game that's being played here."

"Make sure you tell my office to set it in hand with the Cabinet Office."

That signalled the end of the meeting. When we got outside, Woodruffe said nothing and strode away.

"We must have an urgent word," said Seymour. "Could you come to my room after lunch – about quarter to three?"

"Certainly."

I was left with Iain Cogbill. We walked out of the building together.

"A bit of a baptism of fire there," he remarked with a faint smile. "But you said the right things. Remember, whatever anyone tries to do to get you to 'nuance' your report, don't. Your surest defence is that you reported accurately and your analysis and proposals were based on incontrovertible evidence. Once you start down the road of half-truths or misleading statements, when it all goes wrong, the easiest place for the finger of blame to be pointed will be you. If it does, they'll probably try to do it anyway. But if you've been completely straight, they couldn't make it stick."

"That was what I was intending to do anyway. If other people want to lie or mislead, that's their business."

"Quite so ... But you said on the phone you wanted to have a word with me ...?"

"Yes. Rosemary and I flew to Paris for the weekend and while we were there we were convinced that we were being followed. We didn't notice it until the Saturday evening. But as we were followed all the time until we got back to our hotel then and all the time until we left on our coach on Sunday, we assumed we'd probably been followed earlier.....and before you say anything, we didn't do anything illegal, as far as we were aware."

"Did you get a look at who was following you?"

"Yes."

"What did they look like? Russians? French?"

"Neither, I'd say. They didn't look like Germans, for that matter."

"Well, I'll see if any of my contacts know anything about it. I can't imagine it was any of our lot. But I assume word will've got around Whitehall about your work and if it has, it'll certainly have found its way to the ears of the Americans. My guess is that some folk over there don't want us to get this stuff. Some may want us to. Some may even want us to so that we can foul up again. Then they can blackball us in places where we still get through the door and they'd rather we didn't. Most of them are fairly paranoid as well. So it's possible that once you booked a trip to Paris, they suspected that you might have some sort of rendezvous with the Russians, or even the French. More than a few think we are either utterly venal or completely riddled with fellow travellers, so why should you be any different? And they probably know about your father's politics and assume yours are the same, but you just disguise them better."

"That wouldn't be hard! But if it was the Americans, they weren't particularly good. Once we'd spotted them, they were pretty obvious."

"It's always possible they were sending you a message. If they were only using two people, the chances are they weren't taking you too seriously. If the IB are tailing someone, we'd never use less than six people and we'd keep swapping them around."

"If they were trying to send me a message, it was a rather obscure one."

"That's the trouble with us and them – two English speaking countries talking a different language."

I reported back the gist of the meeting to my Section and we agreed that Ken and Morry would go to Gatwick Airport the following day. It seemed likely that I would be needed 'in support' of Nigel Seymour writing the Customs and Excise paper for this Cabinet Office committee.

I went back over to King's Beam House for 3.45. Seymour was already back in his room.

"That didn't go very well this morning," he began. "Wilf Watling would've had little confidence in you in the first place because you started in the Outfield. But then you reduced it still more by that performance."

"So what was I supposed to do – lie to him? Or tell him things that were so misleading as to amount to the same thing?"

"You could be moved from this work, you realise – and revert to HEO."

"I'm only on temporary promotion. I'll revert in a couple of months anyway."

"Not necessarily, if you do well."

"Well, if remaining as an SEO requires me to lie or sugar the truth so much that it becomes a lie, I'd rather revert now and do something else."

"I see you've inherited your father's dogmatism."

"I don't know what my father has to do with any of this. I don't know why anyone has been poking around in my private life. What's going on?"

"You are writing a report that impinges on highly sensitive matters. Your background is bound to be investigated. I was merely tipped the wink by a contact in the Cabinet Office that preliminary investigations into you had revealed a father who was a dogmatic Stalinist…."

"In that case, your informant was incorrect – or perhaps he just has a way of 'nuancing' things. My father is a dogmatic communist. You could certainly call him Leninist, but he believes in the sovereignty of the proletariat, not personality cults or labour camps."

"That's as maybe. You have to realise that you are under close scrutiny. A lot depends on this deal with the Americans. It could help put us at the front of massive developments with computers and modern military technology that could make the country millions of pounds and mean that the balance of payments problem would soon be effectively abolished."

"Yes, but if we tell other departments what they want to hear and they then promise the Americans something we know we can't deliver, what'll happen if the stuff the Americans are giving us ends up in the hands of the Russians?"

"But they're leaky enough. Who's to say it didn't get out through them?"

"I expect they'd wish to crawl all over us – and they'd find out as quickly as I did, that our export systems aren't up to 100% guarantees. It wouldn't matter if they couldn't prove the stuff had gone from here rather than from them. They'd just point a finger to our systems and say we'd lied to them. And they'd be right."

"I doubt we're going to resolve this today. Until we see a fuller version of your skeleton report, along with an analysis of the risks, only then can we take a view on the extent to which we can overcome or manage these risks, depending on the likelihood of them occurring, and whether the potential cost in terms of additional staff or tighter controls is worth it."

"Fine. I must make clear, though, that my name will only go under something I regard as accurate and truthful. If you or Commissioner Watling wish to 'nuance' it, it won't be over my name. And if that means you wish to replace me with someone else, you must feel entirely free to do so."

"I'm sure it won't come to that."

We agreed that, as I had never even seen a paper prepared for a Cabinet Office committee, he would prepare a first draft and I would join him at 10.30 the following morning, "for a factual contribution", as he put it.

When I got home and told Rosemary about it, she gave me a huge kiss.

"Despite your unconventional ways with statements to the police and potential evidence, I've always known what you are really like."

When I told her about what Iain Cogbill had suggested about the people who had been following us in Paris, she laughed and said she hoped they hadn't also bugged our hotel room - or worse, had a hidden camera, as in "From Russia with Love". She doubted her career in the police could continue if what had gone on in our hotel room appeared on the telly. I suggested she might, however, receive offers of openings in a different career, so she threw a wet dishcloth at me.

"I think if you see those sorts of films," she observed, "the ladies are rather larger than I am – and make a good deal more noise."

"Where have you seen films like that!"

"Policewomen are spared nothing of the seamier side of life......Actually I saw about fifteen seconds once, when I was asked to take a message to the CID in Leicester and burst in on them, 'reviewing evidence', as they called it."

"Well, you've seen more than I have....I'm really very innocent."

"In about half an hour, we can test that theory!"

Much of the following day was spent with me sitting in Nigel Seymour's room while he drafted a paper for the Cabinet Office in what was apparently the prescribed format. My task appeared to be to fill in the occasional fact or technical term. My main objective was to prevent anything appearing at this stage that would prejudge the outcome of the work I and my

Section were undertaking. But, when he reached the concluding paragraphs, Seymour announced that there would be 'no hostages to fortune'. As far as I could tell, over some four pages of typescript, the paper said next to nothing. I noted that it promised an 'annexe' to the final report which would set out the primary and secondary legislation which was relevant to export controls and procedures

"Will your contact in the Sols (Solicitor's) Office be able to provide that list of relevant legislation?" I asked.

"Regrettably not. He says he's up to his eyes in Finance Bill work and will cast an eye over what we provide – and certainly he'll happily examine any proposals we might make regarding interpretation of the existing law or for new legislation. So I fear your Section will need to do that piece of work."

Finally, I returned to Custom House and found Paul Barton-Jones twiddling his thumbs. So I set him the task of gathering together all the relevant legislation pertaining to export controls and procedures. In order to avoid causing him too much stress, I explained that he should try and find as much as he could in a fortnight, but he didn't need to be exhaustive. I suggested that the Librarians in the main Library in King's Beam House, or failing them, the Librarian in the Sols Office, should be able to point him in the right direction. I suggested that, if he was amenable, it would be sensible for him to base himself in the main Library and write down all he found out in a notebook. This seemed to please him and he set off at once to begin his task.

I didn't expect Ken and Morry to return from Gatwick airport that day and Bernard was busy sorting out our travel arrangements and contacting appropriate Collectorate offices to ensure they were aware of our planned visits. So I reflected on what we had learnt so far about export procedures and controls. The most obvious point was that there was an inconsistency and a tension between trying to get exports out of the country as fast as possible, with minimal paperwork and expense, to help with the balance of payments problems and the need to control those goods that we either didn't want to export at all, or only under licence. It would be naïve to argue that all you had to do was examine the Tariff heading of the goods in question - and that would enable you to identify arms or nuclear material, for instance, and prevent exports of such things, while letting the rest wing its way through 'without touching the sides'. Quite simply, if you were going to try to export goods which were prohibited or required a licence, you wouldn't use a Tariff heading that identified them. You would use a false description or you would conceal the items in question within a legitimate cargo, accurately described.

So how could you either prevent that happening or detect it when it did? Personally, I didn't see much benefit in merely putting more Customs Officers on the job. The number of export consignments was vast and it would still be like searching for a needle in a haystack. I ruled out anything that would seriously disrupt or delay exports. For all my experience in ports, I was sceptical about the famous "revenue nose", which supposedly enabled experienced Customs staff to detect smuggled goods or passengers engaged in smuggling. It seemed more likely that, possibly unconsciously, they spotted patterns of behaviour or inconsistencies in the paperwork and had the confidence to follow up their suspicions. Quite often they would be wrong, but they'd be right often enough to maintain their self-confidence. And it seemed probable that they learnt from their successes and failures, so that they made fewer of the same mistakes. So what we needed to find out was what evidence encouraged them to challenge a passenger, a consignment or an entry? That might help in trying to work out whether we could control specific prohibited exports better.

But there were other difficulties. Even if we were able to detect fishy exports more effectively, how would we know that they were genuinely prohibited items? It would be easy enough to identify machine guns or anti-personnel mines destined for Rhodesia, for example. But once you got to electrical components – especially obscure, high-tech ones – how on earth would any Customs Officer be able to tell – especially if it was shipped as part of a consignment of thousands of similar items? We lacked expertise – but the question was where might we find it? And could we guarantee that such expertise might be available at short notice so Customs weren't accused of holding up valuable export shipments? You might attempt to exercise some control over the manufacturers or importers of such stuff. But how far would other Government Departments or their Ministers be prepared to allow Customs to tramp our heavy boots all over their long-favoured contractors? How could you prevent stuff you knew nothing about being despatched to sub-contractors or just taken out by employees who could see a fat profit in it for themselves? Would Ministers put up with Customs and Excise operating as a sort of security force round the major British computer makers, for instance? In any case, wouldn't something like that require legislation, which would open up the whole subject of why it was needed? Many Excise and PT traders already regarded our controls as unnecessarily intrusive, yet this would be a considerable step further.

I scribbled all these thoughts down on some foolscap paper in a way that they could be fitted into the analysis section of the report. Then I locked it, as well as all the other relevant documents, into my combination cupboard before I departed for the evening.

When I got home, Rosemary was sitting on our couch, puzzling over a rather strange bit of post.

"This was lying on the floor with the rest of the post when I got in. But the envelope didn't have a stamp on it. Do you know what it means, Nick?"

It was a single sheet of writing paper from, I would have guessed, a cheap pad bought from Woolworths. It read. "Hope you got the message" in capitals, written in blue biro.

"I haven't the faintest idea......what message? What message have we received? I wasn't aware of any?"

"I can't think of anything either."

"Iain Cogbill said that the fact that we were able to spot those two following us in Paris might've been intended to give us a message. But what message? And if it's to do with my work, do they want my report to support getting this American stuff in, or the opposite? If someone's going to send a message, it'd help if it was clear."

"Or perhaps it was the milkman and his message got mislaid?"

"We could ask him when we see him next....But I'll take this into work and send it to Iain and see what he makes of it. The capitals certainly suggest someone didn't want to give clues about their handwriting....."

"Or their handwriting was virtually unintelligible, like yours......if you wrote something like that it could easily look like 'have pan fried the sausage'."

"Let's hope it is just some kind of a joke."

I took the envelope and message in with me the following day and sent them in a transit envelope to

Iain Cogbill with a brief explanatory note. I didn't expect an early response.

The first task of the morning was for Ken and Morry to tell us what they learnt from the export procedures and controls at Gatwick. Essentially it came down to everything being very similar to what happened at Heathrow, though, as even Morry admitted, the staff at Gatwick took a greater interest in exports, especially freight. But, as Ken explained, taking all year round, Gatwick probably took a greater share of freight as a proportion of its overall traffic compared to Heathrow.

As we got through that quite quickly, I asked them about how they approached the task of identifying potential smugglers among the passengers and fishy consignments among the freight. In other words, what was it that tickled their revenue noses?

"Lots of things," said Morry. "With pax, it's generally their behaviour. Either they avoid looking at you or they brazenly stare you straight in the eyes, but for slightly too long. After a while, you see a pattern of how most pax make their way towards the PO or APO. I always try to have more of a chat with those who don't fit the pattern. Sometimes I'm content they aren't trying it on – but I can always ask them to open their bags for a quick rummage. But some flights tend to be more productive than others, of course. And, of course, if someone is struggling with a case that seems to weigh half a ton, it's always worth having a look inside."

"Especially when it chinks," added Ken. "But pax are relatively straightforward compared to freight…"

"Do you mind if we stick to passengers for the moment?" I said. "When it's incoming passengers, those that are smuggling have things like booze or fags or watches or cameras for example. They know they're smuggling and they probably believe, deep down, they're doing something wrong. But on the outward side, all we're seriously checking for is currency. I wonder how many people really think that if they take out more than five hundred quid, it's wrong. After all, it's their money. It's not like coming in, when it must feel a bit like stealing – if only from the Government. Are outward passengers likely to be as revealing?"

"Well, of course, if we're talking purely about the currency restrictions, you're probably right. But if it was the stuff we're talking about in this report, I'd guess their behaviour wouldn't be all that different," replied Morry.

"Though if it really was very important, very valuable stuff, they might use professional smugglers," added Ken.

"Professional smugglers?" I asked.

"We don't see lots of them, but there are a few around. They generally look like businessmen returning from a business trip abroad, somewhere you'd expect, like Paris or Amsterdam or New York. They carry only very high value stuff, like diamonds or possibly expensive watches, for instance. They're well trained and their luggage will always have clever concealments, so nothing would be discovered in the course of our usual quick searches. They're very difficult to spot."

"So how do you?"

"Either an IB tip-off or sometimes, if we have time, we look at schedules of the travel of some of these people. For instance, given the travelling time, would you really travel to New York one day and come back the next and do it once a month, regular as clockwork? Surely you could do business on the phone or by using a facsimile machine? Of course, they could be genuine – but someone like that would always be worth challenging and examining their luggage very thoroughly - and thoroughly search them as well."

"And that would work for both inward and outward passengers."

"Yes. But you'd have to be pretty quick with outward pax. Because the only serious check is for currency, the time available for examination in the airline schedules is much less for outward flights."

"So what about freight?"

"It starts with the documents. Anything that looks a bit fishy or perhaps just unusual. Of course, exporters we haven't come across before or unusual destinations. How the paperwork is done can make your antennae twitch. How much is hand-written or typed? Does it look professional? Does it look too professional? Does all the documentation tie up together? What sort of goods are they? Do the values look right against the Tariff heading?"

"And then when it gets to the PO and APO," added Morry, "it's what the consignment looks like. Does it look like what you'd expect from the paperwork? How well is it parcelled up? Does it look right for the nature of the goods? Does it look too secure or not secure enough? ... But like pax, there's not much time to deal with consignments for export ... and, even if you think you've got a fishy consignment, actually identifying prohibited electric computer parts would be impossible unless there was an expert on tap."

"Is there anything we could do to minimise the risks?" I asked.

"The IB could take more of an interest in potential export fraudsters ... and some sort of arrangement to get expert advice available quickly would help."

"But it wouldn't guarantee that specific stuff wouldn't get out one way or another," added Ken.

As the two of them appeared to have managed the visit to Gatwick satisfactorily, I suggested that both carried out the visit which we had set up for the following day to Biggin Hill airport, which was used for only occasional overseas flights but was the base for several flying clubs whose members could fly across the Channel and back. I explained that, though I would have liked to have gone, my attendance in support of Commissioner Watling at this Cabinet Office meeting appeared to be non-negotiable.

Shortly before I left that evening I received a phone call from Nigel Seymour.

"I hope you can make your own way to the Cabinet Office tomorrow morning, Storey. Wilf Watling doesn't like passengers in the front seat of the Board's car and three would be too much of a crowd in the back. I assume you know where it is? Go to number 70 Whitehall. It's pretty well opposite the new MoD building. Remember to be there no later than ten-fifty."

"I'm sure I'll be able to find it."

Rosemary was probably more enthusiastic than I was about the meeting.

"I bet you never thought you'd ever be at a meeting in the very heart of Government. The Cabinet Office is right next to Downing Street. I had a look in the 'A to Z'. Perhaps you'll see some Ministers. You must tell me all about it."

I made my way there in good time. The classical façade of the Cabinet Office contrasted greatly with the large modern building opposite. Walking along Whitehall, I noticed that MoD appeared to own several rather grand buildings, as well as their vast headquarters. I also noticed some Min of Ag buildings and, on the north side of Whitehall, a rather elegant round classical porch at the front of a building belonging to the Scottish Office.

Shortly after I found the entrance marked '70', the Customs and Excise Board's car drew up, its pennant fluttering elegantly in the light breeze. Out stepped Commissioner Watling and – on the road side - Nigel Seymour. We entered the building and went to the reception desk, where we were joined by Stanley Woodruffe, rising from a nearby chair. We were all formally signed in and given day passes to the building, except for the Commissioner who had a permanent one.

A messenger led us up a flight of stairs and along a corridor, one side of which was evidently part of the original building on the site – Tudor, I would have guessed. Then we reached a lobby with various historic artefacts on the wall – a steel helmet of Tudor vintage, a pike, a halberd, etc – and a man sitting by a door at one side. But we didn't go that way, but out through another door to a lift that took us up from the first to the third floors. Somehow, despite arriving on the ground floor, our brief walk through the building had transferred us to the first floor! Getting out of the lift, we followed a corridor past rooms that were numbered, but with no indication of their inhabitants. I hoped that some of them might have belonged to Ministers, but we saw no-one else until we reached a room whose door informed us it was Conference Room C.

Inside, I found myself in a large, long room of a vaguely Georgian type, with several vast original oil paintings on the walls. They were in eighteenth or nineteenth century classical style, of suitably royal or military themes. The room was almost entirely filled by an enormous polished mahogany table with two dozen chairs round it and similar number against the walls. A messenger ticked off our names as we entered.

"We sit at the far end," explained Seymour in a whisper. "There's a protocol to that sort of thing. The Cabinet Office Committee Chairman sits in the middle by the door, with the Treasury and Foreign Office opposite. The other Departments spread out between them, depending on status. Ours is quite low in Whitehall terms. So that's why we sit where we are. I suggest you go and sit down there. The area by the door tends to get rather crowded."

Indeed, it did. For the next ten minutes it was filled with almost entirely men aged between 35 and 55 greeting each other, mainly as though they were old friends, occasionally with more visible coolness. Then a square faced, dapper man of middling height and slightly receding black hair appeared, accompanied by two younger men, with keen faces and fly-away hair, both looking like former inmates of one of the country's foremost public schools.

Having greeted both of them, Nigel Seymour came and sat down next to me. A further round of greetings continued with the latest arrival. Then he sat down and everyone hastily made their way to their allotted places. The two young men sat next to the Chairman – Sir Rodney Walmesley.

"Are we all here?" he demanded in a gravelly voice, but with a strongly upper class accent.

Evidently there were no formal introductions.

"We have papers from the Foreign Office, MoD, MinTech and Customs. I propose each Department gives us a brief resumé and a general discussion follows."

"I can put the Foreign Office point very simply," said a rotund man sitting almost opposite Walmesley, in a very plummy voice and a belligerent manner, which I thought odd for a member of the Diplomatic Service. "We want to maintain good relations with the Americans, but my masters are equally clear that we wish to avoid being placed in a position where it becomes necessary to join them in their ghastly war in

Vietnam. It's imperative that we don't make a mess of this. If we go for this deal, there must be no possibility that their stuff should leak to the Soviets – or the French, for that matter. Better no deal than that." He glared across the table at Walmesley with undisguised animosity.

"The Ministry of Defence view is more nuanced," added a sleek man with wavy hair, a reddish complexion and a military moustache. "Of course we would like this kit. It could give the defence contractors a massive shot in the arm and give us a competitive advantage over the French, at least – and they're realistically our main competitors. It'd also cement our good co-operation with the Americans. As colleagues will be aware, recovering from Suez has been a long, hard road and they're not very keen on the present Government – though the Defence Minister generally goes down well when he's over there, even though they're aware he was a communist in his youth. The D-Day stuff scores a lot of points. But they don't like us washing our hands like Pontius Pilate over Vietnam. Whatever we do, the one thing our Ministers don't want is to 'piss off the Yanks', as my Minister so graphically put it."

"MinTech has a simpler position. The future is technology. While we are good at the pure science, our ability to turn it into commercial technology is mediocre. If the Americans have technology we can use to give us a competitive technical advantage, it's essential that we grab it with both hands," said a slim, bespectacled woman in her early forties, with long, dark hair tied up into a severe bun.

"The main role for Customs and Excise," began Watling, "is to ensure that sensitive technology isn't diverted from here into the hands of the Soviets. As colleagues will be aware, the Government is eager to export as much and as quickly as possible, in order to help the balance of payments. At the same time, Customs staff endeavour to detect goods the export of which is prohibited or subject to MoD or BoT licensing. We are presently engaged in a review of our controls to consider the extent of the potential risks in our controls and the export licensing and prohibition procedures. At the end of this it is our intention to advise on the nature of any guarantee that might be made to the Americans, taking account of the nature of these risks and what might be done to mitigate them. At this point, it is impossible to prejudge the outcome of this review and therefore whether any guarantee could be given and, if so, of what it might consist."

"I'm grateful to colleagues for their summaries," said Walmesley. "Now I think we might go round the table for any comments.....Sidney?"

A youngish man with thick, dark hair, a jutting jaw, sporting a red, spotted bow-tie spoke.

"The Home Secretary has doubts. He fears that when push comes to shove, the Americans will only give us this technology in return for a commitment to send troops to Vietnam. The Home Secretary considers that the war is deeply unpopular among the young and that the minor demonstrations that have taken place against the war would be like village tea-parties compared to what would erupt if British troops were sent there. He also suspects that the Americans are already trying to filch the technology that we are offering them, initially at least by identifying who developed it and buying them for themselves. But my colleague may be able to add something to that."

The man next to him was the only other person in the room I recognised. When Rosemary and I were summoned to London after pushing the Commercial Counsellor at the Russian Embassy into the Grand

Union canal and tying up his accompanying hoods in their car, he was the man from "Box 500", known only to me by his Christian name "Jacob", who had chaired the meeting.

"What we know is that the Americans are, as usual, deeply divided about this. The State Department and the Department of Defense want to tie any deal to British participation in Vietnam. Commerce don't want us to have the technology. They reckon they'll develop the technology we're offering themselves – or, as John said just now – buy or steal it. They reckon the price is too high. On the other hand, the CIA want us to have the stuff, because they believe we won't be able to stop it going to the Soviets. Then they can finally close all doors to us, just as we had got back in after the Burgess, Maclean and Philby fiascos."

"So why have they offered the deal in these terms?" demanded a hawk-faced man in his early thirties, with incongruous grey hair cut in an extraordinarily old-fashioned pudding-bowl style. "Indeed, why have they offered it at all?"

"Perhaps I could finish, before my colleague from the Treasury steps in," continued 'Jacob'. "Our belief is that State and Defense want to tie us into discussions about this deal, to the point at which we're sufficiently committed - and then drag Vietnam in. On the other hand, our understanding of US Treasury's position is that they want the deal to go ahead. They think our economy is so weak that we need their help. Otherwise this instability in the money markets will keep creating financial crises with the risk of competitive devaluations and rapid inflation."

"And what is your understanding of where the Soviets stand in all this?" asked Walmesley.

"Despite the Americans believing we would let this stuff go, they're as leaky as sieves themselves. So the

Soviets are aware of the deal and have some sort of idea of the nature of the stuff involved. Of course, it's stuff they'd love to get their paws on. But I doubt whether they have a strong view as to whether they'd be better off trying to get it here or the other side of the pond."

"And what about these fronts that are poking their noses in and trying to release all details about every piece of military equipment?"

"There are a couple of organisations which certainly believe that publishing details of all military secrets is the best way to prevent a third world war, because no-one would have any advantage which tempted them to get in a pre-emptive strike. Both are relatively new and as yet we have no firm information about any links with the Soviets – or possibly the Chinese – though, I agree, they have all the appearance of classic Soviet front organisations."

"Perhaps one of you might enlighten us as to who these organisations are? asked a middle-aged man with thinning, greyish hair and a grey, irascible face.

"I realise such matters don't normally arouse the interest of the Board of Trade," replied 'Jacob'. "They are called "Peace Now" and "Peace in our time". The former contains many of our traditional left wing, anti-Vietnam war, CND types. The latter gives off a more religious aura and has recruited a few of the lefty, trendy churchmen to give it a feel of greater respectability. But so far they've been quite good at keeping us at bay, so we don't really know who the guiding minds are – or where they are getting their money."

"I think that's enough on that score for the present," concluded Walmesley. "Over to you, Nigel."

'Nigel' was a bespectacled, thickset man with a crew-cut.

"The DEA is broadly of the same mind as MinTech on this. It is essential that we can give the Americans a sufficiently persuasive guarantee for us to get our hands on this stuff. It's exactly the sort of thing the economy badly needs to drag us out of our outdated Victorian infrastructure." I was struck by his grating Northern Irish accent.

"There's little I need add from the Foreign Office. We broadly share the analysis of the American positions as set out by Jacob. I would just nuance it a bit to say that I believe that State support the deal provided we cheer in the wings about Vietnam. They're canny enough to know how difficult actual participation would be for the British Government, but they don't like to see us sitting on our hands. Unlike the boneheads in Defense." He stared at Walmesley again with undisguised hatred.

"While the Treasury is as keen as anyone to find solutions that would help to tackle our chronic balance of payments problems, this prospective deal won't do anything for us for how many years? Five at least, I'd say. Treasury Ministers are more concerned that the deal might require hundreds more Civil Servants to provide the requisite guarantee of security. They are also concerned about what the American reaction might have on Sterling if we were seen to have messed up."

"The Board of Trade has nothing to add to what has been said already."

"All I need do is re-iterate the view of my masters as stated earlier," added the man from the Ministry of Defence.

"I believe Customs and Excise have nothing to add," said Watling.

"Then I think we can move on to our programme of work. Wilf?"

"We expect to have a preliminary report within a fortnight," began Watling. "We will attempt to provide a picture of the possibilities from our analysis of our fieldwork, but I think it would be imprudent to assume hard and fast conclusions at that stage. But the Committee might wish to have a first pass round the material at that stage."

"On broadly the same timescale, we would expect to have a more in-depth analysis of the value of the American technology and how far our people have got in coming up with something similar," said the lady from MinTech.

"Thank you, Irene. A paper on that would be appreciated."

"Home Office will provide a further analysis of the possible hostile interest and its nature," added the man from the Home Office, presumably speaking on behalf of 'Jacob'. "But it'll have to be given at least 'secret' classification and limited circulation, therefore."

"That's understood, of course."

"The Foreign Office will provide an update on the state of negotiations with the Americans to the same timescale."

"I trust the Foreign Office will keep Cabinet Office in the picture. The PM has expressed an interest in this," demanded Walmesley, regarding his Foreign Office counterpart with contempt.

"And the Treasury. The Chancellor has expressed concerns about this," added the man from the Treasury.

"Naturally. I can see this is going to be a game of tennis with about eight players holding on to the racquet," replied the man from the Foreign Office.

"Then we'll meet in a fortnight. Speed is of the essence. So I'll accept papers 48 hours in advance. I think that settles MISC 38(67) for today. Thank you gentlemen – and lady."

They all started to mill out, a few in conversation with each other. I wondered whether the Chairman and the man from the Foreign Office might come to blows, such seemed the enmity between them. But the Chairman had departed first, along with one of the floppy-haired young men. The other was left, presumably to make sure we all departed. Watling, closely followed by Seymour, strode out, while I was still putting my papers into my briefcase. Woodruffe had made a beeline round the table for 'Jacob'. So I made my way towards the door, almost bumping into the floppy-haired young man.

"Your first time?" he asked in a very posh accent.

"Yes," I replied. "It was quite remarkable."

"A dogfight. They're often like that." He struck me as probably an Assistant Principal given an opportunity to show off to a rustic from Customs. "Do you want some help in finding your way out?"

"I'd be grateful."

"This place is a bit of a warren."

As he led me to a different lift, nearer the conference room, but with a capacity of no more than three people, he gave me his view of the meeting.

"Of course, Walmesley and Roddy Pilkington – that was the FO chap – hate each other's guts. Walmesley got Moscow when Roddy wanted it. He's hated him ever since. And the Treasury hate the DEA…actually they hate all of us for spending money. When that chap said the Chancellor was concerned about extra Civil Servants, he was aiming his gun at you lot, of course. They think you're going to bid for several hundred more staff…"

We reached the first floor and got out. We went back through the lobby with the historic artefacts on the wall and the messenger sitting on a chair by a door on the opposite side.

"That's the door to No 10," explained the young man. "The top brass all have keys, but if any of the rest of us oiks want to go through, we have to be escorted......and this is the Tudor wall...It always makes me reflect on the continuity of government when I see it, though I believe it may have been part of an old tennis court for Whitehall Palace....of course, they played real tennis then....But here we are...."

With that he left me at the reception desk, where I handed my day pass back and left the building. Once outside, I breathed a deep breath of relief, first, that no-one had asked me to say anything and second, that I was back in a world I recognised.

The Board's car had doubtless long gone, so I walked to the Tube and got back to Custom House in time for a late lunch. Then I encouraged Bernard to tidy up the latest version of our plan and send it off for typing. Meanwhile, I tried to incorporate within the skeleton report anything relevant that had been said during the meeting.

I must confess that I was contemplating calling a "POETS day" again, when the phone rang and a woman's voice with a soft Irish accent invited me to attend a meeting with Commissioner Watling in half an hour's time. Having told Bernard that once he'd finished his current piece of work, he was free to go, I made my way over to King's Beam House, with a singular lack of enthusiasm.

"That went satisfactorily," observed Watling, as Nigel Seymour and I sat down. "I assume Stan Woodruffe isn't available?"

"I'm afraid not, Sir," replied the pleasant Irish girl. "His office said there was an operation under way this afternoon."

"Hmm...probably involving the use of a set of clubs, a little white ball and some pleasant countryside walking, if I know Stan....and probably with Jacob Ffoulkes from the Security Service. The IB do love their little friendships with the security chaps!"

"It seemed to me that the Treasury were trying to spike our guns early," observed Seymour.

"That little fart, Michaelson! Yes. But I bet that rubbish about the Chancellor being concerned was a lie. Callaghan's got a lot more on his plate at the moment than bothering about a few hundred more Customs staff. Anyhow, if we need them, there'll be plenty round the table that'll back us..."

"Not least the man from the DEA."

"Of course. But the DEA hasn't got the clout it had under George Brown."

"Was there anything else you wanted us to do about the report?"

"No. Just crack on with it. It'd be a good idea if we have a first draft of the paper by Thursday evening , so we could go over it next Friday. Then we can polish it the following week."

"We won't have much more field work completed by next Thursday," I said. "So any analysis and preliminary conclusions will be largely based on what we've got already."

"Perhaps you may be able to bring forward some of your fieldwork to the early part of next week," suggested Seymour.

"I'll see what I can do. But it doesn't give us much time to think."

"Don't worry about that. Once we've got the basic stuff, then we can start to do the thinking," retorted Watling.

Part of me wondered whether they hadn't already done much of their thinking in advance of receipt of "the basic stuff", but as we were dismissed and Seymour evidently had no desire to set me straight this afternoon, I took the opportunity to escape back to Custom House and, having made sure every paper was securely locked away in my cupboard, I made my way home, my step lighter and happier at the thought of two whole days with Rosemary, rather than in this strange world where ambition, words, politics and power mingled in a shadowy and rather unwholesome way.

FIVE
MESSAGES

As I reached the front door of our flat, my step became a little heavier, when I remembered that Rosemary's parents were coming for the weekend. Not that I had anything against them. They were nice people and pleasant company. It was just at that time in our lives, I wanted that precious time at weekends to be only Rosemary and me together.

Fortunately, they weren't arriving at St Pancras until 11 am the following morning. When I opened the door, Rosemary was already inside, tidying stuff away and beginning to clean the flat.

"I know it's not dirty," she said, "but we were away all last weekend and I'd feel dreadful if my mother saw a dusty surface or something that had fallen under the couch....Are you all right to do the shopping on your own this evening?"

So I changed and went out with our trolley and did the necessary shopping.

"I assume you weren't planning to cook tomorrow evening were you?" I asked on my return. "If you are, we'll need to go out first thing tomorrow to get what you need."

"I thought about doing a spaghetti Bolognese and following it with bananas in custard for desert. We've already got enough spaghetti and we've got quite a few bananas that are riper than I really like, so all we'd need to do is to get some mince tomorrow. Do you think that'd be OK?"

"They're your parents......I'm sure they'll like it. Your mother will be pleased you've learnt to cook so well."

"Well, we have had a few disasters in our time – even with spaghetti. Do you remember the time we let the pan boil dry?"

"How could I forget?....We had our minds on other things, as I recall...."

It was Rosemary's parents' first visit to our new flat. My mother had paid us a brief visit, but my father, true to his communist principles, refused to set foot in this symbol of my progress along the path of capitalism. "All property is theft" he had been heard to mutter – and remained at home, true to his principles in the council house he had lived in for the best part of thirty-five years.

We met Rosemary's parents on time and, as the dutiful son-in-law, I took Mrs Johnson's case. They said that they were keen to see the Temple Church, St Bride and then some of the City churches, before we headed back to Beckenham. We accomplished the first two and had a light lunch in one of the streets near St Bride.

"Have you been in many of the City churches, since you've been working in the City?" Mr Johnson asked me.

"Very few," I confessed. "I've been in St Magnus the Martyr, right by Billingsgate, and All Hallows by the Tower....but the one I like best has remained a ruin since the war, St Dunstan's in the East. When the weather is nice, I sometimes sit there for a few minutes in my lunch hour, especially if I'm going between Custom House and King's Beam House."

"I suppose you don't get a lot of time."

"As far as I can see most people take at least an hour for lunch. I just haven't thought about it. If I go anywhere, I tend to head for Leadenhall Market to do a bit of shopping."

"There are many fine churches, many designed by Sir Christopher Wren. There's even a Norman choir in St Bartholomew the Great and St Ethelburga is the only church to survive both the Great Fire of London and the Blitz."

"I don't think we can expect to see them all today, dear," said his wife. "You'll have to choose three or four."

In the end it was more like six and we got on a train from Cannon Street fairly footsore. It's a curious phenomenon that when you are walking where you want to go, your feet barely notice a thing, but when you are following in someone else's footsteps, they start feeling it almost immediately. And though having parents/parents-in-law as guests cramped our normal Saturday night style a bit, Rosemary cooked the dinner well and I sliced the bananas and made the custard with practiced skill.

The following morning, Mrs Johnson said she wished to attend a church service, as she always did. So we all made the short walk to St George's, a fine example of traditional English church architecture in the centre of Beckenham. Her husband, Rosemary and I all attended - more as a matter of duty than of belief on my part, at least. Afterwards, we took a short walk in Beckenham Place Park before having lunch – cold meat and salad – at our flat.

Mrs Johnson was just opening her handbag to get out a camera to take come pictures of our flat when a plain brown envelope fell out. It was addressed to 'Storey'.

"I don't know how that got there," she remarked.

"I've never seen it before.....I wonder how it got there," I replied, the lump growing in my guts registering recognition of the capital letters written in blue biro.

Inside there was an identical piece of paper with the words "have you got the message yet?" in the same capitals as before. I folded it and put it into a pocket.

"Sorry. It must've fallen from somewhere. It's our milkman about a change in deliveries."

"I suppose with you both working, you don't get much chance to see him," said Mr Johnson.

After we had seen them off at Beckenham Junction, Rosemary said "That was the same as the last one, wasn't it?"

"Yes. I'll send it to Iain Cogbill as well.....I wish these people would be more specific about what the message actually is."

"Where do you think it was put in my mother's bag? Coming out of the church? There were plenty of people hanging around."

"I wonder whether we were being followed?"

"Why don't we go out for a walk and see? We've not seen what Kelsey Park is like yet."

We walked down the High Street and round the park, full of families with children enjoying the afternoon sun of a pleasant Spring day.

"We are being followed, I believe," whispered Rosemary, leaning on my shoulder. "A man and a woman. They've followed us from outside our flats."

"Not the same ones as in Paris, surely?"

"No. Though the woman is wearing a headscarf, I'm sure she's blonde, while the woman in Paris was dark-haired and shorter. The man looks younger and bigger, too."

"Perhaps this is the time to ask them what they're up to," I said. "Perhaps they can tell us what the message is."

We set off towards them, but the moment they saw us heading for them they turned and walked rapidly away. We set off in pursuit, but they got out of the park before us and by the time we got there, a black car was speeding away up Manor Way.

When we got back to our flat, there were no cars parked in the road outside and those in the car park belonging to the flats were all familiar. But when I looked out of the window later on, a black car was parked in the road opposite. I couldn't tell whether there was anyone in it. I promised Rosemary I'd mention all this to Iain Cogbill and ask him to give it some priority. It was unsettling having someone shadowing us all the time.

"If they're still there tomorrow night, I'll give them something to think about," Rosemary remarked, but without being more specific.

So I returned to work on Monday feeling less than refreshed. I managed to have a conversation with Iain Cogbill, explaining that I seemed to be permanently shadowed. Indeed, I couldn't tell whether I wasn't also being followed when I was at work. I also asked him to encourage his contacts in places like "Box 500", not just to discover who was doing this but also for them to make it clear what message I was supposed to be getting. He said he would do what he could.

Ken and Morry told us about their visit to Biggin Hill, which sounded a desperately difficult place to get to, requiring several changes of bus from Bromley South station. What they found was a small airport that had a number of charter flights, which might involve just passengers, but could also involve small quantities of freight. There were also several flying clubs who, in theory, filed flight plans whenever an aircraft was in the air. But most of the aircraft had sufficient capacity to fly across the Channel and back, so could be a route whereby small consignments or technical documents, for example, could leave the country. Customs staff attended on demand - and carried out the necessary

Immigration functions. From speaking to the officer who was present during the visit, it was regarded as a chore and the airport regarded as very low risk. I asked them to flesh out the relevant parts of our skeleton report.

We were due to visit Tilbury the next day and Dover on Thursday. I decided that in order to have fuller information for the preliminary report, we should bring forward our visit to Dover to Wednesday, if it could be managed. So to Bernard fell the unenviable task of contacting the Dover Collectorate office to rearrange. Meanwhile, I asked the rest of the Section to think about what could be done to mitigate the risks in the present system, without worrying about what it might cost or whether it would require changing the law. It seemed better to me to get every possible idea down on paper. We could decide what was sensible and what we would 'prune', in Nigel Seymour's words, later.

At lunchtime, I decided to test whether I was being followed. I had bought a small brochure about the City churches on Saturday and decided to walk to one of the churches that hadn't been affected by the Great Fire of London, St Katharine Cree in Leadenhall Street. It was near enough to visit in my lunch hour, but far enough away for me to try to detect whether anyone was attempting to follow me.

Unfortunately, the City streets were so crowded at that time, it was quite difficult to be certain. I was pretty sure that neither the man nor the woman we had seen in Kelsey Park on Sunday was there, but there were so many men around dressed in suits and women in smart jackets and dresses or blouses and skirts that it was hard to tell someone who might be following me from someone who was innocently enjoying his or her lunch hour. Few people were just ambling around.

Everyone looked as they were going somewhere. And someone following me would look just like that.

I stopped and looked in the occasional shop window, but with all the people walking past, I couldn't really tell whether someone following me had halted too. My best chance was when I went into the church, as it seemed to me my shadow – if I had one – would have to follow me inside. As I entered, I noticed a strange church with what seemed to be to be a mixture of styles – unlike the pure classical design in several of the Wren churches we'd seen on Saturday. I sat down in a place where I hoped I could see people coming in behind me. But for the next quarter of an hour, no-one came in on their own. Moreover, none of them then did what I would have expected someone following me to do. Most either peered round briefly and left or sat - or knelt – and prayed and then went out. I decided that if someone was following me, they were too clever to be caught by a ruse like this. So I went back outside again. There were a few people hanging around outside, but no-one obviously keeping an eye out for me. But then, if they were any good, they wouldn't make it easy for me. Yet if they were trying to send me a message, why didn't they wish to make it more obvious what the message was?

I set off back towards Custom House, but decided to go through Leadenhall Market to pick up some fresh bananas. While I was at the fruit stall, I felt – or persuaded myself – that I could see a young man with longish hair in a dark suit watching me. As I set off, he did too, but he was no longer visible when I crossed Great Tower Street and, after a brief pause to reflect on the ruins of St Dunstan in the East, re-entered Custom House.

I couldn't for the life of me decide whether this was worrying or merely irritating. If it had something to do with my report, whoever it was seemed to have a completely unrealistic view about my place in the great scheme of things. Though I might come up with a report, with lots of details about how Customs controls and procedures relating to exports currently worked, with an analysis of how effective they were and with some ideas as to how any weaknesses might be addressed, the eventual conclusions would say what Commissioner Watling wanted them to say. Whatever I might write, if it was unacceptable to him, it would be 'nuanced'. Indeed, I still recognised the distinct possibility that I might be prepared to sign my name only up to, but not as far as, the conclusions. Did whoever was shadowing me really think I had the influence or the status to determine the outcome of this review? The only thing I could guess was that if I drew up the factual and analysis part of the review in a particular way, any conclusion resulting from it was pre-determined and inescapable. But anyone who knew anything about this matter would surely realise that a black and white outcome was unrealistic in such circumstances? Besides….what did they want? Did they want me to make a deal with the Americans impossible? Or encourage it? Why were these messages so unclear? Was there somewhere a less obscure message that I had somehow missed?

During the afternoon the Section had quite a long discussion about what we might do to make export procedures more secure.

"More staff would enable you to check the documents more thoroughly and faster and also examine more consignments," said Ken.

"But you'd still need someone who knew about this technical stuff to be able to identify it," observed Morry. "So you're either going to have to employ several people with such knowledge, train some staff up or make some sort of arrangement where you could get advice from the right person very quickly."

"That doesn't seem very likely," replied Ken. "You might only need someone with such knowledge a dozen times a year, so you couldn't justify training staff or employing someone full time. And the trouble with getting an expert at short notice is that you're almost always going to have to delay the shipment."

"Presumably we should know where this stuff is going," said Morry. "So we might be able to apply some greater levels of control to them – a bit like excise traders. So we could require them to notify us of anything leaving their premises and we could use our normal powers to check security...."

"But we may not have the powers if they aren't involved with excisable goods. That'd need legislation."

"But if this stuff is so hot, it can't be going to many places and they must be desperate to have it. Surely they'd be happy to accept controls in such circumstances....especially as I guess most of them must be doing stuff for the military."

"It's not clear to me who this stuff is intended for," I intervened. "I agree that it seems likely it'd be restricted and mainly for military purposes. But my impression was it hadn't been developed by the American military, but by commercial businesses. While I suppose they might get enough money from the US Government for a few years, surely they must want to put this technology into computers that are more widely available. So it may be that we might need only temporary controls – for perhaps 5 years – over perhaps a limited number of traders. I do think if we were going to develop controls along these lines, we'd need to know more about how this technology is likely to be used in this country."

"Do you think you can put that in this interim report that's supposed to be going to the Cabinet Committee?" asked Morry.

"I don't see why not. We could set out these ideas while suggesting that we would need to know more before we could firm anything up……..And whether that would provide a sufficient guarantee, I'm still not at all sure."

That evening, I told Rosemary about my excursion at lunchtime and my lack of success.

"Well, at least my father will be pleased you visited a City church," she replied. "That reminds me…." She went on, going over to the window. "Yes, there's that black car parked over there again. I think it's time they had a taste of their own medicine."

She went to the phone and rang the local police station, informing them who she was and telling them about the black car outside, which appeared to be acting suspiciously, possibly with a view to attempting burglary.

We went into our bedroom, keeping the lights off and waited to see what happened next. Within about quarter of an hour, a police car drew up behind the black car. Slightly to my surprise, it made no attempt to drive away. A constable got out and went over to the driver's window of the black car. A conversation ensued. The police car drew away. The black car remained.

About twenty minutes later, the phone rang. I let Rosemary answer it, as I guessed it was for her. After a couple of minutes she returned to the lounge.

"The local police said that they'd spoken to the people in the car. They said they had diplomatic status, but weren't prepared to say where they were from. They claimed they had no interest in us, but were watching a member of a dissident organisation from their country who was currently living under an alias in our block of flats."

"Did they believe them?"

"They didn't really have much choice. The police – local police especially – are very wary about pushing their luck when someone claims diplomatic status."

"But do we believe their story?"

"No we don't. Do you want to go outside and challenge them?"

"No. Not tonight. We've got the registration number and their claim that they've got diplomatic status. I'll ring Iain Cogbill in the morning and add this to what he's supposed to be chasing up for me."

"I hope he regards it as important. I'm beginning to get a bit fed up with constantly being spied on."

"Well, if they're still there tomorrow, perhaps we'll tackle them then."

I took Ken with me to Tilbury, on the basis that, from what I'd seen, Morry was better at putting stuff down on paper and I needed a very first draft of the interim paper to be available for me to look at when we got back. Besides he was working on some mathematical formulae which he claimed would assist in making controls more effective

I recognised a few faces at Tilbury from my stint as a UO (Unattached Officer) there, but no-one appeared particularly welcoming. I could only assume that the local Surveyor or AC (Assistant Collector) had decided to give people the impression that we were some sort of inspection, rather than a review which was making no judgements, merely gathering facts. In practice, it turned out that the port was largely unhelpful for the sort of thing we were talking about. It mainly handled bulk cargoes in large quantities, cars from Ford at Dagenham, live farm animals, grain, etc. If electrical components were exported by this route, they would be in very large quantities and generally be a small number of export entries covering reams of detailed items, at a level of technical detail no-one there could understand.

"Reg Midgley makes 'is own radios and tellies," explained one of the POs, "but even 'e don't understand 'alf of what's on them lists."

As with elsewhere we had visited, it was clear that exports were regarded as of low importance compared to checking imports and few staff were allocated to the work. One had developed quite a bit of expertise in sniffing out dodgy exporters, especially potential arms smugglers to Rhodesia, but even he quailed a bit at the thought of trying to identify certain types of electrical components. He also reminded us that, however effective our controls might be, if someone really wanted to get something through the port – especially outwards where Customs were thin on the ground – there would always be a docker who could be bought. As he hastened to assure us, that wasn't because dockers as a breed were dishonest, merely that among them there was always at least one rotten apple.

We got back to Custom House at half past three. I began to read what Morry had drafted and realised quite quickly from the first paper I'd seen Nigel Seymour draft that it would need to be written in a less down to earth style. Whether I could do it, I was less sure. But I decided I would attempt to produce a ten page interim report, containing a summary of what we had discovered about our export controls and procedures, an analysis of what that meant about their effectiveness and some thoughts about things we might consider to tackle those risks, including seeking greater information about where the American technology would be used. As Morry and I were supposed to be going to Dover the next day, I felt I had to complete it that evening.

By just after six, I put down my pen, satisfied that I had least got everything down on paper in roughly a form I was pleased with. I would have another look at it first thing on Thursday morning.

So I got a later train than usual and was making my way from New Beckenham station, when I saw the black car parked in front of our flats. On the spur of the moment, I went up to the driver's window and beckoned to him to open it. He gestured me away with his hand. So I tapped on the window. But he continued to gesture. I tapped again and he made a very obvious sign of ignoring me, as did his female companion. These seemed to be the two we had seen in Kelsey Park. As he plainly wasn't going to respond to me tapping on the window, I decided that I would return his persecution of us by sitting on his car bonnet. As that got no reaction, I opened my briefcase and took out the evening newspaper and began to read it. After a couple of minutes, the driver wound down his window and called out, in a hoarse whisper, "Will you go away!"

"Why don't you?" I replied, getting off the bonnet and coming over to him. "You've been sitting outside here for days and you've been following me and my wife around. What are you up to?"

"You are mistaken. We have no interest in you or your wife. We are keeping an eye on someone else. We have diplomatic status, as we told the police who set on us last night."

"So if you weren't following us, why did you make such a quick getaway when we tried to approach you in the park on Sunday?"

"We did not want a scene and have our cover blown."

93

"Frankly, I don't believe you. I'll bet it's you that've been sending me obscure messages saying things like 'have you got the message?' And if it wasn't you, I'll bet you know who it was. Anyway, you can tell them from me that Nick Storey doesn't understand what the message means. He hasn't received any message that means anything. Has he got to stop or go? He doesn't know. Encourage them to enlighten me....please!"

"I am sorry. I don't have the faintest idea what you are talking about."

"I find that hard to believe.....But if you don't leave us alone, I'll make sure you can't sit here night after night or keep following us through the streets without being noticed. Calling the police was just the start. I might call the ambulance service and tell them that someone in this car appeared to be having a heart attack. I might report a fire in the neighbourhood. I could probably get some yobs in a local pub to believe that you were a pair of perverts.....Do I need to say more?"

"You would be disrupting important work for our country…"

"Which is?"

"I am not at liberty to say. We shall report this to our Embassy."

"Please feel free to make a complain to the Foreign Office if you wish, but stop following me around.....I'll now go back to my flat and will ring someone to cause you inconvenience shortly."

"You are a fool."

"Possibly. I'd rather you were straight with me, but I don't see what else I can do."

I went into the flat.

"I see you've been having words with our friends in the black car," said Rosemary.

"Yes. They wouldn't tell me anything, of course. But I did tell them that sending obscure messages that don't tell me what they want me to do won't get anyone anywhere."

"I see they're driving away. How did you manage that?"

"I told them I'd find ways to persecute them, like sending the police round....They claimed that they weren't interested in us, but I wasn't convinced."

"Oh well, at least they've gone – for now. How was Tilbury?"

"Unfriendly....I wonder whether they'll be back – or whether they'll be more subtle about it?"

"Oh, I meant to say – we got another envelope with the same message in it – or at least it said 'now do you get the message?' But what message?"

"I just hope they haven't genuinely got me confused for someone else."

However, the black car didn't reappear that night – nor was it apparently replaced by anything else.

I got up early to catch a train to Dover feeling a little more relieved. I met Morry on the train and spent much of the journey getting him to explain how his ideas for providing a more systematic mathematical basis for Customs controls would work.

"It's essentially a mixture of basic data, weightings and probabilities," he began, losing me almost at once. "We know how many export entries go through each port and airport and we could work out how many come from different exporters. That's the basic data. Then you can assess each exporter on the basis of the riskiness of his business and of his previous behaviour. For example, if he's always been as good as gold and is co-operative and, on inspection, appears efficient and competent, and exports stuff that is, let's say, in sealed containers which would be difficult to break into and obvious if you had, and the goods were routine anyway, you might give him a low weighting. Which would mean you'd give his entries a very light touch. So you might just examine one per cent or even less. But if you had an exporter who had a poor reputation, had been caught trying to export prohibited goods before, and dealt with stuff in insecure containers and goods likely to be prohibited or require licences, you'd give him a very high weighting and would check a very high proportion of his consignments. Indeed, whoever was in charge of clearing the goods could probably just look down a table which combined these factors and decide from that whether an export consignment should be examined or not. Part of the control over the unreliable exporters would be that if we gave them a high weighting, they could expect their goods to be delayed for examination more often. That might encourage them to be less dishonest.....And, of course, you'd always need a certain percentage of consignments you checked on a random basis, to test whether what you were doing was achieving what you intended."

"I can see that would make export controls better targeted and make better use of the time of Customs staff, but it wouldn't make it any easier to identify highly technical stuff even if you had stopped the consignment to examine it."

"I agree. My ideas don't get you that far. In such circumstances, I think our best bet would be to clear the consignments at the exporter's premises, with any experts we needed present at that stage. Then the goods could be moved under a Customs seal."

"We probably couldn't do something like that on a widespread basis – but for a small number of exporters using stuff which it was absolutely essential to avoid getting out to the Soviets, it might be possible."

"Of course, all these processes will soon be carried out on computers. The Heathrow people and the agents there are already talking about a computer that would log freight and possibly passengers as well. If we could get our fingers into that little pie, some of this mathematical stuff I've been talking about could be added in, so that we'd be able to manage the clearance process, including physical exams, much better."

"I'll reflect all this in a fairly general way in the interim report which I'm aiming to finish tomorrow morning. If you want to write something in more detail, I'd be happy to fit it into the final report – though it might have to be as one of these 'annexes' Seymour and people like that seem so keen on."

Looking occasionally out of the window, I realised that we were passing through very much the same countryside as Rosemary and I had passed through on our way to Lympne Airport.

At Dover Marine station, close to the Western Docks, we were met by the AC John Peters, an amiable, friendly middle-aged man, whose enthusiasm for what was happening at Dover was immense and infectious.

"This place is booming and it's only just the start," he explained. "The Dover Harbour Board have incredibly ambitious plans to reclaim great areas round the harbour here, so that four times as many ships can dock here, unload – mainly lorries – pick up more lorries and get away within as short a time as possible. They believe that future trade is going to go primarily by road – in large lorries or in containers, though they reckon Felixstowe is better placed to benefit from containers than they are here – purely because of shortage of space. They're constantly on at us to use less space. Ideally they'd like us out of the harbour area altogether and they certainly hate our requirements for physical exams."

"Does much freight travel by rail?" I asked.

"Virtually none. Here it's almost entirely passengers. MIB is tiny and dying. If it's small and so valuable you need someone to keep an eye on it, these days you'll go by air not by rail and sea....You're interested in export controls, I know...Well, here in the Western Docks, it's essentially rail passengers. Our sole interest is the currency restrictions. We ask virtually everyone who exits and do a light search of less than one per cent and we've found absolutely nothing. Your average rail passenger isn't likely to be carrying five hundred pounds. The people with that sort of money go by air."

We made our way round to the eastern docks, where all the great schemes of the Dover Harbour Board were starting to take shape. The Customs offices were in several pre-fabricated buildings with a separate examination bay, where lorries and cars could be searched.

"We don't really have anything that could merit the term 'long room'," said Peters. "Because this is the best accommodation the Harbour Board are prepared to give us, it's all rather crowded and cluttered, as you can see...Our export section is over here."

The export section consisted of a DCA and two DCAs under the supervision of Mike Evans, an OCX. The latter explained that most exports through Dover these days came in lorries. The number of consignments – and therefore entries – for any lorry could vary enormously. Of course, if you pulled one consignment for examination, all the rest would have to be delayed. So, not surprisingly, export consignments were rarely examined. Because the IB believed that this so-called 'roll on/roll off' traffic was vulnerable to smuggling, quite a lot of imports were examined, which meant that the limited space in the examination bays was quickly filled up. It was not uncommon for lorries awaiting examination to be parked all over the harbour. In addition, there were substantial numbers of consignments of agricultural produces from Holland, including my old friends from my Harwich days, cut flowers. Min of Ag requirements hadn't changed, so significant numbers of these also joined the queues for physical checks.

"Frankly, it's a logistical nightmare," observed Peters, in a phrase that suggested an Armed Forces background. "And the Harbour Board don't really want to help. They just want everything out of here as fast as possible. There's little enough space as it is and they're on my back pretty well every day about lorries awaiting physical checks. They may be forward looking, but on a day to day basis, they're a pain in the behind."

"So do you physically check any export consignments?" I asked.

"Unless we had an IB tip-off, frankly, no. I know what it says in Instructions, but we don't have the space or the time – and they just aren't seen as risky enough....I suppose if one of Mike Evans's section spotted something really odd, we might pull it for examination. But it hasn't happened yet in my time here."

Just standing and watching the lorries thundering on to one ship and off another, I could understand why the Dover Harbour Board saw this method of transport as the way of the future. It was quick and neat. Consignments could go to a depot inland and be despatched by a smaller lorry or van to their ultimate destination. Similarly, exporters could send their consignments to a local depot, where they would be consolidated into a load for a container lorry.

"Do we exercise any controls over the places where the consignments are put into containers?" I asked.

"We don't. The controls are still exercised at the frontiers. If you ask me, it'd make a lot of sense in a place like this if all the export stuff was controlled at consolidation depots, so we got all the export stuff under Customs seal. We could then just check the seals as necessary and let them just roll through. If you could suggest that in your report, we'd be eternally grateful….and the Harbour Board would probably buy you an extremely good lunch."

"It's certainly worth thinking about – especially as this seems to be the way things are going."

"If you don't mind…looking at the time, we are invited to join the Harbour Manager from the Harbour Board for a spot of lunch. These chaps have their ears very close to the ground and when they learnt there was someone from Customs HQ coming today, they couldn't lose the opportunity to bend your ears about a few of their main gripes. Take my advice – don't commit to anything. Just say you're carrying out a nation-wide review and though it'll take local issues into account, you can't promise anything specific."

"Thanks. I'm happy to follow your advice."

He walked us over to a rather more salubrious building in the centre of the harbour. The reception area was smart and vaguely naval. As we went up the stairs to the first floor, I looked out of the large glass window. At the edge of the docks – just outside the area where permits were required to enter – was standing a man I felt I recognised. But almost immediately my hand was being grasped by a keen looking man, with dark, brylcreemed hair and a smile that was a little too easy.

"Roger Winstanley, Harbour Manager," he exclaimed, shaking my hand vigorously. "You're from

Customs and Excise headquarters in London, I believe….."

Over sandwiches and fruit juice, he pumped me for information about the report and pressed me hard to include reference for the need for Customs to speed up procedures and reduce the amount of physical examination taking place at the port. Arguing that trade was the country's lifeblood, he told us that Dover would soon be one of the main arteries, indeed, probably the one where the blood flowed fastest. The only thing that could slow this down, he claimed, were the antediluvian processes of HM Customs and Excise. John Peters felt moved to point out that many people wouldn't welcome the country being overwhelmed with drugs or our tobacco industry ravaged by smuggled cigarettes. He also reminded Winstanley that many of the controls exercised by Customs were at the behest of other Government Departments, like the Min of Ag, some of whose requirements were enshrined in law or international agreements. I got the distinct feeling that they had enjoyed similar conversations before. I stuck rigidly to the line which he had suggested. Not that Winstanley wasn't doing his job. It seemed to me he was making perfectly sensible points from his perspective. The only thing I didn't like about the man was his chain smoking.

Afterwards John Peters apologised that we had been required to endure a lunch of that nature. "I had in mind finding a nice local pub," he said, "but Roger's never one to lose an opportunity."

That was that, however. I must say it was nice to meet an AC who was such a decent, friendly man. He looked like my idea of a gentleman farmer and probably voted as an old-fashioned Tory, but he eschewed the discourtesy and rank-consciousness so prevalent in many of his fellows.

101

As we got back on the train at Dover Marine, I could have sworn that the man I had seen earlier followed us on. But as it happened in an instant and in the corner of my eye, just as I was thanking John Peters, I couldn't be certain.

As we travelled back, Morry and I agreed that our experience at Dover reinforced our earlier discussion about encouraging at least some exports to be cleared inland, either on the exporter's premises or at one of these places where consignments were consolidated. If for certain exporters we had some sort of early warning arrangement, it might also be possible to ensure that an appropriate expert was available. I changed at Bromley South for a Beckenham Junction train and arrived home about an hour earlier than usual. Again, I felt that among the people who alighted at Bromley South was the man who I thought was following me, but no-one seemed to cross to the platform and await the Beckenham train with me. Perhaps I had got so jumpy that I was beginning to see shadows!

When I got outside our flats, I noticed with relief that the black car hadn't returned. There was one of those commercial vans with no windows in the back. It didn't have the firm's name, but there was no-one in the front and it was shut up, so I assumed there must be some work going on nearby. It was only when I noticed it was still there as I made my way to work the next morning that I began to ask myself questions about it. But when I peered inside, it seemed to be empty. Indeed, all I could see on the floor of the passenger side was a scrap of paper with some symbol on it. It looked like a circle behind a 'T' with a thick semi-circle coming from the middle of the stem of the 'T'. Presumably some sort of trader's symbol. If it hadn't been for the coincidence of the van appearing so soon after the black car had moved, I would have said it had been abandoned there. Anyway, I noted its number plate, which, along with that of the black car, I passed on to Iain Cogbill - or, more accurately, one of his Section – shortly after I arrived at work.

I spent the first part of the morning revising my draft of the interim report and then got Bernard to take it over to the typing pool in King's Beam House for urgent typing in duplicate. By lunchtime, it was ready and he went back and collected it, the top copy going to Nigel Seymour. The carbon copy I retained for my inevitable discussion with Seymour about the finer points of drafting. I wasn't therefore surprised to be summoned at around 4 pm.

To my surprise and slight pleasure, my draft had considerably less blue biro on it than I had expected.

"A lot of this is purely factual," he explained, "so all I've done is tighten up the drafting a bit. But I'm rather concerned about two aspects. The first is where you are seeking to know more about the American stuff. At the moment, we can keep this on a 'restricted' basis, but once we start mentioning that, we'll have to re-classify it as 'confidential' and then we'll have to follow all the procedures like double-enveloping and anything will have to be typed in Division. Do you think it's absolutely necessary?"

"That depends on what you want," I replied. " If you want to say we've got various options for mitigating the risks of this stuff being exported, but we couldn't give a guarantee of at best, say, sixty per cent, you could leave it out. On the other hand, we believe that if we could exercise the controls primarily at the premises of the firms who'll be using the American stuff, we could probably increase the level of the guarantee significantly."

"To a hundred per cent?"

"I wouldn't ever give such a guarantee. If this stuff really is small, it'd only take a corrupt person working for the firm to walk out with it in his pocket or briefcase. Of course, if the firm has rigorous security procedures, that would eliminate some of that risk. But suppose the Managing Director is corruptible – do you believe he'd be stopped and searched every time he left the premises?"

"I can see your years in the Outfield have left an indelible mark of cynicism."

"I prefer to call it realism. If this stuff is as valuable to the Soviets as we're being told, it's presumably worth their while to offer the right person a very large amount of money to get their hands on it. Or they may be able to blackmail someone. Indeed, I assume it's something the security people are thinking about. If the Soviets know there's someone here in a convenient place who they know they can blackmail, they may actually be keen for us to get this stuff...."

"But that's no concern for us.....I'll leave it in, but I think it could be worded more elegantly. My second concern is about the conclusions. The draft doesn't really set out a firm conclusion. We're not really giving the Committee any kind of steer."

"That's because it's an interim report and I don't feel confident we can draw a firm conclusion. I believe we need to know more about where this stuff is going, as I've said. Also some of this has implications for staff numbers and locations and I've no idea whether we have the legal powers needed to make our ideas work."

"Why don't we set out some options? That might encourage the Committee to agree we could dismiss some and concentrate on the others. That would save time in drawing up the final report."

"That's possible, though in some cases it might not be 'either-or', but 'both'."

"Let me see what I can do with it."

So I sat there while he scribbled away, sometimes amending his own draft. He plainly had a very fast mind, but I also felt he was thinking too quickly, without giving himself enough time to reflect. Moreover, some of the alterations to my draft seemed to me to be fussy or entirely a matter of personal taste, without foundation in grammar or comprehensibility. After about twenty minutes, he pushed the papers over to me and I read them through. By and large, he accepted any suggestion I had which I could base on fact or evidence, but anything to do with the organisation of the draft was ignored. At the end I felt, as someone like Seymour might put it, not dissatisfied, but not really satisfied with the outcome. But anyway, this peculiar process was over and the papers passed to the Divisional typist to type as a 'confidential' document, to be sent to Commissioner Watling that evening. Seymour suggested that I should expect to be summoned to the Commissioner's office the following day and that, rather than send my copy of the draft over to Custom House, with all the security 'fiddle-faddle', I should collect it on my way to the fourth floor.

I had left my Section to continue filling in the flesh of the full report. It seemed increasingly important to me that we should have a document that set out exactly what we had seen and learnt, what our ideas and suggestions, analysis and proposals were and that it could be placed on record somewhere. However, now that it appeared it contained material deemed to be 'confidential', I explained that we would need to handle it rather more carefully, in accordance with the Instructions for handling such material. That sent all of us to our Instructions, to find out what that entailed.

The van was still parked outside our flats when I got home, but with no visible sign of life. Rosemary had snooped round it as well and had come to the same uneasy conclusion as me. But at least we seemed to have been spared any more of the anonymous messages for the past two days. So perhaps they had been posted by the people in the black car.

As Seymour had predicted, we were summoned to see Commissioner Watling at noon the following day. For over an hour we - or more accurately, I should say, they – picked over the draft virtually word by word, often discussing the appropriateness of a particular adjective or adverb. At the end of this process, Seymour was bidden to go away and produce a 'clean copy' in the light of their endeavours, which we would all consider on Monday morning. Meanwhile Seymour was bidden to draft a 'covering paper' for the Committee. This task he happily delegated to me, saying all I needed to do was describe what was in our interim report, 'headline' any conclusions and set out any actions we wished the Committee to undertake, including which aspects we wanted them to discuss or merely 'take note'. I took this task away, fully confident that virtually every word I wrote would be changed when my draft landed on his desk sometime later Monday morning.

But at least I had the weekend to look forward to. It would have been even better, if I hadn't received another envelope containing the familiar message "Have you got the message yet?". I felt like opening the window and shouting out "No! I bloody well haven't!" as loudly as I could. But all there was out there was this apparently abandoned Commer van.

On Saturday night Rosemary took me to a concert at the Royal Festival Hall. Though her violin had travelled with us to Stoke Newington and then on to our new flat in Beckenham, she had barely touched it. But she owned several LPs of classical violin music which she listened to sometimes. The only knowledge I had of classical music was attempts by music teachers at school to interest us, which had failed. At home, if any music was played at all, it was light music on the radio – generally abused by my father as 'candy floss', while he regarded classical music as bourgeois. But as Rosemary was desperate to hear this virtuoso young violinist Itzhak Perlman, I was content to go along with her, even though I feared I wouldn't really appreciate it.

Our seats were in a strange place behind the orchestra, but when Rosemary had booked, they were all that were left. The first item was an overture to a Mozart opera, which was lively and jolly. Then everyone clapped as Itzhak Perlman made his way on to the stage. I was amazed to see that he walked with crutches, but Rosemary whispered that he'd had polio as a child. But when he started playing a violin concerto by Bruch, it was clear that his handicap meant absolutely nothing. I couldn't imagine that a violin could sound so wonderful or that classical music could move me so much. I could tell that Rosemary, with her head resting against my shoulder, had tears streaming down her cheeks and even more prosaic I had tears in my eyes.

"It's really when I hear violinists like him that make me not want to pick up my violin," said Rosemary during the interval. "When I play, it sounds so dismal by comparison."

"On that basis, there'd only be about half a dozen violinists playing anywhere in the world," I observed.

"The trouble is, the longer it gets, the more out of practice I know I'll be and the worse it'll sound....Besides, I can't imagine you'd want to hear me scraping away."

"I'll admit there are other things I'd rather get up to when we're together…"

"Perhaps I'll get it out when we have children. I think it's important children should appreciate music – and not just pop."

The second half consisted of a symphony by Tchaikovsky. Though it had passages that failed to maintain my interest, it contained several haunting tunes and made me realise that perhaps I should be rather more open minded about this area of music than I had been. Inevitably, during the less gripping passages, I wondered whether we had been followed, but the one place you could be sure you would be unable to tell was a concert like this. And the crowded late evening train back to New Beckenham was no better.

"It was nice of you to come to the concert, especially when you're not interested in that sort of thing," said Rosemary, as we lay next to each other on our sofa having a mug of tea.

"I enjoyed it – more than I expected to. So if you want to book concerts in the future, I'll be happy to come along.......It'd be nice to see the front of the orchestra sometime, though!"

Sunday was rainy, but we went for a long walk under a large umbrella through the quiet leafy streets of our part of Beckenham and along Brackley Road to Beckenham Place Park. If we were followed, they did it much more professionally than the couple the previous weekend, because we saw no-one. On my own, I would never have chosen to do this, but with Rosemary, it felt that the umbrella and the rainstorm kept us in a little world where there was just the two of us

As always, the weekend was too short. I arrived at work with the feeling that I was about to spend a couple of hours producing a draft of which, if a quarter remained in the final version, I would have done well. By mid-afternoon, I was again in Commissioner

Watling's room to sit through a meeting that consisted purely of discussion about words, often, in my humble opinion, with little connection to the substance. At any rate, a paper and interim report which satisfied Watling and Seymour and to which I couldn't object, was completed by about 4.30, to be re-typed that evening and sent – in the correct format and under the appropriate security measures – to the Cabinet Office the following morning.

In summary, what we were saying was that current export systems fell between the two stools of facilitating exports and attempting to control a small number of prohibited and restricted items. For many of these items, this system was probably good enough, but for the sort of small, extremely high value items that we were concerned with, the current system could not provide an adequate guarantee. The main risks were that these items could be easily concealed, including being hidden among large consignments of apparently indistinguishable items, and transported out of the UK by many different routes, many of which would be difficult to control a hundred per cent of the time. There were, however, things we could do to improve this position. Controls more targeted on the individual exporter appeared to offer the best chance for improvement. But before we could be more categoric (a word particularly favoured by Commissioner Watling), we would need to know more about the prospective usage of the US technology, in particular the number and nature of the firms that would be involved. If we were given this information, we could proceed to the next stage of our report, which would be to work with these firms to identify the nature of their controls and whether or how Customs might be able to provide a greater guarantee against any of this critical technology leaking out to 'hostile interests'. As Watling explained, that was common parlance within Whitehall to cover not just the Soviet bloc, but also the Chinese and the French.

That appeared to be that for now. I was able to return to working on the main report. But, in practice, there was only a limited amount more we could do. We had added all the material we had gleaned from recent visits, as well as the results of various conversations about possible ways of improving controls over exports. Morry had added several pages on how a more quantitative approach could improve our effectiveness in dealing with exports.

I decided that I would let Ken and Morry do the visit to Newhaven on Wednesday. I guessed it was not dissimilar to Harwich and felt I'd seen enough of that sort of environment to know pretty well how exports were managed there. Really we needed to go to a regional airport, like Birmingham or Manchester, and somewhere like Hull. But I was beginning to feel that the law of diminishing returns was rapidly setting in. These would involve overnight stays, which would add to the cost of the report and I had grave doubts as to whether it could be justified. I concluded that I would await the outcome of the discussion at Committee MISC 38 on Friday before making any further plans. If we got approval to learn more about what was expected to happen if we got this American technology, it would be sensible to plan the rest of our time in relation to that. In particular, the most helpful thing, so it seemed to me, would be for us to visit the premises of those firms who would be using the technology and both inspect their controls and see how willing they would be to be subject to some degree of control by Customs at their premises.

As we were all at a bit of a loose end, I suggested that Ken and Morry, assisted as necessary by Bernard, should start turning the rather unwieldy and amorphous beast that the full report had become into something that might resemble a typical report better. To start off with, I suggested they might want to look at some of the reports that were stored in the King's Beam House Library, so that they could see how such reports were structured and the sort of language they used.

While they continued this work on the Wednesday, I went over to the King's Beam House Library myself, first to check that Paul Barton-Jones was getting on with the task I had set him. Eventually I caught up with him in the Sols Office Library, where he told me he expected to have completed his work by the end of the week. I suggested that he then wrote it up in a form that could be a factual annex to the report and arrange to get it typed. Afterwards I went back to the main Library to learn more about Cabinet Office committees and also about computers. I realised that I was woefully ignorant about the latter and if I was going to visit the premises of firms engaged in this business, I needed a greater understanding of what they were, what they could do – and also of the jargon. I realised that Rosemary already knew a lot more than me, but neither of us regarded our evenings as time to teach each other about our work. The more I read, the more I was both interested and also realised the tremendous depth of my ignorance.

I left work slightly later than usual – mainly because I had spent so much time in the Library in King's Beam House that I hadn't realised how late it had got. And then I felt compelled to go back to Custom House to check that all our documents had been securely locked away in the combination. Of course, they had – but I wasn't prepared to take a chance. And I was further delayed by a couple of phone calls – evidently wrong numbers, as the caller hung up the moment I answered. I just missed a train and the next one was cancelled. So with mounting frustration, I eventually got a train over an hour later than I had intended. I just hoped Rosemary hadn't planned to cook something that might be spoiled.

I was walking towards our flats from New Beckenham Station when I realised that there were several police cars outside the flats blocking the road and an ambulance standing in the car park. I hastened my steps. Just as I got to the building next to our flats a policeman stopped me.

"What's going on?" I demanded.

"There's been some sort of explosion in one of the flats next door," he replied.

"I live in one of them," I said.

"I'm sorry. You can't go through."

I crossed the road, in order to get a better view of where the explosion had occurred. At that stage I was thinking about the gas central heating installed in all the flats. But the moment I looked over, I could see there was an immense hole in the front of one of the flats – our flat! The lounge window was completely smashed and the surroundings seemed blackened with smoke.

I ran over to the nearest policeman.

"That's my flat where there was the explosion!" I cried out. "My wife may have been in there. I must go in!"

"I don't think you should…" he began, but I ducked round him and ran up to the flats.

There was another constable standing by the front door.

"It's my flat where this explosion has happened," I said, as calmly as I could. "I insist that I'm allowed up to see what has happened. My wife may well have been in there. I must see how she is."

"I don't think you want…" he began, but I pushed past him and ran up the stairs.

The scene that greeted me in our flat was practically indescribable. The explosion had completely wrecked the lounge, smashing the furniture and the glass wall at the back into smithereens. The walls were blackened and much of the ceiling had fallen down. There were craters in the blackened floor as well. I couldn't imagine this was just a gas explosion.

Then I saw it, a blackened, bleeding, mutilated body – just a torso. Much of the clothes had been blasted off it, but I could see bits of the shiny black plastic mac which I'd bought for Rosemary the Christmas before last. I noticed a leg lying incongruously by the shattered door of our store cupboard. I sank to the floor, in shocked disbelief.

"Who are you?" demanded a man in plain clothes, presumably a detective.

"I'm her husband," I croaked. "What happened?"

"We think it was some kind of missile – about an hour ago now."

"I think it was intended for me," was all I could say.

I knelt there, by the last remains of my darling Rosemary. Her body had been torn apart, desecrated, obscenely smashed into pieces. I couldn't even see her head. In the very place where we had been at our happiest, she had died, suddenly, horribly and for what? The realisation dawned swiftly - it wasn't her that was supposed to have been killed. It was me. My poor Rosemary had been brutally murdered instead of me. Why hadn't I taken those messages more seriously? Why hadn't bloody Cogbill done more about them? Why hadn't I come home at my usual time? Then it would be me lying there and Rosemary might still be alive. That was what should've happened. That battered mound of flesh should be me, not her.

Then I couldn't help myself. I collapsed into tears, immense heaving tears that poured out from my soul like a tidal wave. My throat was aching, my stomach burning, my heart aching with a pain that nothing could heal. I howled in anguish. I rose and tried to batter my head against the wall, beat my hands against the wall. It took two policemen to restrain me.

I stood stock still. I couldn't believe that was all that was left of my Rosemary, now covered under a blanket. How could I have let this happen? How could I live on after this? Rosemary was my world, my life, my heart, my soul. Without her, I had nothing. Without her, the world was utterly empty, completely barren. I couldn't continue to live in such a world. I would kill myself – and I would do it now.

Without thinking, I rushed towards the window, thinking to throw myself out. But a couple of policeman grabbed me and held me, kicking and shouting that they hadn't the right to stop me. But they held me firmly until I felt the sharp jab of a needle in my arm and I remembered nothing more.

SIX
SEARCHING FOR ANSWERS

When I awoke, I realised I was in a strange bed. I looked in front of me. Evidently I was in a hospital. Then I remembered. My heart sank. I closed my eyes. I wanted to keep them closed – to life, to everything. My Rosemary was dead, killed in the most horrible way, her lovely body torn apart. And it should have been me. I was doubly guilty. Not only was the missile aimed at me. I should have done something, anything to prevent it. Rosemary was more precious to me than my own life. Now I had got her killed. With cold certainty I vowed to myself that I would kill myself the soonest an opportunity arose. I suspected that I would be prevented from doing it for a time. I'd already alerted people to my state of mind. But I could dissemble. I'd tell them that all I wanted to do was to find the people who'd killed my wife and kill them. Indeed, it was just possible I might do that and then kill myself. But there was not the slightest possibility that I could continue to live long in a world without Rosemary. The light had utterly gone out of my life. My life had died with Rosemary. I remembered that battered, burnt, half-naked torso on the floor of what had been our home and almost retched with horror and self-disgust.

Suddenly I felt someone stroking my hair. I turned to look. The person doing it resembled Rosemary. I could only assume that whatever drugs they had given me were giving me hallucinations. This was presumably just a nurse. Or was I, despite my beliefs, already in heaven? No – I was just seeing what I wanted more desperately than anything I'd ever wanted before.

115

"Nick," her voice spoke. "I really am here. It wasn't my body in the flat."

I sat up and looked at her. It really was her. She gave that smile that had bewitched me when we first met. I couldn't take this. I clung to her shoulder and wept and wept. Tears coursed down my face and I shuddered with the pain of my emotions.

"They said you tried to kill yourself," she added sternly. "You should know I'd never want that."

"You're alive!" I croaked, my mouth and throat dry and sore. "But that looked just like you...your coat...."

"It was somebody else. I got delayed. I didn't get to the flat until after you, and they wouldn't let me through – even though I told them who I was and it was our flat. It was only when I saw them taking you out that I was able to be with you. A constable told me you'd tried to kill yourself and they'd given you a knock-out drug so you wouldn't wake for at least twelve hours."

"So what time is it?"

"Just after 9.30. Don't worry. Both your work and mine know what's happened, so nobody expects us in today."

"I can't believe it. You're alive. I thought my world had come to an end!"

I held her close to me, both of us close to yet more tears.

"You know you are the light of my life. Without you, my world would be completely empty," I said.

"Please don't say things like that," she replied, trying to smile through her tears. "It's so wonderful, but it hurts so much.....I was sitting here watching you during the night. You looked so peaceful. But I knew what agonies you must've gone through. If I'd been in your position, I couldn't't've borne it either.....and I kept

116

thinking, what would've happened if the police hadn't stopped you."

"Well, I think I was trying to jump out of the lounge window," I explained. "I don't think I'd've done a very good job."

"No – from the first floor, I think it would've been a broken leg and collar-bone and a few cracked ribs."

We both started to laugh and continued to laugh hysterically. A nurse came in, presumably thinking such behaviour was out of place. After all, an unknown woman had been horribly murdered in our flat.

"I see you're awake, Mr Storey. As you can see, Mrs Storey wasn't the person killed in your flat."

"I'm sorry for her – though I don't know what she was doing inside our flat. But I can't tell you how I feel knowing that Rosemary isn't dead."

"From what I heard last night, I think I can guess…..I suggest that you give some thought to how you don't suffer the same misfortune again – but perhaps for real next time…..I believe a detective would like to talk to you about that."

"Please ask him to come in."

The detective who entered turned out to be Mike Elliott, who we had last seen at a meeting in an obscure office in Bloomsbury more than two years previously. Though I had no idea of his present rank or job, I knew he was working in Special Branch then.

"The moment I heard the name Storey, I knew there'd be trouble," he remarked. "You two seem to have a knack for attracting it. Do you know anything about this? You realise someone fired some sort of highly explosive missile directly at your flat with the clear aim of killing whoever was inside?"

"I did notice that much…… I can tell you what I know. I started work a few weeks ago on a report looking into how effective Customs controls on exports are. There's the possibility of some deal with the Americans about some high tech stuff which depends on our ability to give a guarantee that the stuff won't leak out to the Russians. All my part is to produce a report on the Customs controls, in what ways they could be strengthened and then to give a view on the level of guarantee that we might offer. But all my stuff gets a thorough going-over by various senior people in the Department, who are quite likely to substitute their own evaluation and recommendations for mine. Not long after I started work on this, we started to get envelopes posted through our door – without a stamp, of course – with a series of notes written in blue biro in capitals saying things like 'have you got the message?'. But we never got any message to tell us what the actual message was. Also when we had a weekend in Paris, we were sure we were being followed and we also think we've been followed round here. For several days, a black car parked outside the flats every evening, but when I confronted them last week, they went away and haven't come back. There's been a Commer van there, but I could never see anyone in it."

"It wasn't there when the police got to the scene after the missile had been fired. I think you should assume that if you were being watched, they were doing it from inside the van.....But why didn't you report any of this?"

"I did – to Iain Cogbill. He's the one with the contacts and I assumed he'd get on with it. He certainly said he would."

"I haven't heard anything. But it could easily have gone to a different area – or even to the security people."

"I set the local police on the people in the black car," added Rosemary, "but they claimed they had diplomatic status and that they were watching someone else."

"That's really all we know" I continued. "I've never received any message in relation to the work I've been doing. I could understand it if I'd had a message telling me to make sure my report prevented the American stuff from coming here – or made sure that it did. But I've never even had a whisper. The messages stopped last week. Since then, the only thing that's happened is that we've sent an interim version of the report to the Cabinet Office for a committee to discuss on Friday….tomorrow."

"It's all very strange…." remarked Mike Elliott.

"Do you know the name of the poor woman who was killed was?"

"You wouldn't have seen last night, but apparently she had with her some equipment for bugging your flat. I imagine she was dressed like WPS Storey so that she wouldn't be suspected. But whether whoever fired the missile was aiming at her in particular, but just waited until the light was switched on in the lounge, isn't clear….We're not absolutely certain, but it's highly likely that she's an employee of the East German Embassy. We've informed them and asked for her dental records."

"You don't think the missile might've been aimed specifically at her?" asked Rosemary.

"We can't really say at the moment."

"At least her being there doing what you think she was doing might explain something," Rosemary went on. "I had a curious evening yesterday. I was just packing up to go home when my phone rang and a woman's voice asked me to go and see a Chief Superintendant I'd never even heard of in Old Scotland Yard, which is quite a walk. When I got there, no-one knew anything about the call. So I had to go all the way back to my office. Then there was a message left on my desk by someone from Reception telling me that my husband had called and asked me to get some tea on my way home. I'd already missed a couple of trains and then had to get the tea from the late shop in the High Street after I arrived in Beckenham, which was why I arrived so late. I assume that this woman needed to look like me arriving home, so she wouldn't be noticed, so I had to be delayed."

"I'm sorry for the woman, but thank God for that!" I exclaimed, atheist as I was.

"Well, you clearly can't go back to your flat," said Mike Elliott. "And it seems likely that you're still at risk. If these people – whoever they are – were intending to kill one or both of you, they'll realise before too long that they failed. So they may well try again. I'll get on to my people to find a safe house for you – and some protection. If they were really professional, someone will've stuck around to see what happened. So they may know already that you're both still alive. Your bedroom was virtually unscathed, so when you're ready, we can take you over there and you can get some clothes and anything else you need that isn't damaged and bring it with you to the safe house. I should warn you though – it's likely to be much closer to central London."

"I don't think we care where it is at the moment," I replied. "Just as long as we're together.."

"..and safe," added Rosemary.

I found my clothes and managed to have a shower and dressed. Then a policeman drove us to our devastated flat and we collected as many clothes as we could and put them in suitcases which fortunately had been stored under our bed. I also packed anything else I thought might be useful in the coming weeks.

"I wonder when we'll get back here?" mused Rosemary.

"Are you sure you want to, after all that's happened?"

"Yes. Of course. No-one must be allowed to push us out of our home. I want our babies to start their lives here, where we've been so happy."

I took her in my arms and stroked her hair while she wept on my shoulder. The shock of seeing our ruined flat and the realisation that it could so easily have been her there when the missile was fired suddenly overwhelmed her. She had been so brave for me. Now it was my turn to comfort her.

"Once we've finished with it as a crime scene," said the constable uncomfortably, "you can get on with getting all this sorted out. It's amazing how well these things can be repaired. After fires...."

"I assume people will know how to get in touch with us?" I asked. "I don't know whether this has got into the press, but I expect it will sooner or later and we've got parents and friends who we'll need to contact."

"You'd best discuss that with Chief Inspector Elliott," he replied. "We're just guarding the place. Special Branch are in charge here now."

"Do you mind if we stay here on our own just for a moment?" I said. "We'd like to be alone just for a while. We aren't going to do anything foolish."

"All right. I'll be just outside."

"What's the matter?" asked Rosemary, drying her eyes on the corner of the bed-sheet.

"I want to do something. And I want to do it today," I replied. "Do you trust me, Rosemary?"

"Of course....Well, generally....What are you up to?"

"Just standing here has made me angry. I don't get angry often. And I don't get hot-angry. I get cold-angry. I get energetic-angry. I don't want to spend the next few weeks hidden away in some safe house guarded by the police. I want to get some answers. I want to know who did this. And I have to do something today. It's possible that it's the only day I may be able to get some answers and I'm probably the only person who can ask them."

"I don't understand what you mean."

"I need to get to London. I've no doubt I can get away from this young bobby if I need to. But I need you to tell Mike Elliott where I'll be. I'll be by the Kent platforms at Victoria station at 4 o'clock and I'll come quietly. But you can tell him I'm not going to be a prisoner. If they want me to attend this Cabinet Office meeting on Friday, I intend to do so. Similarly, I intend to complete my report. If that means I have to have a bobby shadowing me all the time, so be it."

"How can you risk yourself again after this?" she cried, tears filling her eyes.

"Because this bit – at least what I've got to do today – only I can do. I'm not going to sit around waiting for them to take another shot at us. Do you really believe we can be completely safe in one of these safe houses? I think we're better off doing our damnedest to find out who these people are who tried to kill us."

"You know I trust you, Nick. But please remember what you felt when you thought I was dead. I don't want to feel like that. So be completely careful. Don't be brave and take risks, just because you're angry."

"I promise I won't."

We set off back to the police station, but just as we were at the traffic lights by Beckenham Junction station, I opened the car door and leapt out. I ran down to the station and tried to conceal myself as best I could in case the policeman came after me, but I knew he would be unable to leave his car at the traffic lights and would have to wait until they changed and then find somewhere to park, always assuming Rosemary didn't try to hamper his efforts or talk him out of following me. Anyway, I never saw him before a London train appeared.

Suspecting that telephone calls might be made while I was on the train, I slipped off at Herne Hill and got a couple of buses into the centre. I found a telephone box with a phone book with the address of the East German Embassy. I made my way there by bus, not least because I reckoned that if I was being followed, it was the easiest way to tell. However, I didn't think I was being shadowed.

When I got to the embassy, I was, inevitably, stopped by a security guard.

"I have information about the death last night of one of your embassy officials," I said in German. "I need to see the appropriate person about it."

He spoke into his walkie-talkie.

"Go ahead to the reception desk," he said.

I went through the revolving doors and into a large lobby, where an unfriendly middle-aged woman with badly-dyed red hair, awaited me.

"Your name?" she demanded, in a thick German accent.

"I'm Nicholas Storey. Your colleague was killed in my flat last night. I have some information about it. I wish to speak to the appropriate person."

"I wasn't aware that anyone from our embassy had died."

"Then perhaps you will check with your security colleagues. I understand the British authorities have been in touch with you about dental records."

"I know nothing about this. What is your purpose in coming here?"

"I have what I consider is useful information for your colleagues. If you wish me to go away without speaking to them, I can do so."

"Wait. I will telephone."

She spoke rapidly into the phone in German, with her hand in front of her mouth in an attempt to prevent me from hearing what she was saying. In vain – but I chose not to comment at that stage.

"You must wait."

I waited for about ten minutes, then a military attaché came out of a door on the far side of the lobby. Of course, he wasn't in uniform, but the haircut, gait and general manner betrayed his profession. He had the broad face I associated with northern Germans.

"You are Storey? You claim to know something about the death of a colleague from this embassy?" He spoke in English. His accent betrayed him as a Mecklenburger.

"I am and I do." I replied in German.

"You can tell me what you have to say." He reverted to his native tongue.

"No. You and I both know why your colleague was where she was. We shall share information – or you will get nothing from me."

"Why should we do this? What can you possibly tell us?"

"We have a mutual interest in discovering who killed your colleague – unless you already know, of course."

"And what if you have nothing of interest to tell us?"

"Then you can tell me nothing. But unless you give me your word as an officer that if what I tell you has some value and you will reciprocate, I shan't tell you

124

anything. I came here to be helpful. I'm sorry your colleague was killed – not least because I believe the missile that killed her was meant for me or my wife. My only concern is to try and find the bastards who killed your colleague and tried to kill me. Do you understand that?"

"I think we had better come through … You speak German quite well …"

"I lived in West Berlin for a while."

He took me into a small, sparse office, with a black and white photograph of Walter Ulbricht on the wall behind his desk.

"Very well. What have you to say?"

"You and I both know why your colleague was in my flat. The equipment she was going to install was found by her body. I believe you wished to listen to my conversations because of work I am doing for Customs and Excise in relation to export controls regarding certain items of American technology. The British authorities are aware of this and have a good idea who the lady was. I have also informed them that I have received certain anonymous messages and have been followed, both in this country and abroad."

"I know nothing about any messages or following you. You will pardon me saying so, but you are a relatively low grade target. The requirement was merely to install listening equipment in your apartment. You do not rate surveillance and it's not our practice to send anonymous letters."

"I assume that you do not believe that your colleague was the target of the missile?"

"We do not know. This was carried out at the request of Russian colleagues. You will understand that when something like this happens, we ask ourselves questions."

"But if the people watching me and sending these letters weren't you, who were they?"

"You are too low grade for the Russians to bother with you. Perhaps it was the Americans or one of their stooges."

"You believe that the Americans would use a missile against a British Government employee? ... Sorry, that was a foolish question. Of course you do."

"In fact, I would find it surprising. But when we use stooges, some of them cannot be controlled in the way you can control your own people. Some of the people you use may not be people you would choose to use."

"I think I understand....For some days before this attack, there was an unmarked and apparently empty van outside my block of flats. In the front was a scrap of paper with a particular symbol written on it. I'll write it down for you, if you like."

I wrote down what I had seen.

"Does that mean anything to you?"

"I'm surprised you don't know it. It's been on your British television often enough. It's the symbol of an organisation called 'Peace in our time', who have been active in demonstrations by your working people against the imperialist American war in Vietnam."

"Well, you may like to ask yourselves what someone connected to them was doing outside my block of flats, right up to the time the missile was fired. They replaced people watching me who used a black Ford Zodiac and when challenged, claimed diplomatic status."

"You realise your people will know you've been here. Everyone who comes here is automatically photographed."

"Yes. But I believe we have a death in common. I am used to having to explain actions which my seniors consider unorthodox."

"If I find anything out which I believe would be appropriate to let you know, I will inform you because of your visit here today. How can I contact you?"

"I suggest you write to me – N V Storey – at the main HM Customs and Excise address in the City or this telephone number 01 626 7963......May I ask what your colleague's name was?"

"Ute Hoefgen, Lieutenant Hoefgen. She had a young daughter."

"I am truly sorry. Until this morning, I thought it was my wife who'd been killed. I am especially sorry because I feel sure it was me or my wife they were trying to kill and it was the measures you took to delay my wife that probably saved her life."

"That is generous of you. You could reasonably feel that Lt Hoefgen wasn't rightfully there."

We shook hands and I was escorted out of the building.

I needed to find a public telephone that wasn't in a too public place, so I took a bus to Holborn Public Library. I needed to get information from Nigel Seymour and Iain Cogbill.

When I got through to Seymour, he said he understood that there'd been an accident at my home. As this was presumably how Special Branch wished to describe it, I didn't give any more details. I asked whether I was expected to attend the meeting of the Committee MISC 38 the following day and he confirmed that I was, assuming I could make it. I told him I could and that I would make my own way there. He showed no interest in what sort of accident had occurred.

Then I rang Iain Cogbill.

"I'm extremely sorry to hear what happened," he began. "Mike Elliott has been in touch – mainly to chase up the stuff you sent me. He told me what happened. Most of your stuff had already been copied and sent to Special Branch and Box 500, but I'm afraid they didn't give it much priority. I believe they'll be taking it a lot more seriously now."

"Has anyone been able to trace the car numbers which I gave you?"

"The black Zodiac was bought new, for cash, by a man who gave a false name. He appears to be using a false driving licence under the name of 'Martin Jones'. The Commer van has had several owners. The latest claims to have sold it, again for cash, to a 'Derek West'. Neither vehicle has been spotted anywhere, so we can assume these people have several secure lock-ups."

"Has anyone been able to shed any light on these messages? Not least, what they mean?"

"I'm afraid not. They are as obscure and unhelpful to us as they undoubtedly have been to you.....I can tell you that whoever did this is extremely careful. There are apparently no fingerprints anywhere."

"Do you know any more about this deal with the Americans than you've told me so far? It just seems weird to me that so much effort should be put into getting at me, in view of my severely limited influence in all of this – and to go to such an extreme!"

"No. I probably know less than you do now. The IB interest so far has turned out to be minimal....Elliott said they were going to get you into a safe house....are you ringing from there?"

"Not exactly. There were things I needed to do."

"Hell's teeth! For God's sake be careful, man! Think of that pretty wife of yours! Try not to be so rash!"

"It's too late for that. Anyway, thanks for your help."

"Take care!"

I decided I'd better ring my Section, just to ensure work was proceeding in my absence and that they were aware what was going on. Morry answered the phone.

"Have you heard about the accident at my flat yesterday evening?" I asked.

"Yes. Mr Seymour phoned us mid-morning. He told us to get on with whatever we were doing. So basically Ken and I have been writing up yesterday's visit to Newhaven. Not that there's a lot new to add."

"I shan't be in today. Too much to sort out. I'll go straight to the Cabinet Office tomorrow morning then I may come back to Custom House or not. It depends how much still needs to be done. Our flat was pretty much destroyed, so we're going to have to live somewhere else for quite a while.."

"Good Lord! What on earth was it?"

"An explosion. I don't think they're certain yet exactly what caused it....Anyway, I suggest you and Ken, with any help Bernard can give you, should start to consider, if we were to control a small number of firms using this stuff, how we would do it and what questions we would need to ask them. Basically, it's to prepare ourselves for the next stage of our work."

"OK......Oh, I should have said – there was a letter hand-delivered for you round about midday."

"Any stamp or indication who it was from?"

"No. Just your name and the Custom House address in capital letters, written in blue biro."

"Could you open it carefully please and tell me what's inside?"

"Gracious God! It says 'Was that not a sufficient message? Next time it will be you or your wife, probably wife.'....... What the hell is going on?"

"Morry, I'm sure you know there are times when you don't ask questions someone can't answer. Please put the message back in the envelope. Stick it in a sealed envelope and get Bernard to deliver it personally, by hand, to Iain Cogbill in the IB in Fetter Lane, as soon as possible. Tell him to tell Iain that it's extremely urgent. Thanks."

I rang off, so I wasn't placed in a position of having to lie to Morry, as opposed to mere prevarication.

I had a while before I needed to make my way to Victoria Station and I felt I would be more exposed there than in the library. So I picked out a book on computers and started to read it. Or, more accurately, I pretended to read it. In fact, my head was in a whirl. Clearly, one of those who had attempted to kill Rosemary or me had remained at the scene to see what happened. That was the only way to explain how they knew neither of us was dead. When we had gone back with the policeman to gather clothes from our devastated flat, there had been no cars parked – other than police vehicles. In any case, it would have been next to impossible to have seen us then and got the letter to Custom House by noon. Moreover, if we had been seen in Beckenham, what would have been the point in sending a letter to me in London?

I began to think about the latest message. It was no clearer about what message I was supposed to be getting, but the second part – 'next time it will be you or your wife' began to raise questions. Was this just telling me that they knew they hadn't got us this time? Or had they spotted that Lt Hoefgen wasn't Rosemary and had killed her deliberately, to reinforce the seriousness of the message? Evidently it had been the East Germans who had used ruses to delay Rosemary's return. But that was explicable. If they were trying to plant these bugs unobtrusively, it was better to use someone who resembled Rosemary and appear at a time of day when she would be expected to be there. As Rosemary wore the shiny black plastic mac most days

130

at this time of year, a woman with short dark hair and the coat would probably be enough disguise. But to do that, the East Germans must have been observing us. Someone must have known roughly what time Rosemary returned and that she wore that sort of mac. If they had carried out probably a brief observation over a few days, presumably the people watching us in the black car or, more likely, the plain Commer van, would have seen them as well. So it wasn't implausible that poor Lt Hoefgen was their actual target. To encourage me to act on the message that evidently they thought I had received. It was yet another chilling reminder of the utterly cold-hearted brutality of these people.

But what on earth was the message I was supposed to act on – and where? The deeply troubling thought struck me that if this was being carried out by someone's stooges and, as the East German had told me, stooges weren't necessarily either controllable or the sort of people one would choose to do this kind of work, was it possible that this activity was being carried out by several different groups, one of whom had got its wires crossed? For example, the people who fired the missile at the flat and had been sending me all those messages appear to assume that I had received a message, but wasn't acting on it. What if some other group were supposed to deliver the message but for some reason hadn't? In that case, Rosemary and I remained in grave danger.

But why had they moved from threatening messages to something so extremely violent and brutal? Surely, the rational next stage might have been a car narrowly missing one of us or perhaps a bullet shot through the flat window? Or a dead cat on our doorstep? What could have prompted such an extreme reaction? As I racked my brains, the only thing I could think of was the interim report that was going to be discussed by Committee MISC 38 the following day. That had been around within Customs from the previous Thursday and had been sent to the Cabinet Office on the Tuesday morning. So it would have been circulated – under a 'confidential' classification – to all members of the Committee that day, presumably. From what I had read of the rules of Cabinet committees, you weren't supposed to make any copies of committee papers – but I guessed that people probably did. In any case, presumably underlings like Seymour and me would be expected to provide notes – 'briefing' – on other Department's committee papers, so they would need access. I realised that Seymour had done that for Commissioner Watling for the previous meeting. So that meant the ideas we were putting forward for reducing the likelihood of the American stuff leaking and therefore increasing the likelihood that a deal could be done with them were potentially quite widely available within Customs from the Thursday and within the rest of Whitehall from the following Tuesday. It seemed to me difficult to reach any other conclusion that someone had passed the word about what our interim report proposed either directly or indirectly to the people who fired the missile at our flat, deliberately killing Lt Hoefgen.

So what about Watling and Seymour in Customs? As far as I was aware, neither had been subject to the threats that I had received. Yet on any objective view, they would be far more influential in the ultimate decision on what sort of guarantee we could give in relation to the American stuff. So why me and not them? What did I know about them?

The rumour mill had it that Seymour had started in an OGD (another Government Department) as a CO, but had risen rapidly, due to his intelligence, hard work and single-minded ambition, to transfer to the Administrative class as an Assistant Principal, from which grade he had been promoted within three years, an unusual achievement. I knew nothing of his home life, whether he could be bribed or perhaps blackmailed…..But then it came to me. His contribution would never be decisive. Though he would happily 'nuance' the findings of my report, he would do it to his master's bidding.

And that master was Commissioner Watling. I knew even less about him. He was known to be ruthless, with blood of ice and obsessed with rising to the post of Deputy Chairman before doing something rare for a Customs and Excise official, becoming Chairman. Normally, that post was handed to outsiders, often senior Treasury mandarins who needed to be pushed aside for their aspiring juniors. Indeed, the present Chairman, Sir James MacDonald, was exactly such. It seemed unlikely that such a man could be bribed and from what I knew about him, he struck me as not being the sort of person who would ever have laid himself open to blackmail. He was undoubtedly the most unpleasant person I had ever met. Beside him, the late and unlamented Jock Imrie was what the Chinese would call a "paper tiger". But surely he could be threatened, just as I had been? But perhaps he was too prominent to be threatened in such a way? If he or his wife were killed in the way poor Lt Hoefgens had been, there would be an almighty hoo-hah in the press which might compel the police and the security services to be a lot more thorough than if it was just Rosemary or me. I recalled only too well the superficial investigations into the deaths – murders rather – of Neville Davenport and his wife. Could they possibly have been so sloppy if it had been a Commissioner that had been killed?

So, though I didn't entirely rule them out, they didn't strike me as obvious candidates for leaking out details of our interim report to these assassins. But all that did was take me into Whitehall Departments I knew practically nothing about. But in theory at least there should be a trail which would enable Special Branch to check who had access to the interim report. But would it include secretaries and typists? I suddenly realised that, within Customs, the interim report had been typed by a Divisional typist and certainly passed through the hands of Commissioner Watling's assistant, the pleasant Irish girl. At a guess, we were probably talking about as many as sixty people. Moreover, knowing who they were was just the first step. Each one would have to be thoroughly investigated and, assuming that one of them had leaked information about the interim report, if – as seemed likely – they had any brains, it was likely to be extremely difficult to identify that they had done it.

And who was behind all this? Though I had been thinking loosely about 'stooges' - in whose pay were these stooges? Did the Russians want this American stuff to come to Britain or not? Logic suggested they would. Apart from adding to the possibilities of getting their hands on it, it also potentially added distrust between Britain and the US, notably between their respective secret services. So, logically, the Russians should welcome the direction the interim report was going. On the other hand, from what I had heard at the first meeting of Committee MISC 38, the Americans were generally against a deal. They should, therefore, be uncomfortable with my interim report. But would they really get involved in this sort of thing with arguably their closest ally?

And how did this 'Peace in our time' group fit into the picture, if at all?

A lot more questions than answers. But I had no time for more. I needed to get myself to Victoria Station and keep my wits about me as I did so. Fortunately bus queues are good places in which to remain unnoticed and buses are quite good for spotting whether someone is following you. I did not believe I had been shadowed getting to my destination.

I stood apparently browsing in WH Smiths until I saw Mike Elliott arrive from one of the side entrances.

"You're a bloody fool!" he exclaimed. "Let's get out through here!"

He led me at a fair pace down the side of platform 2 to a side exit where a black car was waiting.

"What the hell did you think you were doing?" he demanded.

"The East German Embassy, I suppose?"

"That's right. You must've known you'd be spotted going in there."

"Yes. But I thought there was something I could do there – and it had to be done today and I was the only one who could do it."

"And was it worth it?"

"I believe so."

"Then you can tell me about it when we get to your new abode."

We drove in silence along Vauxhall Bridge Road, then before the bridge turned off into John Islip Street and into Erasmus Street. We stopped outside one of the red brick blocks of flats and got out.

"The whole of this block is under surveillance," Mike Elliott explained, "and you can only get in with a pass-key. You wife has a couple upstairs."

He let us in and we went up to the first floor. As he opened the door, Rosemary rushed to meet me and flung herself into my arms.

"I wasn't really worried, you know," she said. "But it's a relief just to see you, all the same."

"You might be less relieved if you knew what he'd been up to," remarked Elliott.

"Perhaps you'd like some tea before you start explaining yourself?" asked Rosemary.

"Actually, if you have anything else – a sandwich, toast, just something. I realise I haven't had anything to eat since yesterday lunchtime," I said.

"That might explain why your brain has been working as it has," commented Elliott sourly.

After I had wolfed down some marmite on toast and started my mug of tea, I explained what I had been doing and why.

"After what happened I couldn't just sit around. I know you'd like me to, but I can't. When I realised that it was likely someone from the East German Embassy had been killed instead of us, I thought I might be able to catch them off balance, off their guard, if I went there today to find out a few things. It had to be me. Only I could tell them that I was sorry Lt Hoefgen had been killed when it was supposed to be Rosemary or me. I felt they would be in shock and today was the only day they might exchange some information and only with me."

"At what possible risk to your reputation, presumably never entered your head! But I see you learnt the name of the woman who was killed."

"Yes. Ute Hoefgen. She had a daughter. The East German bloke I met confirmed that she had been placing listening devices in our flat, at the behest of the Russians. He said that showed I was a pretty low grade target. He also pretty well confirmed that it was them who delayed Rosemary coming home, so Lt Hoefgen could plant the devices as unobtrusively as possible, posing as Rosemary. He also told me that it wasn't them who had sent the warning letters or them who'd been following us. All they'd been asked to do was plant the bugs."

"Did you believe him?"

"Yes. Of course, they must've done some surveillance of us – if only to know when Rosemary and I got home and that Rosemary wore a mac like that. He said he didn't believe the Russians had ordered the attack...."

"But then he would, wouldn't he."

"Quite so. But logically, why would they? What he did say was that both sides use stooge groups to do some of their dirty work for them and that they can't necessarily control what they are up to. I'm beginning to wonder whether the real message for me has been given to some group that's failed to deliver it, but the another one thinks they have.....I got another message handed in at my workplace earlier today. I've had it delivered to Iain Cogbill. It showed that whoever has been doing this knows we're still alive and that it will be one of us next if we don't heed the message.....It made me wonder whether Lt Hoefgen was actually the intended target. After all, if we were being watched from that Commer van somehow, they would presumably have spotted the East Germans doing their recce. It also shows someone was hanging around after the missile was fired to see what the effect had been."

"So the East Germans think some group of American stooges did it?"

"The man in the Embassy didn't go that far.......But he did tell me something I should've known. When I peered into the front of the Commer van to see if anyone was there, I noticed a scrap of paper with a logo on it. Apparently it's the symbol of an organisation called 'Peace in our time'. I don't think he expected that. My impression was that he saw them as having Soviet bloc connections."

"It could've been left there to lead us on a false trail."

"Of course. But why? Besides, though whoever's doing this is cautious and persistent, they've scarcely been terribly competent. Rosemary and I and the police have seen their faces and their shadowing of us has been poor. Their attempts presumably to stop me going in a certain direction in my interim report haven't succeeded. I've never got the 'message' I'm supposed to have received. But I think we should ask ourselves why they suddenly decided to use such extreme violence at this particular time, just a couple of days after my interim report was copied round Whitehall?"

"I think you should ask yourself whether you aren't likely to be suspended for going to the East German Embassy. If you got information from them, what did you tell them in return?"

"I told them what they already knew – that the UK and the Americans were negotiating about a deal in relation to some high-tech stuff. They wouldn't've been bugging our flat if they didn't know at least as much as that."

"I suppose we could argue you were suffering from delayed shock. And you certainly got information faster than we would've done. It's possible they would never have confirmed the woman's name – just admitted she was one of theirs and asked for her remains."

"So who knows I went there?"

"We do – and the Security Service."

"I'm due to attend a meeting of this Committee tomorrow in the Cabinet Office. It'll be interesting to see whether Jacob Ffoulkes objects to my presence."

"You plan to attend?"

"Of course. In the latest message, the greater threat is aimed at Rosemary. If she's safe here, I believe I must get out – and be seen to be out and about. After all, if I disappear from view, I can hardly be doing anything to achieve the aims of those who keep sending me their messages. In which case, it seems to me Rosemary's life is in even more danger. The most important thing is to try and find out who these people are and how they were informed about the contents of my interim report."

"That's a job for us, not you. I realise you're upset and angry, but you could very easily get in the way and either blow our chances of discovering these people or get yourself killed."

"I'm aware of that. But you'd better figure me in your plans as someone who is out and about, doing my job, not out of sight here."

"And I'm not going to sit around here all day, either," added Rosemary. "It must be possible for me to get to my work without too much baby-sitting or too much risk."

"Let's talk that over between us," I said. "The latest message is very clear that they see threatening your life as the best way of getting me to do what they want. Indeed, I'm more and more convinced that was why they took the opportunity to kill poor Lt Hoefgen."

"Either neither of us takes any risks, or we both accept some risk."

"You two really are a pain in the neck!" exclaimed Elliott. "But I'll see what we can do. Despite what you did today, you still have quite a large balance of goodwill in our part of the world. Just don't spend it all too quickly!"

"May I ask what you know about these people 'Peace in our time'?" I asked.

"Not a great deal. Unlike 'Peace now', where we're pretty clear some funding comes from the Soviets, their finances are more opaque. There's a religious side to them - several of their leading lights are clergymen – which might be less attractive to the Russians. But they'll use anyone they can. Both claim to be non-violent, but whenever they've had rallies – usually against the Vietnam war – there's always been some violence. But even with CND, there's often a bit of that. All sorts of small, nastier organisations get in on the act. They tend to be smaller, less public, with membership that is recruited on the streets and in pubs, often with people who just want an excuse for a fight. They can be very tight-knit, but small, or so loosely-organised, like some of the anarchist groups, that getting to know much about them is extremely hard. Of course, we've been looking at 'Peace in our time', but we haven't got very far, I fear."

"Well, if the man from the East German Embassy was right, I think we might need to be looking out for stooge groups, rather than the official people from the embassies."

"That may well be so. But please don't go sticking your oar in without letting me know. I'll give you my phone number, so you don't have your usual excuse that you had no way of getting in touch."

He left us to get used to this strange new flat. It was comfortable enough, though inevitably lacking anything that made it ours. The kitchen and bathroom were rather old-fashioned, but the food cupboards and fridge were well stocked and the bath enormous. We could undoubtedly put that to good use. However, that particular day, making love was far from being on our minds. That night we lay in bed, Rosemary's head on my shoulder, profoundly grateful we were both still alive.

"Really, after yesterday evening, I'd like to find a place hundreds of miles away from anywhere like this, where we'd be completely safe, just you and me, and stay there with you for ever," I whispered. "I know it's not possible, but...."

"I just keep hoping it'll all go away ... But it won't until this report is completed, will it?"

"I don't know. If the Committee agrees with the interim report tomorrow, we'll've moved quite a long way towards a deal with the Americans and I doubt whether there'd be anything I could do in the next bit of work to change that direction....The trouble is, we seem to be getting one set of messages where I feel there should be two ..."

"You will be careful, won't you? ... And I mean really careful ..."

"I'll be as careful as I was today ... I knew I'd be seen at the East German Embassy, but I made my way around central London without being followed, I'm certain. I think I've just got to take special care at certain places where they could expect to see me – like Custom House, for instance."

"Do you think we're really safe here?"

"Mike Elliott may find what we do exasperating, but I trust him to do his utmost to keep us safe."

"Well, let's make sure we don't let him down."

SEVEN
DEMONSTRATIONS

In the downstairs flat there was a sort of concierge who apparently made all the necessary arrangements. At 10.15, an unobtrusive Morris Minor drew up outside and I got quickly into it. We drove as far as Victoria, where I alighted and took a bus along Victoria Street and into Whitehall. I knew that buses almost invariably slowed down near the entrance to Downing Street, so I made my way to the exit and jumped off on the corner of Downing Street and Whitehall, making my way rapidly to No 70. I was about twenty minutes early, so I got myself signed in, took my day pass, and sat down in a moderately comfortable chair in the entrance lobby. At least I hadn't been barred so far.

Various people came in and took the lifts in front of me or followed the route we had taken on my previous visit. I got up and looked at various engravings of the buildings that made up the Cabinet Office and its neighbour, the Privy Council Office. I began to realise that these were, in fact, several separate buildings constructed at different times and subsequently conjoined, which explained why the floor you were on at any one time wasn't necessarily what you expected.

Stan Woodruffe arrived and sat down, studiously ignoring me. Shortly after ten to eleven, Commissoner Watling and Nigel Seymour appeared. Watling eyed me as though I was something brown and smelly he had just trodden in. Seymour muttered a good morning. I wondered whether any of them knew what had actually happened at my flat – or my excursion to the East German Embassy. We were escorted up to the same conference room and the same rituals took place. The attendees appeared to be the same, except a younger man with black-rimmed glasses and a bushy beard and moustache replaced the man from the DEA and the Board of Trade appeared not to be represented at all.

"I see we're all met," observed our Chairman. "I trust everyone has received the papers. I fear the Foreign Office paper was somewhat tardy – but I understand that was because of the need to provide the latest gen on the state of negotiations with the Americans, such as it was. And we may have to ask a few to leave the room when we discuss the Home Office paper – anyone not cleared to see 'Secret' material. But we'll take that paper last to avoid undue disruption.....I think we should take the Customs paper first."

While Commissioner Watling gave a brief summary of our paper, I glanced round the room. It seemed I had been allowed in, despite my previous day's escapade. But then I suppose it was possible it hadn't reached such senior levels yet. Or perhaps Mike Elliott had been able to explain it away as a momentary aberration due to delayed shock?

"......So, in conclusion, we ask the Committee to take a view on whether they agree that, if this seems the correct direction, Customs and Excise would be authorised to enter into discussions with those firms who it is anticipated will receive this technology to ascertain whether appropriate controls can be established and whether these would be acceptable," Watling concluded.

"Comments, gentlemen – and lady?" exclaimed Walmesley.

"The Treasury supports this approach. It should maintain a tight ceiling on costs and on the need for additional Civil Servants. We are also intrigued by the suggestion in the report about controlling exports at

143

inland locations where goods are consolidated. This, too, may be a way of reducing costs and should be considered in relation to imports as well, in our view."

"A working party is presently examining that very matter," replied Watling sharply.

"This will have to be handled with extreme care," said the lady from MinTech. "These are generally businesses that have little or nothing to do with HM Customs and Excise. The Department's reputation, however, is for heavy-handedness and intrusiveness. There may also be concerns about security within the Department's own employees."

"I believe that is the point of engaging in discussions along the lines proposed," suggested Walmesley.

"MinTech isn't against this proposal. Merely that it will need to be handled with diplomacy and sensitivity."

"I believe most members of the Department have now descended from the trees," remarked Watling, to general smirking.

"I believe what's more important is the extent to which HM Customs and Excise staff will need access to highly sensitive information about the technologies involved," remarked Jacob Ffoulkes. "I imagine the firms involved will have considerable concerns about the security of their technology."

"I cannot see that is really a problem. The details which we would need to see in the next stage of the work would be agreed with the firms themselves. If they had any problems, we wouldn't proceed. Of course, it's possible that would mean we couldn't adequately complete the next stage and would therefore have to limit the nature of any guarantee we might be able to give," replied Watling.

"I'm not sure that this provides us with a satisfactory way forward. We don't really want to reach a stage where we can't give a satisfactory guarantee because Customs haven't got enough information," said Walmesley.

"If I may say something," I said. "There is no reason why the next stage of work should require any details of the actual technology. What we would need to know is about the firms' own systems for keeping track of their components, their security systems preventing staff from walking out of the premises with components or documents, their ability to identify this high-tech stuff, its size and portability and if it closely resembled other components. I think we would expect them to check their own export consignments themselves. It seems to me we would more likely want to check they were doing it thoroughly. We don't have the knowledge to tell one component from another."

"I see.....Does that resolve your concerns Jacob....and Miss Tyldesley?"

Both nodded.

"Thank you for your intervention. It was helpful.....Now, who else?"

"DEA have no objection," said the man with the bushy beard.

There appeared to be no other comments.

"Then subject to the caveats that have emerged during our discussions, Customs have clearance from this Committee to proceed as proposed in MISC 38/5 (67)," concluded Walmesley. "Now, the MinTech paper 38/6 (67). Miss Tyldesley. Over to you."

In effect, the MinTech paper, which I read over Nigel Seymour's shoulder, advanced little on what they had said on the previous occasion. The new technology would evidently make computers go much faster and would enable much smaller computers to be made.

There were evident 'spin-offs for the military' that were not further explained. The main point seemed to be that the technology couldn't be kept secret indefinitely. It was estimated that within 4 years, it would become widely available – not through any leak to the Soviets, but because the US inventors of these high-tech components would insist on putting them into computers that would be widely available. At that stage, the Soviets would be able to 'reverse-engineer' the key components. The essential point was that this technology wouldn't stand still. It was dynamic and more developments could be expected over the forthcoming years. But getting this technology now would mean that Britain was in on the ground floor of developing a radically new technology and could therefore hope to continue to be several years ahead of our commercial competitors (other than the US), provided we first 'got the kit' and second used our well-known scientific skills to keep improving and developing it.

The man from the Treasury asked about how realistic the time-scales were and about our ability genuinely to keep up with the Americans and the Japanese in this area, but the paper wasn't asking for endorsement, just for the Committee to note. No-one else had any comments.

The Foreign Office paper on the current state of the negotiations with the Americans was solely notable for a venomous spat between Sir Rodney Walmesley on the one side and his Foreign Office counterpart, Sir Roderick Pilkington. Insofar as any light emerged from the heat, it appeared that until Britain could give a satisfactory guarantee about security of the technology, the negotiations were going nowhere.

146

"Home Office paper next," said Walmesley, sipping a glass of water. "Those not cleared for 'Secret' material will need to depart, I'm afraid."

Nigel Seymour and I rose, along with several others, including the man from DEA. However, as I reached the door, just behind the Chairman, Jacob Ffoulkes leaned across the table to him and said "I'd like Mr Storey from Customs to stay. Though he isn't cleared, I'm prepared to vouch for him.....His clearance is being progressed as we speak."

"Very well," replied Walmesley. "Mr Storey, you are allowed to remain."

I returned to my seat, deliberately avoiding the poisonous looks from Commissioner Watling.

"Jacob, I assume you'll speak to this paper?" asked Walmesley.

"Yes. But I would like to say something first. I've asked Mr Storey to remain because the Committee should be aware that, as a result of his involvement in this work, someone fired a missile into his flat on Wednesday evening. It's believed that the intention was to kill him and possibly his wife. As it happened, there was a woman from East German security planting listening devices there at the time and she was killed in an extremely destructive explosion. I mention this in introduction because it illustrates graphically how important and sensitive this matter is to some people."

Everyone had turned to look at me – except Jacob Ffoulkes. I kept staring at the wall opposite me. I wasn't sure where he was going with this.

"We don't know who did this. All we can conclude is that it wasn't the East Germans. Direct Russian involvement is improbable. It seems likely that the organisations that are actively being employed are irregular groups who may be less amendable to control by their principals. By that token, we shouldn't rule out some arm of the US Government – notably the CIA – from willing the result, if not the methods employed. This is an extremely muddy area. Many of these groups form, dissolve and reform in a different guise rapidly, specifically to avoid identification and penetration. As we have seen, they are potentially extremely dangerous and, in all likelihood, uncoordinated and chaotic. We are currently doing our best to establish who we are dealing with, with valuable help from Mr Storey. But I think we should assume that anyone involved in key aspects of the matter we are considering is a potential target. Specifically, if anyone round this table or your principal supporters receives any anonymous messages, you should report it to my office at once."

"I take it that Mr Storey has received such anonymous messages?" asked Stan Woodruffe.

"I can confirm that," replied Ffoulkes. "I understand your people have passed them to Special Branch and to my organisation, as is right and proper."

"Are we allowed to ask what the anonymous messages contain?" asked the hatchet-faced man from the Treasury.

"So far they have conveyed menace, but in an opaque way. Putting it a little more clearly – they appear to expect certain action, but haven't specified what. That's why I mentioned about the uncoordinated nature of these groups."

"So why should Storey be the target of such a violent attack?" asked Pilkington. "With the greatest respect, he doesn't have a seat at the top table. Far from it."

"That isn't entirely clear. It would seem that his report is considered critical as to the nature of a guarantee we could give the Americans and therefore whether this stuff will come here or not. That's the best I can surmise. Regrettably, these hostile elements have not seen fit to divulge which direction they wished Mr Storey's report to head in."

There followed a brief discussion of a list of about a dozen known groups who might be involved, including 'Peace in our time' and 'Peace Now'. But it seemed to me a case of the nearly blind leading the blind. Equally, it was possible that Ffoulkes didn't wish to divulge too much to colleagues who, if he had reflected on it, might include someone leaking information, directly or indirectly, to one or more of these groups.

That discussion concluded the meeting.

As we all stood up, Commissioner Watling turned to me and said icily, "Monday morning. In my office." He then turned his back and left.

"I assume you put all this through Cogbill," added Woodruffe.

"He has oversight over this work," I replied. "So naturally he was the person I would go to."

"And you thought not to inform us about what happened at your flat?"

"I've followed the line indicated by Special Branch, who are in charge of the case. I hope Mr Ffoulkes had cleared what he said this morning with them."

"Do you believe that they may try to attack you again?"

"A message delivered by hand to Custom House yesterday said so. But I am currently under some form of police protection – in a safe house, that sort of thing."

"I'd advise you to tread warily – and not just with whoever tried to kill you."

He departed and I followed. As I went out of the door, Ffoulkes turned from his conversation with Walmesley and said, "Storey. It'd be helpful if we could have a word soon. Do you think you could get to Bloomsbury sometime on Monday?"

"If you wish. It'll have to be in the afternoon as my Commissioner wishes to see me in the morning. I shall be on my work phone on Monday, if your office wishes to arrange a convenient time for you."

"Have a safe weekend."

I made my way downstairs to the lobby. It seemed unlikely that someone would try to kill me on the steps of the Cabinet Office, in the middle of Whitehall. But it wasn't inconceivable that they would know I had attended this meeting and might be waiting in order to follow me and find out where Rosemary and I were now living. I sat down for a moment to make a plan of escape. Then I handed my day pass in at the reception desk and went outside, heading towards Trafalgar Square. I walked up as far as the Whitehall entrance to Horseguards, where a couple of soldiers from the Household Cavalry kept guard, mainly for the edification of tourists. I walked through the yard and the covered way under the building. The moment I was out the other side, I hared off at top speed across Horseguards Parade towards St James's Park. I never looked back, just ran like the clappers. I ran between the traffic going along the Mall and up the Duke of York steps. I turned back for a second and couldn't see any pursuer, but, of course, they might well have got into a car. Quite breathless – I'd run at my top speed for longer than I'd done for years – I walked as fast as I could to Regent Street and got on the first bus that came along. The moment it stopped along Oxford Street, I got off and made my way east along the back streets roughly parallel to Oxford Street as far as Tottenham Court Road. There I caught a bus to the City, confident that I was not being followed.

I was trying to see whether someone was watching the Custom House. It seemed likely that when they lost sight of me, my watchers would return to places where

I could be expected to turn up at some point. If I could identify them without them spotting me, I might be able to get Special Branch on to them. In order to get some sort of vantage point, I made my way to the Monument and climbed to the top. Immediately I could see that it would be difficult to be sure I could see my watchers before they saw me. Though Billingsgate was pretty well closed down at this time of day, Lower Thames Street was too open. Wherever I might come from, I reckoned I could be observed, even if I could make them out as well. Of course, I reckoned I could always outwit them so they would be unable to follow me back to the safe house, but equally it would be hard to turn the tables on them.

I decided not to go into the office. I'd had enough running and dodging for one day. So I took a couple of buses back to Holborn and ate lunch in a sandwich bar. Then I returned to the Library and read various books and magazines about computers. I even looked at a book about what were called 'programming languages', but it could easily have been in Greek, as far as I was concerned.

At about 4 pm, I rang the Special Branch number and arranged to be picked up by the British Museum. A green Morris Traveller met me there and took me, in a circuitous route, back to Erasmus Street. There an anxious Rosemary was waiting for me.

"I believe it's possible to get out and do something a bit like our normal work," I said, after we'd kissed and cuddled. "But it'll require a bit of ingenuity and sometimes being quite nippy on your feet. Clearly, the one thing we can't do is be dropped off and picked up by Special Branch cars at our workplaces. We need to plan routes where we can get away quickly on foot and know where some of the local buses go, so we can be met in places where we haven't been followed. What I did today was pretty well made up on the spur of the moment - and I'm sure we could do it better."

"How long do you think this will last?"

"Well....the Committee meeting agreed that we should move to the next stage of our report. I guess that'll take a couple of weeks. I think that's when the next meeting is – and they expect another interim report. After that, I'm not sure what more we'll have to do. So it could be only two or three more weeks. After that, my part in all of this will be over - and since I believe someone in or around the Committee leaked information about the interim report to those people, they'll know that by then, killing either of us would be pointless."

"So you weren't barred from the meeting."

"No. Indeed, that man from the security service we met that time in Gower Street asked me to stay when they were talking about secret stuff, when I should've been booted out by rights. He then told them what'd happened. But he didn't seem to know any more about these people than Mike Elliott – or us for that matter. But he asked me to go over there on Monday afternoon, so perhaps he knows more than he was letting on. On Monday morning, I've got to go and see Commissioner Watling. He seemed very put out at me being allowed to stay and then hearing about the attack on our flat from Ffoulkes – that's the man from the security service we met that time in Holborn. As Jim Round used to say, it's probably exercise book down the back of the pants time."

"So what are we going to do this weekend – just stay here? I'm already feeling cooped up."

"I don't know whether Special Branch would allow us to go out of town – to Brighton or Oxford or somewhere like that? ... You could always go and demonstrate against the war in Vietnam. I heard

152

someone on the bus telling her friend that there was going to be a big demonstration in Trafalgar Square on Sunday."

"That's not really my sort of thing."

"Hmmm ... I wonder who's organising it?"

"Why what difference does that make? ... Oh, I see! What if 'Peace in our time' were involved? ... But we'd be just asking for trouble if any of their people were there and recognised us."

"But what if we were in disguise? If you wore a caftan and a long blonde wig and dark glasses ..."

"And you had a hippy wig and a droopy moustache! And a 'ban the bomb' t-shirt and leather trousers!"

"And dark glasses as well. After all, everyone seems to wear them these days."

"Do you think they'd recognise us?"

"Not a chance ... Do you think they've got any pop music here to get us in the mood?"

"No. I've looked. It's all light orchestra and crooners. If you want 'Strawberry Fields' or 'Baby I need your loving', you're going to have to ask the nice people from Special Branch to get it for you."

"I think I'd better pass on that. I've used up enough credit for the time being ... Actually, I was half-expecting Mike Elliott to be here sometime."

"I expect they keep away as much as possible, in case they're being followed."

"Well, it's going to be a quiet weekend, Mrs Storey. Just the two of us with nowhere to go and nothing to distract us."

"I think we can find things to do that'll keep us occupied....have you seen the size of that bath?"

At around 11 am on the Saturday morning, the concierge informed us that if we provided a list, our weekly shopping would be done for us – but encouraged us to be 'sensible'. I noticed there was a

Central London telephone book in the hall and discovered a couple of theatrical outfitters which seemed to be what we would need for our disguises. Then we asked the concierge to get us a car. A grey Austin Cambridge appeared shortly afterwards and took us to Long Acre. There we dived out and went to a nearby theatrical outfitters, returning to the car again in Dury Lane, and heading back to Erasmus Street. We spent the rest of Saturday lazing around, much of the time, with out arms round each other, silently grateful that we were still together. Sometimes I wanted to hold Rosemary so tightly to me, fearful that she might escape me again. Unlike when we had been in Paris, out mood was autumnal. It seemed we had too long to endure, contending with an unknown and uncomprehending enemy, whose cold-blooded brutality appeared to have no bounds.

Early on the Sunday morning, we got into our disguises. I had a dark wig of hair about shoulder-length, with the drooping moustache that Rosemary insisted on, which I attached with the substance recommended by the man in the theatrical outfitters. I also put on a CND t-shirt and black jeans with a pair of walking boots, which I reckoned would add at least an inch to my height. Rosemary had eschewed a blonde wig, which didn't suit her complexion, and now wore a long wig of black hair, with a headband, a mauve caftan and yellow jeans, with sandals, which probably made her look slightly shorter than she normally did. Both of us had the latest line in sunglasses. Thus attired, we left the flat and headed for Trafalgar Square.

Quite soon we met other young people, similarly dressed and heading in the same direction. We joined them. Calling ourselves 'Chris' and 'Suzie' from Battersea, we were quickly accepted. I could revert to a South London accent with ease and Rosemary's

154

musical ear meant that she could mimic the accent without difficulty. Clearly, the people we were with were mainly out for a good time. They didn't particularly like the Americans – though they liked some of their music – and were against war. "Peace, man" was commonly uttered. Indeed, it was almost a password into this group of well-meaning, but essentially non-violent youngsters. All seemed to be young couples, who ten years ago would probably have spent their Sundays going for a quiet stroll while they courted. Today they were going to watch left wing politicians, radical clergymen and possibly a pop star or two harangue them about the Vietnam war. Then they would join in the singing of familiar anti-war songs, perhaps led by the pop stars. If the police allowed it, everyone would march along Whitehall and stop outside Downing Street shouting slogans at the Prime Minister, who almost certainly wasn't there and who wanted to keep Britain out of the Vietnam war anyway, and would pass into Parliament Square for a final round of speeches, singing and the shouting of slogans.

"Then we go in a pub and 'ave a few beers or, if it's nice, we go to the park and smoke dope," explained a young man with a mod haircut called Jez. "Issa good day art, innit!"

I agreed. I wondered what the organisers of the rally felt about those like Jez – probably the majority of those attending it.

The young couples seemed keen to wind themselves round each other, something Rosemary and I required no persuasion or acting to do.

As we walked up Whitehall to join the masses in Trafalgar Square we passed No. 70 Whitehall. I wondered what the mandarins who had attended MISC 38 (67) 2nd meeting would make of me looking like this? I wondered also what Mike Elliott, Iain Cogbill and Jacob Ffoulkes would have said about our Sunday activities. But neither Rosemary nor I were good at sitting around waiting for things to happen to us. And though we certainly didn't feel we were invulnerable, we didn't believe that any of those who had been watching us could possibly spot us in these disguises, among so many others similarly attired. Indeed, as I started to reflect on their modus operandi, as Rosemary called it, it seemed to me that they would be staking out places where they had a good chance of spotting us and would then attempt to follow us from there. I doubted whether their resources were large and they would have to concentrate them where they could be most effective.

Trafalgar Square was already filled with thousands of people, mostly young, but with a fair smattering of older people – often, judging by their badges, members of CND, veterans of many such events. We made our way nearer to where the speeches would be made. I wanted to try and find out whether 'Peace in our time' were involved and, if so, where their people were located.

Various anti-war or protest songs were being played through the loudspeakers. Long time favourites like "Blowin' in the wind", "Where have all the flowers gone?", "Chimes of Freedom", "The times they are a-changin'", etc followed each other in quick succession. They were interrupted by a harangue from an elderly Scottish politician, with a Glasgow accent so strong that I doubted whether more than one in a thousand of his audience could understand what he was saying, though there was no mistaking his passion. It was followed by "Masters of war", "Turn, Turn, Turn" and "A hard rain's gonna fall" before a plump, middle-aged clergyman, a veteran of CND, told us in a very plummy, Oxbridge voice of the iniquities of war, any war. Someone was clearly observing the reactions of

156

his audience, as it seemed to me that he was cut short and more music put on. This time we got "Eve of Destruction", which I had always regarded as truly dire, "It's all over now, baby blue" and "Guantanamera", which I could listen to all day.

Then the main speakers started. The first was a youngish left winger, an MP for somewhere in the North Midlands. He gave a rabidly anti-American speech, accusing them of imperialism and colonialism, often in terms that would have been deeply familiar to Mao Tse Tung. He was given great applause when he finished. He was followed by a fairly well-known actress, notorious in the press for her 'Trotskyite' views. Somewhat to my surprise, she wasn't a particularly eloquent speaker and her phrases seemed to have emerged from some sort of Trotskyite manual for all-purpose anti-American, anti-Capitalist speeches. As she finished, she was given a decent cheer, presumably because people knew vaguely who she was. (Of course, Rosemary and I clapped and cheered just like everyone else). Then a black American clergyman gave us the perspective of the oppressed American blacks, denied their civil rights, but still drafted into fighting a war against people they were more likely to see as their brothers resisting oppression. He was an impressive speaker, using the rhythms of the evangelical church, in the way familiar to us from the speeches of Martin Luther King on the radio. The pop singer who followed was at the other extreme – barely articulate, but plainly filled with great rage. Both got an equally warm reception from the crowd, the latter I assumed on the basis of his performances as a pop-star rather than as an orator.

Then a youngish clergyman took the microphone. He explained he represented "Peace in our time" and, along with the usual ritual condemnations of the

Vietnam war, he urged us all to do our bit to find out all the military secrets and make them public, so that war could be prevented, because each side would know everything there was to know about the other and would all have equal access to the technology of war? "Would the USA be attacking Vietnam if the North Vietnamese had B-52 bombers and long range nuclear missiles?" he asked us rhetorically. He explained PIOT's mission was to "make war a level playing field so that there would be no wars". I imagined that there would be undercover people from Special Branch and the Security Service spread out among the crowd, but I didn't think this would add to what they knew about the organisation already.

He received lukewarm applause. Perhaps it was rather too theoretical. Another pop-star, a drummer with a well-known band, spoke next. Given that he appeared to be drunk, he gave an entertaining performance attacking the Americans for their attitudes to drug use and sex with teenage girls, presumably subjects he knew most about. Eventually he got on to the script and noted that the Vietnam war was "uncool, man" – and was greeted with a rapturous reception when he finished. At that point it appeared to be time for the assembled throng to march past Downing Street and on to Parliament Square. Led by a group of guitarists playing "We shall overcome", we set off.

Rosemary and I kept as close an eye as we dared on the PIOT speaker. It was reasonable to assume that he would join the fellow members of his group. At first the people we saw him talking to were unknown to either of us. Most, however, didn't look like the sort of people you would associate with this sort of protest organisation. They were short-haired and tidily, soberly dressed. Though it was a pleasantly warm day, all wore dark jackets. It would not have surprised me if that was to disguise the guns they were carrying. Of course, it was possible that PIOT expected to meet trouble and these people were merely well prepared for it. And after the assassination of JFK and the death threats against numerous other American politicians, security probably was quite high in their minds. But the speaker had been British and this was London. For an organisation so opposed to war, they seemed to have a rather military approach.

We began to make our way across Trafalgar Square. Rosemary and I gradually let ourselves be caught up by what seemed to be the PIOT element.

"Are you with 'Peace in our time'?" demanded a young man, suddenly and sharply.

"No," I replied. "But we were very interested in what your speaker had to say and would like to get more involved…"

"Why?"

"Most of the other speakers were either just spouting old claptrap and not proposing to do anything. At least you seem to be suggesting that we can do something against the war."

"Here's a leaflet. If you ring the phone number, they'll be able to tell when we meet. We don't publish in advance, for obvious reasons."

We continued to walk with them, Rosemary and I reading the leaflet. Apart from the phone number and a couple of names of the leadership, it told us nothing new.

"Oh," said the young man. "Your names?"

"Chris and Suzie…Bentley….We live in Battersea…"

"It's OK. We'll get all your details if you come to a meeting…You understand the pigs try to get in everywhere to spy on us."

"Of course…..Would we need to bring any identification to a meeting?"

"No. Just turn up. We'll tell you want you need to do, if and when you turn up."

"We'll definitely come along," added Rosemary.

He drifted away. We kept a wary eye on those around us. Most were like us, but there were small groups of tough-looking young men in jeans and combat jackets that looked as though they were here for more than listening to a few speeches and singing protest songs. And over to one side were these neat, short-haired men who looked as though they provided security for the PIOT leadership, who were walking - a group of five or six men, mostly clergymen – about thirty feet to our left.

Then Rosemary nudged my arm

"Don't look now, but over to the left are the two people who were following us in Kelsey Park…and I'm sure were in the black car outside our flat."

"Are they definitely with the 'Peace in our time' lot?"

"I think so. What do you want to do?"

"Nothing. The main aim of coming today was to see what the 'Peace in our time' people looked like and whether the people we'd seen were associated with them. I don't think these are the sort of people we'd want to tackle unarmed, especially when there's such a lot of them about. Let's just keep our eyes on them – discreetly of course. We might be able to get some more information."

"I reckon there'll be Special Branch undercover people here as well."

"Yes. But we're the only ones here that can recognise these people. You never know, when they're leaving we might be able to get a car number or two."

160

We were now in Whitehall, opposite the theatre which had made its name for "side-splitting farces", which my mother adored and my father, typically, despised as "bourgeois pap". I wondered what he would have thought about today's demonstration. I felt he would probably have regarded it as a sideshow by Trotskyite fellow-travellers that diverted people's attention from the importance of the class struggle. Personally, I doubted whether more than a quarter of the people were there for anything other than an amusing day out. A few people were plainly angry – but for most, it was someone else's war, on the other side of the world.

We continued slowly along Whitehall and then the front of the column stopped opposite the entrance to Downing Street where a line of police, eight to ten ranks deep, blocked passage into the street. People at that side of the column started to press against them. Whether they wanted to or whether it was just the force of those behind was impossible to tell, but they clearly were being shoved against the police, whose line gave a few feet and then held firm. The tough-looking young men began to weave through the ranks of those who were just there to have fun. Some had stones or other missiles in the pockets of their jackets and they began to hurl them at the police. Someone started shouting out, "Down with the pigs!" and even "Kill the pigs!" It was taken up by a few voices, but it was also noticeable how plenty of people were trying to move away from the front of the column and the confrontation with the police.

A couple of policeman were hit by the missiles and had to be taken behind their lines with blood streaming from their faces. More of these aggressive young men slipped past us, with missiles in their hands. I noticed that one of the PIOT people who provided security for

161

their leaders was using a walkie-talkie. Was he perhaps organising these thugs to attack the police? More missiles were hurled and a couple more policemen were injured. Weight of numbers continued to press people against the police lines and scuffles erupted between some of the policemen at the front and the more aggressive demonstrators. The cries of "Down with the pigs!" and "Kill the pigs!" were taken up by more people, as a couple of the demonstrators - one of them a young woman - were taken away, bloody and shaken.

"That's what they're after, of course," Rosemary whispered to me. "Any over-reaction from the police. Then they hope they can stir people up and it'll all get a lot nastier."

More tough young men appeared from behind us and made their way forward, throwing missiles at the police. Some had got hold of some of the placards and were thrusting them at the police. Several more police were injured. The PIOT man continued on his walkie-talkie. I noticed several TV news vans had arrived over by the huge new MoD building and cameras were being set up on their roofs. The crowd continued to press against the police. More people were getting angry and more scuffles were occurring between the police and the crowd. Every time someone from the crowd was injured, the collective anger grew, especially when a woman was hurt.

Then, just as I felt the police line was at risk of giving way, dozens of police appeared on the south-west side of Whitehall. Presumably they had been massing on the Embankment near Cannon Row police station and now poured through past the MoD building and began to press the crowd back up Whitehall towards Trafalgar Square. These police were considerably less restrained than their colleagues guarding Downing Street. If people didn't move back, they were unceremoniously belted with truncheons and several were dragged away behind the police line. Angered by this more of the demonstrators attacked this new foe, using whatever weapons lay to hand – mainly the placards on their wooden poles.

Police sirens were heard coming up Whitehall from Parliament Square. A dozen or more police vans appeared, with policemen in special riot gear, with water cannon and guns, which Rosemary informed me were for firing tear gas. A big man with silver hair under a peaked cap got out of a large black car. He took up a loud-hailer.

"Listen to me. I am Assistant Commissioner Reilly. By the powers granted me under the Public Order Act, I herewith order this assembly to dissolve. If you do not go away within five minutes I am authorised to use water-cannon and tear gas to compel you to move away. Be on your way!"

Some people started to move back, but others just became angrier and shouted their defiance. A few stones were hurled in his direction.

"Kill the pigs! Kill the pigs! Kill the pigs!"

A group of tough young men hurled themselves at the police guarding Downing Street. At that point, their restraint snapped. They started to fight the demonstrators with truncheons and their fists and boots as necessary. A nasty little battle ensued. Evidently someone in command behind the police line informed AC Reilly who promptly ordered the water-cannon to fire on the crowd. Immediately people started to scatter. Rosemary and I moved alongside the PIOT people against the front of the Cabinet Office. They appeared unperturbed, indeed, if they showed any emotion, it was one of quiet satisfaction.

The police at the Parliament Square side of the crowd began to press forward. Anyone in their way was grabbed and arrested. If they tried to resist, they were beaten. Slowly they came alongside their colleagues in Downing Street and a large group peeled off and weighed into the demonstrators who were still fighting, but were now well and truly trapped. The rest of the crowd retreated, but continued to shout insults at the police. The PIOT man with the walkie-talkie was active again. Within a couple of minutes, several older women emerged from the back of the crowd and sat down in the road. They started singing "We shall overcome" and others quickly joined them. Soon several hundred were sitting there, singing defiantly away. As the rest of the crowd chased past them, fleeing the oncoming mass of police, they continued to sit there. Some of those fleeing sat down with them. Soon they were directly confronting the police.

"We're not moving!" cried out a grey-haired woman. "You've no right to move us!"

"We shall overcome!" called out another.

The police hesitated. The people sitting in the road were right in front of the TV cameras. They didn't want to be seen dragging struggling elderly women off to police vans. The handling of previous demonstrations had proved an embarrassment for the Commissioner. They halted.

AC Riley picked up his loud-hailer again.

"You are committing an unlawful obstruction of the public highway. If you do not disperse within five minutes, you will be dispersed by water-cannon. Be on your way."

At this point, the PIOT people began to make their way back towards Trafalgar Square. I imagined that this was the final element in the day's plan. I guessed

164

they wouldn't want to get caught up in any of the ensuing melee and risk getting arrested.

Without it being too obvious, we followed in their wake. Quite a few had decided they didn't wish to spend the rest of the day soaked to the skin or in a police cell, so they were doing the sensible thing too.

Then Rosemary did something quite extraordinary. She suddenly rushed over to a tall, stringy man with long blond hair, dark glasses and a denim suit.

"Rocky!" she exclaimed. "It's so good to see you!"

Then she embraced him and, from where I was standing, appeared to mutter something into his ear.

"I'm sorry, dear," he replied, looking startled. "I think you've mistaken me for someone else!"

"I'm terribly sorry. You do look just like him!"

She returned, looking visibly perplexed.

"What was that all about?" I whispered.

"I'll tell you later... You may even see for yourself."

The man with the long blond hair had moved back into the retreating crowd and disappeared from my view. We had now got practically back into Trafalgar Square. The PIOT leaders and their security people suddenly moved rapidly towards Northumberland Avenue, pushing their way through the crowd. They were too busy trying to ensure they got away to be watching us following them. Once in Northumberland Avenue, they walked quickly down towards the Embankment. But as they reached the junction with Great Scotland Yard, four police appeared round the corner and arrested the man who we believed we had seen following us in Kelsey Park and in the car outside our flats. His colleagues started to protest, but the man with the walkie-talkie evidently gave some sort of order and they all set off, quickly turning into Whitehall Place, where they were out of our sight. Within half a minute, two vehicles turned right out of Whitehall

Place towards the Embankment and then turned left under Hungerford Bridge eastwards. One of the vehicles was a black Ford, the other a light blue Commer van. We noted both registration numbers. We hoped that a canoodling couple on the pavement coming along Northumberland Avenue hadn't become too much of our trademark for our behaviour to have aroused their suspicions.

"It'd've been nice to have followed them," remarked Rosemary. "But we've not done too badly."

"Besides, they look a very cautious lot to me. I reckon they'd spot a car following them…..Do I take it you got the man who followed us arrested? Was that tall man with the blond hair someone you know from work?"

"No. He was one of the Special Branch detectives who took me to the safe house. He's called Geoff French."

"How on earth did you recognise him, especially at that distance?"

"Oh, that was easy. He actually looks like that normally. I suppose he must do a lot of under-cover work."

"And what exactly did you ask him to do?"

"To detain that man and get him photographed and fingerprinted, if possible. At least get him to show his diplomatic papers, so we know where he's from - or whether they're fake."

"Very quick thinking. Brilliant!"

"I hope they don't get too suspicious."

"What reason would the police give him for arresting him?"

"The grounds would be that they'd seen him directing the people who attacked the police. Of course, as there's no evidence, they'd have to let him go."

"I expect they must always run a risk of something like that happening."

We had reached the Embankment and turned west, walking through the gardens and out into Horse Guards Avenue. Almost directly in front of us, on the opposite side of the road was a man leaning against the bonnet of his car smoking a cigarette. It was Chief Inspector Mike Elliott. In his other hand was a walkie-talkie.

We crossed the road towards him and together began to chant fairly quietly "Kill the pigs! Kill the pigs!"

Mike looked momentarily furious and then his face relaxed into a big grin.

"I should've know you two couldn't keep away from trouble for long….At least dressed up like that no-one's going to recognise you – even your own mothers! I'd hoped you'd taken my advice and stayed out of sight, but when Geoff French told me that WPS Storey told him you'd spotted two of the people who'd been following you and pointed one of them out and suggested we should arrest him to get some better info about him, I realised that you have your uses."

"They were definitely part of the 'Peace in our time' group," I said. "They seemed a strange sort of organisation. Not really what I'd expected. They gave us a leaflet and a phone number to ring if we wanted to attend one of their meetings."

"I hope you're not seriously thinking of going, are you?"

"No. these disguises may work on this sort of occasion. After all, no-one is really going to pull your hair in the street to see whether it's a wig or try to test whether your moustache is real or just glued on. I don't think they're the sort of people who have the wool pulled over their eyes very often."

167

"Good. Leave that sort of thing to the professionals – for once, eh?"

"Did your people get the numbers of the cars they were using?" asked Rosemary. "We've memorised them....I reckon they've repainted the Commer van and given it new plates."

"It's all right. We got all that....You've been very helpful today. You're the only ones who could recognise the people who'd been following you. And putting them with these 'Peace in our time' people gives us something to get our teeth into......Do you want a lift back?"

"No thanks. While we're in disguise, we might as well enjoy the open air," she replied.

We wandered slowly, enjoying the warm sun, along the Embankment, past the Houses of Parliament and along Millbank until we reached the Tate Gallery. Conscious that we were hungry and the Tate had a small café, we went inside and ate a fairly mediocre lunch and then wandered round the gallery for an hour or so. I had to admit that, although I had lived in London for most of my life, I had never been in the Tate – or any other art gallery - before. I should also confess that many of the paintings left me cold. Paintings of countrysides, sometimes with mythical scenes, plump pink naked women or disembodied shapes did nothing for me. But when we reached the paintings by Turner, I was spellbound. The light, the texture, the incredible way just a few brush strokes could create such a powerful impression astounded me. I stood in front of a dozen or so pictures for ages, in awe.

"We'll make a culture vulture of you yet," remarked Rosemary.

I put my arm round her shoulders and kissed her head. Those wonderful paintings made me realise just

168

how much there was for Rosemary and me to do together – and how fragile and precious was our time together. My mind leapt back to when I'd seen what I thought was her devastated corpse and I shuddered. Guessing what I was thinking, she turned towards me and kissed me far too passionately for our aesthetic surroundings.

EIGHT
STITCHING A NET TOGETHER

We had planned our journeys the following morning so that we neither left the safe house together, nor did we arrive at our place of work in the same vehicle we had left the house. Rosemary would arrive by bus. I took the Tube to Monument and walked by way of Fenchurch Street to King's Beam House in Mark Lane. I had no idea what time Commissioner Watling might wish to see me, but I decided I did not want to be seen coming and going too often into Custom House, as I reckoned that was the most likely place my watchers from PIOT would be waiting.

I went up to the fourth floor and found the office where Watling's assistant, the pleasant Irish girl, was located. I explained that he had told me on Friday that he wished to see me on Monday morning, so I awaited his convenience.

"He'll be a bit of a while. Are you sure you want to wait?"

"Is there somewhere I could wait where I could use a phone?"

"There's a waiting room just round the corner."

The waiting room was small, but it had what I needed – a chair and a phone. I rang my office and got Ken Gray on the other end. I explained that I would be in the office later that morning, but that I had been asked to see Commissioner Watling. It was also possible that I would be summoned to a meeting in the afternoon. Meanwhile, I could confirm that the next stage of work had been agreed by the Committee MISC 38 (67) on Friday and I hoped by the end of the day to have a better idea of what firms we would need to meet. We would have to get our skates on as the

Committee wanted another report in a fortnight. Finally, I checked whether there were any other messages for me. To my relief, he said there were none so far.

About forty minutes and most of the "Financial Times" later, the Irish girl appeared and announced that Commissioner Watling would see me.

"Well now," he began, eyeing me with cold distaste. "Where shall I start? When I got back here, I decided to have a look at your file. It makes interesting reading. You appear to believe you can build a career on being difficult, unorthodox. You seem to think that if you acquire friends in strange places it will help you get on. You appear to have acquired a talent for getting in the way. You have itchy feet. The sooner you're in one job, you scuttle off to do another. You fly by the seat of your pants too often for me. In fact, you're a bit too fly generally...."

"Do you expect me to respond?" I asked coolly. I had vowed that once I escaped my father's bullying at the age of sixteen, I would never let anyone bully me again – and that included during National Service. I wasn't about to break that vow now.

"And you have no respect for your betters."

"I respect my betters and I hope I always treat those of senior rank with the respect due to their rank."

"I see your time in the Outfield has turned you into a typical barrack-room lawyer."

"I don't believe that's what I am, but I don't do grovelling or servility either."

"There you go again ... Tell me, why wasn't I aware before Friday's Committee meeting that you had received threatening messages and had a missile fired at your flat? Why was I made to look an ignoramus and a fool in front of the whole of Whitehall by Ffoulkes

171

and you? Did you plan to show me up as not knowing what was going on in my own Department?"

"Not at all. The messages were vague and uttered no specific threat. I gave them to Iain Cogbill in the IB, as he seemed to be the best person to investigate them or pass them on to contacts who would do it. The attack on my flat was unheralded and it was Special Branch who contacted the Department about what had happened. For most of Thursday I was in a state of shock after believing on Wednesday evening that my wife had been blown to pieces by the missile. After I discovered she wasn't dead, I followed the advice Special Branch gave me. I had absolutely no idea Mr Ffoulkes was going to mention what had happened. Indeed, I had assumed that I would have to leave the room for that item."

"Very plausible. You're a sight too plausible for me, Storey."

"Does that mean you are calling me a liar, Mr Watling?"

"Very good. Very good. How could I possibly know what goes on between you and these people! ... And another thing, what possessed you to break all the accepted rules and speak from the back seats at the MISC 38 meeting? Surely even you realised your intervention was bound to make your seniors appear ignorant and foolish in front of the rest of Whitehall?"

"I didn't know anything about such a rule. I assumed I was brought along to provide advice to the Committee on factual matters. I was merely trying to be helpful."

"And in the process make a Commissioner of Customs and Excise look a fool!"

"That wasn't my intention. I believed I could help the Committee with some detailed information which more senior people couldn't be expected to know. If I wasn't supposed to speak from the back seats, perhaps someone should've informed me."

"Well you bloody well know now! Not that I expect to take you along in future after Friday's performance. Indeed, I'm seriously considering taking you off this work altogether."

"Indeed. And for what reason?"

"Because your life is evidently in danger if you continue to do the work … At least that's the cover story. The real one is because you're insubordinate, disrespectful, untrustworthy and ignorant of important aspects of the work you're undertaking. What have you to say to that?"

"I'd say that you'd have a great deal of difficulty proving the first three. And as for the fourth, that could be remedied by training and being kept properly informed. As to replacing me, that's your decision. But I think if you let it be known that you're replacing me because my life has been put in danger by doing this work, you may get few takers as my replacement."

"So why are you prepared to keep on with it now? Seymour told me you'd offered to move on a couple of weeks ago."

"That was different. I wasn't prepared to have my name on a report that was changed by him and you into something that misrepresented what I and my Section had found. I want to stay with the work because I believe in seeing things through to the finish. Now we've got a better idea of who we're up against, we can be better protected."

"So you believe that we would misrepresent what your report said, do you?"

"'Nuanced' is the word, I believe. From what I'd seen at the time, it seemed to me that you would use your skill with drafting words to alter the sense of what we'd come up with to suit how you wanted the outcome to be. And as neither of you have ever suggested that what comes out from my report will be sent forward essentially as it is, I still believe that is possible."

"I think you misunderstand the need for us to polish the drafts that you submit."

"I may have little experience of this, but I can tell the difference between polishing and altering the sense of a draft, Mr Watling."

"That will be all, Storey. You will learn your fate in due course."

I left, feeling that I had at least left this poisonous man with something to think about before he decided to move me off the work. In fact, I suspected he never had any real intention of moving me. He just wanted the opportunity to be unpleasant to me to salve his wounded – and extremely fragile – vanity.

As I left his office, the Irish girl asked if I could call in on Mr Seymour before I left the building. So I headed to his room.

"I take it Wilf Watling has given you his two penn'orth?"

"Yes," I replied. "He indicated that he might well be moving me off this work."

"I expect that was just Wilf. He'd have to explain to rather too many people in Whitehall why he'd done so. The fact that your life has been put in danger through this work won't cut any ice with them. Those in the know will be aware you've got police protection and just substituting someone else wouldn't make the threat go away, but it would delay the work. Obviously, he didn't like what happened on Friday …"

"He made that extremely clear …"

"Plainly, you don't like him. But he can exert a considerable influence on your career."

"To be candid, I don't give a hoot about what he can and can't do to my career. If he feels the need to do me down because of his wounded vanity, I've got more important things to worry about – not least, that my wife and I remain alive. Perhaps if he'd seen what he thought was the body of his wife ripped to pieces by a missile, as I did last Wednesday evening, he might realise that for me, there are a vast number of things more important than all this bollocks."

"We do ... perhaps ... live in a rather rarefied world here, I suppose ..."

"Yes, you do ... Was there something you wanted to say to me?"

"Yes. Cabinet Office have sent over details of the four firms you'll need to meet before the next meeting of the Committee. You understand that's on Friday week, so we'll need to get an interim paper, at least, over to them by next Wednesday."

"How much we can get done will depend on how willing these firms are to accommodate meetings with us. We'll need to visit the premises where this stuff is going to be used – at least some, so we can get a general picture of their procedures and so on."

"So what you're saying is that it may be very interim."

"Yes. And you many need to fit in some time for me to fill you in on the details, as Commissioner Watling appears set on not taking me along to the next meeting."

"Hmmm ... I suspect if he tries to do that, he'll have to answer some pretty pointed questions from Cabinet Office and others."

My next step was the short walk from King's Beam House to the Custom House. Somewhere in good view of the entrance to Custom House would be people watching out for me, I was confident. Though I didn't believe they would attempt to kill me on the doorstep of an official building, I would still have preferred to have been able to get inside without being seen. Though there were side entrances, they were accessible only from Lower Thames Street, just like the main entrance. On the other hand, using the downstream entrance at least reduced any risk that my belief that they wouldn't try to kill me was misplaced. So I made my way towards the Tower, reaching the eastern end of Lower Thames Street, and approached Custom House from that side. The Revenue Constable on the gate wasn't unduly impressed at my wish to enter this way as it was an entrance mainly used by London Port staff, but on production of my Commission, he couldn't really deny me entrance. I traversed the long corridors belonging to London Port Collection before getting to the central lifts and on to my room. I reckoned it wasn't impossible that I had got into the building unseen by any watchers. I looked out on to Lower Thames Street from the fourth floor lobby of the lifts and could see several cars parked, a couple black, one blue, one grey. I couldn't really tell from there whether anyone was there, but I felt there was a fair chance there were a couple of people in one of them.

When I arrived, Ken Grey greeted me with a message that I was invited to Gower Street for 4 pm. I asked Bernard to get in touch with the people whose names we had been given at the four firms to arrange a full day visit to premises where they expected to use the American stuff. Ideally, I wished to carry out two or three visits that week, with another one the following Monday or Tuesday. I then had a look at what Ken and Morry had produced as the basic information which we would need for our visits. Unlike the senior people in King's Beam House, I felt no need to amend it for the sake of it. Though I wouldn't have chosen all the words

176

and phrases, the order in which we would seek the information seemed logical and the scope of that information was precisely what we needed at this stage. I asked them to get it typed, so that we could send it to the four firms in advance of our visits.

Eventually, Morry asked the question that I suspected was in all their minds.

"Is this work likely to be dangerous?" he began. "There's a rumour going round that someone tried to kill you because of it."

"To put it precisely," added Ken. "Are our lives in any danger?"

"No." I replied. "I'm the only one who's received any messages. As you will have seen, they are unspecific about what I am supposed to do. I believe I was attacked because the interim report reached the conclusion that it did. But it seems I'm seen as the author of the report and therefore the one who has to be influenced....By the way, I don't believe whoever it is meant to kill me – just to encourage me to do what they want."

"Which is – to produce a report that says the American stuff shouldn't come to this country?" said Morry.

"That seems to be the logical conclusion."

"But how …?"

"That's what my meeting this afternoon is about. You must all realise this is very sensitive stuff. Don't tell anyone about it, not your wives or girlfriends or any other colleagues or friends. The less anyone else knows, the less risky this'll be. Is that understood?"

Everyone nodded. I don't know whether they were convinced they weren't at risk, but no-one said so. In any case, as I suggested to them, it was likely that I would travel separately from them to the locations of the premises of these firms.

I used the rather unexciting canteen for my lunch and spent the first part of the afternoon sorting out what Paul Barton-Jones had done with the legislation relating to exports. It was pretty comprehensive, but I suggested that he spend a little time organising it so that the most important legislation covering exports was separated from the much more numerous elements which dealt with relatively minor aspects. This would take about a week, but it seemed to be the sort of thing that would keep him contentedly occupied. It would also mean that he could man the phones while the rest of us visited the four firms.

By 3 pm, Bernard told me that he had been able to fix up a visit for us to BCC, the British Computer Company, in Bracknell for Tuesday. The other firms hadn't got back to him yet. I decided I needed time to make my way to Gower Street and told everyone that I would not be coming back after my meeting, but that I expected to be at around my normal time the following morning. No doubt they wondered why I had to leave so early, but their imaginations would probably work it out soon enough.

I decided to leave the building by the same way I had entered it and then make my way towards King's Beam House. Anyone who saw me and was following me might be fooled into thinking I was following a predictable route. But I walked beyond the Customs Building to the next one and then turned into it and dashed down the stairs to the "Manorial Rooms" restaurant. I had learnt during my time in the City that one could walk past the restaurant and, following various underground corridors, some of which were probably private, emerge in Fenchurch Street. I walked smartly across Fenchurch Street and, by way of back streets and alleys, ended up in Aldgate where I caught several buses, before arriving in Gower Street.

Assuming the people watching me were only using a single car, it seemed to me that their chances of pursuing me successfully were quite small.

I was a little early and had to sit for about ten minutes in the gloomy lobby. Then a young woman, of the type generally described as a 'blue-stocking' , appeared and escorted me to the second floor and along a corridor to a small room evidently set up for meetings. Just as we entered, I heard footsteps behind me along the corridor and Jacob Ffoulkes and Jones, with whom I was previously acquainted, joined me.

"Grateful to you for coming over," Ffoulkes began. "Coffee? Tea?"

"I'd have the tea if I was you," advised Jones.

"I'll have tea then." I kept on thinking that Ffoulkes always looked out of his element behind a table. For all the world, he resembled the skipper of a yacht, with his natural place behind a ship's wheel. Perhaps he had begun his career in the Navy.

"Have you started on your visits to the firms getting the US stuff?" asked Ffoulkes.

"We've got a visit to BCC on Tuesday and I'm planning to get as many as I can in before next Wednesday."

"Good. It'll be interesting to see what you make of BCC … Would you mind awfully if Eric here or one of his colleagues tags along with you? I'm sure you can guess why without asking."

"I don't see any reason why not. I'll just introduce him as one of my colleagues."

"That wasn't the main reason for asking you over here, however … I suppose you've been mulling over why your flat was attacked?"

"Yes – and about the timing."

"I suspect we may have been thinking along the same lines. From what I understand, you've been

179

receiving a series of rather vague messages, which actually made no threat of violence. Then suddenly someone fires a missile into your flat, possibly intended to kill your wife, more likely, in my view, to kill the East German woman as a warning to you. Does that make sense to you?"

"Perfectly."

"It raises a number of questions. First – why send you messages that don't tell what you should be doing about them? Second – why the sudden change from opaque messages to extreme violence? Third....Well, I'll come on to that in a moment … Now as far as one is concerned - the messages – the most likely explanation is that there's been a cock-up. You were evidently supposed to get a message to make sure your report either stymied or, at best, reduced the likelihood of this US kit getting here. I think we can assume that from the reaction to the outcome of your interim report. And that, of course leads us to two – why the sudden violence? Answer – because you'd put your interim report in. Whoever did this must've known about what was in the report, but also knew that there was still a chance that your report could go the way they want. Are you with me?"

"Completely. It seems to me that someone in or around that Committee must be tipping them off, directly or indirectly."

"Yes. That's why I skirted round that aspect last Friday. I hope that whoever is doing this hasn't been put on the alert."

"Unfortunately, when I thought about it, there seemed to be a lot of potential suspects."

"Less than you might think. Your MISC 38 paper didn't get circulated until later afternoon on Wednesday, so it wouldn't've reached recipients outside the Cabinet Office before 6 pm. Personally, I don't think it's credible for someone to have set up the attack on your flat in that timescale. So that rules out everyone except people in Customs and the Cabinet Office. Of course, it's possible that they spoke to colleagues in other Departments, but I think we should concentrate on them for the moment."

"I hadn't realised that….It reduces the numbers quite a bit. I believe you could reduce it a bit more. In theory all of my section knew what was in the interim report, but they'd known it for the best part of a week. Besides, apart from the fact that I'd be astounded whether any of them had the necessary contacts, they got into the Section in an entirely haphazard way, without any volunteering for the work. It seems to me that whoever is doing this has a longer term motivation and is in a job because of its value in achieving the goals of whoever is trying to stop the American stuff coming here."

"I wouldn't disagree with you. The problem is that we need to narrow it down further - and also discover who exactly is behind this. Whoever it is within the Civil Service isn't the lynch-pin. They're merely working for someone – I guess either the Soviets or the Americans. But at present we don't know which. Moreover, we don't have anything like enough to be able to pin anyone down. So if we started to check up, going backwards, into who might've tipped these people off, all we'll do is put them on the qui vive without being able to identify them. So next time, they'll be doubly careful."

"I can see that. How many people are we talking about?"

"I reckon about eight or nine in Cabinet Office and three in Customs."

"Watling, Woodruffe and Seymour? I think you'd have to add Watling's PA and presumably Woodruffe has someone who opens his post – even 'confidential' stuff. And the paper was typed by Seymour's Divisional Typist."

"I'm always a bit doubtful as to how much such people actually read - but we should include them, if only to discard them as quickly. I doubt whether most have either the motivation or the contacts."

"So where do we go from here?"

"That's the most difficult bit – and why we need your help, Mr Storey. Special Branch and I want to set a trap. It probably won't enable us to put our finger on a particular individual, but it will enable us to get them in and give 'em the third degree. My purpose is to start a chain of events that will not only unmask this person, but also the nature of the organisation which carried out the attack on your flat and the people who stand behind them. But we can't do this in a single step."

"I understand. And I assume it's the next stage of my report that is going to be the cheese in this trap?"

"I see you're ahead of me again. Yes. What we need to do is for you to indicate to certain selected people after your second visit to these firms, say, that it's clear that we could give an excellent guarantee to the Americans that their kit would be safe here. But then, I'm afraid, comes the more difficult bit. We need your flat to be attacked again. You or your wife will need to appear to go into your flat, knowing that you've been followed there, so that they have the opportunity to do what they've threatened.....Of course it won't be your flat – or the safe house you're currently in. It'll be a flat in a place of our choosing where we can observe these people and catch them in flagrante."

"I'm not prepared to let Rosemary get involved in this. I don't mind doing it myself. But their last message was aimed at her. If you're going to do this, you'll have to find a substitute who looks like her."

"That's exactly what she said to Special Branch when they spoke to her just before lunch – only the other way round. She says she's prepared to do it, provided we can guarantee that the cheese doesn't get eaten before the mouse is trapped, as she put it."

"I'll kill her myself!" I growled. "That woman has got even less sense than I have!"

"I can assure that this will be set up so that it looks as though you are in the flat, but actually you'll both be entirely safe out of sight round the back. The only possible risk would be if they tried to kill you when you led them there, but Special Branch and I believe we can manage the timing so that when you reveal the location of the flat, your deaths aren't in their immediate plans."

"You don't think they mightn't be suspicious about such convenient timing?"

"My impression - from observations on those who've been watching your wife and you at your places of work, is that they are getting very frustrated at their inability to discover where you're living….and their plans have been disrupted by the work you two did on Sunday."

"With the 'Peace in our time' people?"

"Yes. Of course, the police had to let the man they arrested go. But they did manage to take his photograph and get a set of fingerprints, as well as his so-called diplomatic status. It turned out to be fake Irish and his name, for what it is worth, is William Ormonde. But it seems that our activities have been enough for them to cut their losses with him and his partner. A William Ormonde and a Deirdre Anderson have been booked on a flight to Shannon this evening. We'll do our best to see they're tracked wherever they go from there. The fingerprints are still being checked, including with Interpol. It does seem that these 'Peace in our time' people are pretty heavily mixed up in all this, but

183

they're a very cagey bunch. They're being ultra-cautious at the moment – no doubt because of their involvement in this matter."

"When do you want all this to happen?"

"Ideally, I'd like you to do your visits on Tuesday and Wednesday – and then perhaps allow yourself to be followed to our bogus flat on Thursday evening. Then you inform Watling and Seymour - probably a short memo perhaps – by mid-morning Friday that it looks as though we could give the guarantee to the US."

"No-one else? Not Cabinet Office?"

"No. You haven't done that before, so it'd be bound to look suspicious. I don't think either Watling or Seymour will be able to resist telling their oppos in the Cabinet Office. Then we can expect fireworks Friday evening. But we'll talk about the exact details – either us here or Special Branch – on Friday afternoon – because it will need to be very precisely done."

"I think you can guess I'll be extremely interested in the details."

After my circuitous route back to the safe house, I found Rosemary cooking cauliflower cheese.

"You never said you were going to see Special Branch!" I demanded.

"I didn't know anything about them until my Inspector told me there were two men from Special Branch who wanted to have a word. One was Mike Elliott, of course, and it was him who put this plan to me."

"And you went along with it! Haven't you been in enough danger already?"

"I knew you wouldn't turn it down. I wanted to be with you, perhaps it's better – either neither of us gets killed or we both do. You don't think I'd want to remain alive if you were killed do you?"

She burst into tears, sobbing on my shoulder.

"We could still not do it," I said, stroking her hair. "They could still use substitutes."

"I think those people would spot it....and that's pretty well what Mike said earlier today....At least it'd end it and we could get back to living normal lives."

"As various people have said – we are complete fools!"

"But anyway, let's be two fools together ... The skin above your upper lip looks really red and sore ..."

"It's that bloody gum Arabic from that bloody moustache ... It's been plaguing me all day."

"And now I've put cheese sauce in your hair."

"Can you be arrested for dangerous spooning?"

"Only if it's indecent."

NINE

PREPARING THE GROUND

Only my Section, the Security Service and BCC knew of our visit the following day, so I felt sufficiently confident of my destination not being known to make the train journey with them. I joined them at Waterloo and introduced them to "Mr Jones from Whitehall" and left it to their imaginations to speculate who he was. We spent the journey agreeing who would ask which questions and how we might split up and examine different aspects, if that possibility was made available to us. I hoped my Section didn't feel too uncomfortable travelling with someone who might put their lives at risk – and probably thought Jones was my rather improbable-looking bodyguard.

On arrival at Bracknell station, a white minibus with 'BCC' emblazoned on it in large blue letters along with the company's logo awaited us. I hoped that Berkshire County Council used a different set of colours, otherwise there was considerable potential for confusion. We were driven a few miles to the outskirts of the town, where a new office block stood before us. We were met by three men in identical black suits, white shirts and blue and white striped ties, all with crew-cuts. I wondered to myself whether the company also produced robots.

"Hi, Greg Lester," said the first man, a little taller and burlier than the others. He had a North American accent. "Tim Nicholls and Trevor Pickles." A vague wave indicated his companions. "Delighted to meet you. We've got a conference room at your disposal. But we thought we might start with coffee and a presentation."

Having introduced ourselves, we trooped inside. The building appeared ultra-modern, in a Scandinavian style, with lots of highly-varnished light pine. The conference room had modern – and not very comfortable chairs, each with their own table – and a large cinema screen at one end....and a roof made of pine slats. Immediately coffee had been given us, Greg began his presentation, which was illustrated by a series of slides projected on to the screen behind him. They were, inevitably, about the company, its business, its financial position, its main products, customers and its 'ethos'. It took about forty minutes – but felt longer.

"Any questions?" asked Greg.

"We have a lot of questions," I replied. "Your presentation was extremely helpful in giving us a general background to the company, but our interests are quite specific. I hope you received our note setting out the questions which we would like to ask you and your colleagues. It is also necessary for us to see the premises where the components from the US would be used."

"No problem. Our factory is a few miles away. The guys there are prepared."

"Can you explain what you expect your procedures to be for bringing these items from the States?" asked Morry.

"Sure," replied Greg. "Trevor?"

Trevor was evidently the operational manager and he was able to answer many of our questions about how procedures would work. Tim, despite looking like everyone's idea of a boffin, was apparently the head of security. Jones and I grilled him quite a lot about his responsibilities, both in relation to premises and personnel.

"Before we mosey over to Popeswood, I suggest a spot of lunch," proposed Greg.

He pressed a button under his table and within five minutes, trays of sandwiches and collations of cold meats appeared on a long side-table, with a couple of bowls of salad and several bottles of fruit juice and mineral water. This was followed by fruit or fruit salad and more strong coffee.

Then Greg bid us farewell and Trevor and Tim accompanied us on the BCC minibus to Popeswood, where the 'manufacturing facility' was to be found. From the outside, it was quite impressive.

"It looks like a modern gaol," remarked Bernard. As I told Jacob Ffoulkes that my staff weren't security risks, I hoped he had never seen the inside of either an old or modern gaol.

It was surrounded by a wire fence, with barbed wire liberally entangled round the top. There appeared to be only one entrance, with an electric gate, controlled by a security man in a gatehouse. We got out and asked how they managed traffic in and out.

"All vehicles 'ave to be logged in and out. Nothing comes in unless it's on my checklist," said the gateman. "If you work 'ere and drive to work, you 'ave to 'ave a permit and you 'ave to be checked in to be working 'ere every day. If you 'aven't got a permit and you aren't logged in for the day, I won't let you in. Simple as that."

"What about people on foot or bike?" I asked.

"Everyone 'as to 'ave a pass. For people like you just coming in for the day, it's a day pass. Everyone else 'as a monthly pass, except management 'oo 'ave three monthlies. You 'ave to show it whenever you come in and whenever you leave. If you don't show it on your way in, I don't let you in. If you don't show it when you leave, I don't let you out. These gates are controlled from 'ere and you can't get in and out without the gateman's say-so."

"Supposing someone had a pass but was taking stuff out which he shouldn't?"

"I'd only search someone if I was told to by management – Mr Nicholls or one of 'is managers."

"Let me explain that when we're inside," added Tim Nicholls.

The entry formalities having been concluded – including our pictures being taken on a Polaroid camera. Apparently these were stored so that the gateman could check both regular and infrequent visitors, to ensure no-one attempted to masquerade as someone else. In practice, the gateman said he knew most of the regulars. Nicholls explained that the company was considering putting photographs on all monthly and three monthly passes.

Inside, Nicholls and Pickles took us to what they called the 'operations module'. This was a large room with an internal window looking over the factory floor, where dozens of people, all in blue or white overalls and wearing the sort of headgear one normally associated with surgeons in hospitals, were busy constructing the company's computers. In the room were several metal cupboards painted a shining white, with "BCC" and the company logo on each. More interesting were several TV screens and things that looked like typewriters with only the typing keys. There were also several machines I recognised from the computer books I had been reading – essentially ones where information could be fed into the computer and for other information to emerge. The typewriter thing was ... a terminal ... At least, I think that was what it'd been called in the book.

"With this kit we can keep track of every component," explained Trevor Pickles. "Quite simply, if any component fails, the computer is likely to be faulty and our reputation is on the line. When you're competing against the American giants, you've got to maintain a reputation for reliability and speed - which is what we're hoping this American kit will give us. Reliability depends on quality control. If any of the workers drops a component or damages it any way, they have to announce it – by putting their hand up – and the quality control staff will check it and replace it, if necessary. The component is then written off and the component database updated. At any time, I can tell you how many units we have of each and every component – whether they are out on the factory floor, whether they're in the holding area or whether they're in store. The store is accessible only by a few staff who have personal keys and the six-button entry system is updated on a random basis daily. I can assure you it would be impossible for someone to take any component out without us knowing it."

"How do you physically know the items are where you say they are?" asked Morry. "Presumably someone picks out, say, 20 diodes from the store and takes them to the holding area. What happens? Does he key that into the computer to update the database?" ("Good Heavens," I thought to myself, "Does Morry speak computer?")

"Essentially yes. But we do run regular random scans of most components, where security staff actually check the numbers in the holding area or the stores against the numbers that are said to be there according to the database."

"And how often are there discrepancies?"

"Very infrequently – and so far explained by human error, not by any apparent desire to steal anything."

"In any case," added Tim Nicholls. "We realise the high-level security issues surrounding these American components. They will be manufactured in a completely closed facility in small numbers and employing only thoroughly vetted staff."

"Can we see this unit?" asked Jones.

"I'm afraid it's still in the relatively early stages of construction. It's nearer Priestwood, a couple of miles from here. You're welcome to look over it at any stage. Indeed, we'd be happy for you to vet all the security protocols and procedures."

"That's extremely helpful."

"But to add about the American kit. When it gets here from Priestwood, we propose to control it under even tighter procedures. It will be kept under separate lock and key in the stores, and will require double key and two separate people to access. Every time any stock is used, there will be an immediate independent stock count. We will know how many are required per day and each one will be identified after installation in our machines and subject to independent check. From what we can gather, these things could make a phenomenal difference to the next generation of computers and if we don't seize this opportunity, we'll be left desperately behind. We'll do practically anything to get our hands on this kit."

"Will you be doing R&D with it?" asked Jones.

"Yes. We have an R&D lab over towards Swindon. They shouldn't need more than fifty or so pieces of kit to work with. But as they're where we're trying to get a leap or two ahead of the competition, as you might imagine, security's as tight as a drum there. I'll bet we could show Porton Down and Windscale a few things about security there....But, of course, not many people work there and traffic in and out is tiny."

"We might need to have a look there at some point," said Jones.

There were more details to go into and we had a walk round - dressed in overalls with a surgeon's cap on to prevent hair or hair follicles from contaminating the work area – to see the controls actually in operation. Then Nicholls and Pickles took us to the managers' restaurant for a cup of tea and a biscuit or two and we were taken back through gate security and dropped at Bracknell station by the BCC minibus.

"That was pretty impressive," observed Ken. "They're clearly desperate to get hold of the American stuff."

"They also have strong business reasons for running a very tight ship," added Morry. "It's a competitive business and they can't afford to let any secrets get out to their competitors."

"I agree," I said. "But I'd be grateful if you could use your 'revenue noses' to think how you might work your way round that system and get a piece of the American kit out. It may be fool-proof and it certainly looked good. But they knew we were coming and were well prepared. If we are going to give them the thumbs up, we need to step back a bit and reflect before we do so."

I got home a little before Rosemary and, when she arrived, was reading letters which had been passed on to me by the concierge from a bogus address we'd had to give to people who needed to contact us.

"You'll be pleased to know that the management company for our flats and the insurance company have reached an agreement and work will start in the next week or so on repairing our flat," I announced.

"I'm fed up!" she said. "I hate being cooped up like this! I like going out for walks with you and doing things like playing squash. Friday can't come soon enough for me! I don't like nipping down alley-ways and catching buses in the wrong direction just to stop someone following me."

"That's not really it, though, is it?"

"No. You're going out and helping to make this thing happen and get everything in the clear, I just go to work and do the same old thing. I want to be able to do more to help … I know it's not practical, but that's how I feel!"

I held her in my arms while she wept. Rosemary wasn't normally weepy – and I knew what was causing it. She was worried about Friday – and her work gave her too much time to think about it. But I also knew she wasn't worrying about herself, she was worrying about me.

"I know there's nothing that can be done about it," she sniffled. "It's just I get so annoyed and frustrated. I loved our nice airy flat and I detest this gloomy place where I feel like a prisoner. You're much more phlegmatic than I am."

"I probably had to keep my head down more as a child. I'm more used to putting up with things, I suppose."

"So you don't mind about this flat?"

"I'd far rather be back in our flat … But this place? … I suppose I don't care much what it's like because I'd be happy being anywhere when it's with you. I wouldn't want to be in our flat if you were somewhere else."

"Now you've made me feel bad …"

"Not at all … we're different in some things …"

"You do know I'd rather be here with you than anywhere and apart?"

"I know we love each other sufficiently to risk being killed together rather than be separated for ever. I'm just sorry that if it all goes wrong on Friday, you won't've been very happy in the days beforehand."

"Sometimes, you are far too nice, Nick Storey …"

"If I ever feel low, I just have to remember seeing your face in that hospital room last Wednesday morning. It was like dying and coming back to life. You are so precious to me …"

We held each other for a long time in silence. Love is a curious thing. You feel it ought to make you happy all the time, but it doesn't.

The following day we paid a similar visit to Laurel Computing Ltd (LCL) who were based in Cambridge. This was a much more English company, that expected us to make our own way from the station and left us waiting in the traditional wood-panelled lobby of their headquarters for several minutes before a pert secretary with long blonde hair and long slim legs took us to their boardroom. There we met Gus Jarvis, Technical Director, Meurig Hughes, Operations Manager and Elwyn Strevens-Davis, Head of Security.

Jarvis, who looked like a typical University science don – all floppy hair and thick-rimmed glasses – explained the company's business and how the US kit would fit into their 'future product profile'. Hughes and Strevens-Davis then gave us a theoretical response to the note we had sent them previously. They seemed slightly surprised when I told them that we would need to see how these procedures actually worked on the ground in their factory.

"We could, of course, go over to the Cherry Hinton site," said Jarvis, "but you will have to take us as you find us."

"That's exactly what we want," I replied.

We were driven over in their cars. The factory looked like a newly-built secondary school, but it did have a perimeter fence about ten feet high and made of steel, but lacked the ferocious barbed wire we had seen in Bracknell the previous day. There was also a gatehouse and electric gates not dissimilar from those we'd seen at Popeswood.

"All the regulars have passes," explained the cheery, middle-aged woman in the gatehouse. There were a couple of men with her, sipping at large mugs of tea.

"We get a daily schedule for cars and lorries going in and out, including employees. Anything else has to wait and be checked with Security. Most people have permanent passes, with their photos, like this," she said, showing us hers. "Day visitors get a day pass."

"Do you photograph people who get day passes?" asked Morry.

"No. But they're escorted everywhere by someone from Security or the person they've come to see."

"Do you do any checking of people taking stuff out that they shouldn't?" asked Ken.

"Not unless Security asked us to. I know most people here. We've all been here a long time – many of us ever since it opened here."

Having received our paper passes, we went into the factory.

"We might start with lunch," suggested Jarvis.

We ate in the management restaurant – a choice of four hot dishes and three hot deserts. I was told the food was the same as in the works canteen. It was decent, stodgy, typical English fare. I had a steak and kidney pie, peas and chips followed by baked apple and custard. I would need to get back to my regular games of squash with Rosemary if I kept lunching like this!

We were then taken round the factory floor – having attired ourselves in a more assorted set of overalls and headgear than the previous day. LCL clearly didn't see the need to dress everyone the same or emblazon its name and logo everywhere. As a result, it seemed a more relaxed place, but also less dynamic and potentially less secure.

"How exactly do you ensure that components don't go missing?" I asked them. "As I'm sure you're aware, this stuff that may be coming from the US will need to be treated with absolute security. Indeed, if adequate systems aren't in place, it won't come here at all."

"There's a fairly generic, computer-based stock control system that we use," explained Hughes, in a lilting Welsh accent. "It was actually developed over in the States. I helped to develop it actually when I worked over there for Zeetronix Inc. It basically counts flows in and out and relies on periodic physical stock checks. Of course, there's a necessary human interface - an operator has to update whenever stock is moved from the store to pre-pro, as we call it, and then into production. Part of the stock in store is checked daily, after anything unused is returned at the end of production. We reckon to check every item over a ten day period – though we include a random element, so no-one can be sure what items will be checked until moments before the check starts."

"How is access to the store controlled?"

"Six digit keypad, with the numbers changed randomly on a daily basis. The most valuable kit is stored in a special secure store within the main store. That's on a separate keypad, with different numbers and a key, held by a security manager. We'll use that system for any really sensitive stuff, like this American kit. We'll have to treat it like gold-dust. It's that sort of thing that keeps us ahead of our competitors."

"We can't afford to be slack," added Strevens-Davis. "If our competitors get to know our secrets, we're dead and buried."

"But can't they just get hold of one of your products legitimately and take it apart?" asked Jones.

"We make large computers for large organisations – like Government Departments and the military. Our contracts include a security requirement. For commercial customers we have an even more powerful penalty clause. If we discovered it was through them, by design or negligence, that one of our products fell into the hands of a competitor, they'd be required to pay us enormous sums in damages."

"But my understanding is that for the first few years, this American stuff won't be allowed outside Government?" said Jarvis.

"If you get this American stuff, presumably you'll be manufacturing it yourselves?" I asked.

"Yes. We've got a small plant near Huntingdon. It's presently manufacturing certain high-spec diodes and resistors, but if we get this kit we'll be turning the plant over entirely to manufacturing them there. It's like a small fortress. You're welcome to visit it, but I can assure you the diodes and resistors are our top differentiators from the competition and it's as tight as a nut there."

"I think we would want some of our team to visit. If possible in the next week or so. What will happen to these diodes and resistors?"

"As we understand the nature of the American kit, it'll render these diodes at least partly obsolescent – and we're not sure about the resistors. Once we get the kit, we'll need to get it to our lab here in Cambridge and work out how various pieces of our kit will need to be modified to work with it. Then, of course, we'll want to start taking the whole thing a lot further. This is only the first step in what appears to be a new technology. We want to be at the forefront of developing it."

"Where is your lab?"

"Round the back on site here. Only certain staff with keys and a daily password for the entry key system are allowed in."

"Of course, you can't stop people retaining information in their heads and walking out with it," observed Jones.

"That's undeniably true. The human factor – you'll never get that 100%," said Hughes. "It's the bane of the American companies. And they pay a much higher whack than we do over here. We rely a lot on loyalty, giving our best people what they want to work most happily and allowing them space to do some of the things that interest them, but may not be immediately what the Company wants. So if Joe Bloggs, say, wants a vintage car instead of a bonus and wants to be able to listen to the Beatles at work, we'll do what we can to oblige him. But we also expect meticulous records and file loads of patents, so that if someone did try anything on, we'd have a better chance of identifying them."

"Isn't that shutting the stable door after the horse has bolted?"

"To some extent. But if we could prove it, their contracts would make them liable to extremely heavy damages – a good deal more than they'd earn in a couple of years for a competitor."

"Proving it would be the hard thing, I guess."

"And we also maintain discreet – very discreet – security checks on all personnel, but particularly those critical to the company," added Strevens-Davis.

We looked round a bit more of the site, including the entrance to the lab, but we had seen and heard all we really needed to. They graciously dropped us off at the station on their way back to their headquarters.

"Well," I said, as we sat down in the London train, "what did you make of them?"

"Better in substance than in display," observed Morry. "It's not as showy as the other lot, but I doubt it's any less effective."

"It's not surprising," added Jones. "They face essentially the same commercial pressures and have competitive advantages they don't want to leak. Besides, both of them do masses of business with

198

Government, especially the military. It'll be interesting to see Qomputix who operate mainly in the commercial marketplace and are only included in this because of some small, but important contracts for MoD. I imagine they'll have to run a segregated operation in some way."

"We haven't got a visit now until Monday, when, by chance, it's Qomputix," I said. "I'm going to have a first shot at what our next interim report might look like based on these two visits. I'd like the rest of the Section to pool your notes and your reflections and start fleshing them out in the appropriate sections of the full report, please. But, in general, I think we're all agreed that we could give a pretty positive view about procedures and systems at these two firms...I think it's certainly worth making the point about people walking out with information in their heads and passing it on and whatever they're doing, that'll never enable us to give 100% guarantee and that'll have to be made clear to the Americans. But it seems to me they must suffer from exactly the same risk. I didn't think how these two aim to tackle the risk could seriously be improved on, do you?"

"From my experience," replied Jones, "I'd say that the Americans are a lot more at risk than we are. Trying to build loyalty rather than buy it seems to be to be more effective."

"But it might be difficult to convince the Yanks of that," remarked Morry.

To some extent, I reflected, my next draft interim report would be exactly what I had argued against doing. I would necessarily be more positive about the security of these firms than if I was committing myself in a real, final version. But I understood that it needed to be so positive that those who wished to prevent it would feel obliged to take speedy action. I just hoped this three or four page note which I would draft the following morning wasn't, in a sense, my suicide note!

At least when I got home, Rosemary was in a more cheerful mood. When I heard why, I was a good deal less cheerful.

"Mike Elliott thinks I should lead them, at least part of the way towards our new flat," she said happily. "He thinks I shouldn't go all the way, but get them into the right area. I'd perhaps get to a couple of streets away and then disappear inside a shop and escape round the back. Then when you lead them the rest of the way tomorrow, it'll look more plausible."

"If I was them, I'd think I was being set up," I growled. "I don't know why Mike Elliott wants to put you in any more danger than you already are!"

"It was my idea....You know how I was feeling yesterday. Then I had this great idea!"

"And if they decide to shoot you when they get the chance?"

"But they won't know about your latest report, will they?"

"No. I suppose that's true. But you be bloody careful tomorrow!"

"And you. You've got to lead them all the way there."

"Do you know where 'there' is yet?"

"No. I didn't ask and Mike didn't say. I think we're going to get some instructions tomorrow afternoon."

I spent the following morning drafting. I used the way into Custom house that I'd used on Monday and still felt reasonably reassured that I hadn't been spotted. But even if I had, the fact that I was using a side entrance ought to have reassured my watchers that I was on my guard. It seemed inconceivable to me that they wouldn't assume that I knew they would be

200

watching my work place and also that they wouldn't expect me to use devious ways of getting by them.

I was struck that I'd received no more messages. I thought they might have sent something more to Custom House, but presumably they felt the last one had been clear enough – and the attack on our flat certainly seemed to have shown what direction they wanted my report to go. From their point of view it would be whether I heeded their warnings and, if not, could they locate Rosemary or me at a time and in a place where they could wreak their vengeance and presumably send a warning to everyone else?

By lunchtime I had completed my draft of a first go at a Committee paper covering my next interim report. Indeed, I had completed two – the one I would pass to Nigel Seymour and Commissioner Watling the following day and the real one which would be clearly indicated as such in a note stuck on an envelope in my combination safe – just in case … .

Mike Elliott arrived at the Custom House on a police launch. I must confess I hadn't thought of that as a way of arriving unseen by my watchers, but then I lacked his access to water-craft.

"Right," he said cheerily. "Are you ready to become the cheese? Not a big cheese – just a tempting morsel?"

"I hope, for Rosemary's sake and mine, this afternoon is not about being any kind of cheese, but merely showing the rat where the cheese can be found!"

TEN

VARIOUS CHEESES ARE DISPLAYED TO TEMPT VARIOUS RODENTS

At my usual time, I left Custom House by the exit to which I had become accustomed. Anything else might well have put my watchers on their guard. However, in order to ensure they saw me, an unmarked police vehicle came along Byward Street at some speed and made its brakes squeal and hooted at me as I crossed the road. Having gestured at the car, I nipped over to the other side of the road. A black car pulled out from further along Lower Thames Street. I turned the corner into Great Tower Street and stood for a couple of minutes at a bus stop with several other people. The black car halted. I got on to the next bus going west and took it as far as the bus stop by Mansion House Tube station. From the upper deck I was able to observe from the corner of my eye that the black car was following at a discreet distance and that they should be able to see me. At Mansion House I took a bus which went round the eastern end of St Paul's on to Holborn Viaduct. I alighted at the bus stop just before Chancery Lane and noted the black car pulling over as I got off. My next bus went down Holborn Kingsway and along the Strand. I got off at the bus stop for Charing Cross Station. The black car still had me in their sights. I walked past the front of the station and into Northumberland Avenue, where an unmarked Special Branch car was waiting to take me to the safe house.

As I got in, the driver said, "A black car has just turned the corner. Is that the one that's been following you?"

"Yes," I replied, peering, I hoped not too noticeably, in the driving mirror.

We set off, along the Embankment and over Westminster Bridge, the black car continuing to shadow us without ever getting too close. We made our way along Lambeth Palace Road and the Albert Embankment and into Wandsworth Road.

"Is Red Leicester out of the way?" asked the driver on his radio.

"Yes. Done and dusted. Rat 2 is currently in Old Town, presumably hoping for a sighting. You can proceed."

"And what am I?" I enquired. "I take it my wife is Red Leicester – and that she's safe."

"She'll meet you in the safe house … You're Blue Stilton … You'll have take it up with the Chief Inspector. He thought them up."

"I probably will. Who does he think he is – the bloody fondue chef?"

After a while, we turned off into North Street in Clapham and right into Charlotte Row, where there was a terrace of early Victorian houses of fair size, but little architectural merit. As I got out, I could see the black car halt opposite the turning into Charlotte Row. I went into the house and the Special Branch car turned and shot away.

Mike Elliott was in the lobby.

"Blue Stilton has arrived," I announced. "Rat 1 has followed his scent."

"I hope he's going to drive up outside," said Mike Elliott. "I want him to see you're both here. Your flat is on the first floor. WPS Storey is already there. Once I give the word, I suggest you make yourselves discreetly visible."

I went upstairs and found Rosemary drinking a cup of tea in a large stuffed settee with a ghastly floral cover.

"Hello Red Leicester," I said as we hugged each other and kissed.

"Uh?"

"That's your code-name … I'm Blue Stilton. I think Mike Elliott must've chosen yours first somehow."

"Ok 'Blue'. Do you want some tea? Do you know how long we've got to stay here? This place gives me the creeps. It even makes me nostalgic for the place in Pimlico."

"Yes, it's not exactly us, is it."

"They've driven up outside," said Mike Elliott in a loud whisper from half way up the stairs. "Given them about five minutes then let them see you both – but don't make it too obvious please!"

About seven minutes later, I turned on the light in the lounge to reveal Rosemary and me, apparently examining some papers at the table. Within about thirty seconds I dashed over to the switch and turned it off. Then made my way as unobtrusively as I could to the window and drew the curtains. Then I turned the light back on again.

"That looked fine," said Mike, a couple of minutes later. I've got a couple of chaps upstairs in the pub on the corner and they said it looked just about right."

"Do we have to stay here much longer?" asked Rosemary.

"No. You can come down here and learn all about the special nature of this house."

We finished our cups of tea and went downstairs into a large kitchen in the back.

"We got this place after we convicted a man called Ambrose Figueroa. He was a very successful confidence trickster and this house was one of his little tricks. If you go down into the cellar – which we shall in a moment – you can see that there's a door at the far end. It leads into a passage he constructed between this house and one directly behind it in Lillieshall Road, which he also owned, under another name, of course. It provided a very convenient means of concealing his exact whereabouts and was an excellent way to avoid capture."

"Although it isn't to my taste, I'm surprised you're going to allow these people to fire a missile into this house," I said.

"It's scheduled to be pulled down in the next year or so anyway. And, as you've already given your opinion of it, you may imagine that it's shared by others who are placed in it for their own safety. Most of the other residents have moved out already, so it's also becoming a bit more exposed … But for a couple of days it doesn't matter."

"You're not expecting us to stay the night here are you?" demanded Rosemary.

"No. We'll use the passage into Lillieshall Road and get you back to the real safe house shortly … But I would like you to leave from here tomorrow morning, if you will. Otherwise, your watchers will think it very strange."

"OK. You'll just drive us back to the building at the back?"

"Yes – and drive you both away separately as usual, with the usual rigmarole about getting you into work."

"And then we return here tomorrow evening?"

"Yes. But that will require some very careful timing and stage setting. We'll be in touch with you about that after lunch tomorrow.

We were led into the cellar, through a door and along a narrow, low, damp and dank passage to the cellar of the house behind. There were a couple of men and a woman there who bade us 'Good Evening' and showed us through to the front door, where a Harrods delivery van was parked outside.

"That's your transport for this evening," said the woman. So we got in, discovering that there were a couple of perfectly comfortable seats in the back, well-nigh invisible to the casual observer.

Back at Erasmus Street we ate and I asked Rosemary about her part in this deception.

"Usually I dash round the corner into St James Park Tube station or cut through into Birdcage Walk through the little alley that's closed to cars, so by the time they've sorted themselves out, I'm on a bus and they've no idea where I've gone. But today I rushed into Victoria Street and had to wait for a bus for a couple of minutes, which gave them enough time to follow me. I changed buses a couple of times and then got picked up by a Special Branch car and they dropped me off outside a grocer's in Northside. It has a side door into an alley and I was directed through it and taken up to the place in Charlotte Row. I was told that after three or four minutes, a man came into the shop and asked where I was, claiming I'd stolen his wallet. The shopkeeper told him that I'd made a few purchases and then left the shop by the side alley, as I had been doing quite often over the last fortnight or so. Apparently the man seemed quite annoyed."

"Let's hope all of this has worked. Otherwise whatever Mike Elliott is planning for tomorrow could be a complete waste of time."

"I must say, having been there, I feel rather more confident about tomorrow. I'd be a lot happier if an unmarked Commer van or something similar is there by then."

"I'll be a lot happier when I know exactly what his plan is and how he's going to make sure you don't get killed."

"I think others are going to have to do a bit of masquerading. Didn't you think that the woman in the

206

house behind was rather similar to me in build and hair cut?"

"What worries me isn't so much if they use a missile again. But suppose they just decided to shoot you between the time you get out of the Special Branch car and go into the house. Before you set off anywhere tomorrow, please make sure that he's got that bit completely covered. I don't think we should assume they'll do exactly the same thing again – and I hope he isn't either."

It was a strange evening. I doubt whether either of us truly believed that it was our last night together, but we knew well enough how things could go wrong. Perhaps that was why we made love passionately and then lay in each other's arms silently until the early hours of the morning, feeling the love and companionship without needing to put it into words.

We were up early and driven round to Lillieshall Road in an "Interflora" van. We made our way straight through into the house in Charlotte Row and, with the lights off, I drew the curtains and ten minutes – and a cup of tea and a slice of toast and marmalade – later, two cars drew up outside the house and we made our way quickly out. A few yards further up the road on the opposite side was a light blue Commer van.

I carried out my usual routine of getting into Custom House, though I wondered whether my watchers would bother to spend all day waiting outside now they knew where I lived. It was difficult to tell without being too obvious, but I got the impression that the car was no longer there.

However, presumably it had been earlier as within ten minutes of my arrival, a messenger brought me a familiar envelope addressed to me in blue biro. The message inside said "Surely you understand the message and know what to do." I stuffed it in my briefcase to give to Mike Elliott when I saw him later that day.

Because my draft interim report was classified 'confidential', it would have to be typed by Nigel Seymour's Divisional Typist. So I sought his permission to get it typed, then sent Bernard over with it, to stay with the typist while she typed it, and to see whether she read it. When he returned with the typed version, Bernard confirmed that in his opinion she hadn't read it. He appeared to have chatted her up while he was there, as he was also able to inform me that she had two young children, looked after by her mother, because both she and her husband had to work to afford a small house they were buying in Hornchurch. Otherwise, her conversation was entirely concerned with the Beatles, notably Paul McCartney on whom she had a sizeable crush. For a Small Faces fan like Bernard, this was practically heresy. But, all in all, she sounded an extremely unlikely person to have been leaking material to 'Peace in our time' or whoever was masterminding their operations.

By this time, it was almost lunch-time. Bernard was busy making the final arrangements for our visit to Qomputix on Monday and Ken and Morry were in the final throes of incorporating what we'd learnt from our visits earlier in the week into the main report.

Bernard had brought back a top copy and two carbon copies of the interim report. Timing meant that they needed to get to Commissioner Watling and Nigel Seymour quickly. Rather than take a chance, I rang Mike Elliott.

"Is Rat 1 keeping an eye on Blue Stilton?" I enquired. "Blue Stilton wishes to give the mice their scent of the cheese." I was glad I had my own little room where my Section couldn't hear these idiocies being spoken.

"Rat 1 paid Blue Stilton a brief visit earlier, but now both Rat 1 and Rat 2 are back wherever rats go when they're not sniffing around," replied someone who was evidently not Mike. "Blue Stilton should expect a visit from the Fondue Chef shortly after 2 pm."

I smiled to myself. I wondered how Mike had ended up with that code-name?

But the information meant I could walk freely over to King's Beam House and deliver the drafts personally. Seymour had a couple of people in with him, so I dropped the double-enveloped document on his desk. He already knew what it was, of course. Then I went to Commissioner Watling's personal, assistant and told her what I was delivering to her boss. I explained that I hoped if he had any comments, he might be able to let me have them by Monday. She said she would hand the envelope over to him the moment his meeting finished.

I called in for lunch at the King's Beam house restaurant, mainly on the basis that I wasn't sure how long the evening might go on and it seemed best to be prepared with a stodgy English lunch. Of course, as it was Friday, I got fish cakes, chips and peas. I joined a couple of former colleagues from my previous job, who eventually asked me whether it was true that there had been an explosion at my flat while my wife was there. I confirmed that there had been an explosion, but that my wife hadn't been there at the time. Otherwise, we talked about how former colleagues were doing, how their work was progressing and how there seemed to be several big units being formed to work on betting and gaming, on new Customs freight procedures and on possible replacements for Purchase Tax. I wondered whether I would get to work on any of these after my present report had been completed. If Commissioner Watling had his way, I'd probably be banished to the

Valuation Branch. On the other hand, if a different Commissioner was responsible for some of these areas of work, I wasn't sure how he could block a move there. I supposed he would, as they say, "have a word in someone's ear". But I didn't have time to concern myself about that now.

I returned to Custom House at about 1.30. All my Section had gone to lunch. I suspected they'd gone to the pub and were discussing the peculiarities of their T/SEO and all the extraneous strangeness associated with this report. I certainly wouldn't've blamed them.

About ten past two, Mike Elliott arrived with a colleague and I took them up to my room.

"You understand that this afternoon's work depends on very close timing," he began. "There'll be little point doing much if the people in the van outside the Charlotte Row house haven't been given any instructions to do anything. We've got a couple of men on your switchboard, so we can check outgoing calls from Seymour and Watling's numbers. Watling also has a CRESTA phone which gives him a direct link to senior officials in Cabinet Office and other parts of Whitehall. We're monitoring any of his calls on that too. We've not heard anything yet – but these chaps eat lunch late. I feared Watling might go to his club, but apparently he wants to go home early. It's his wedding anniversary this evening….It's all right, I haven't got a source in his office. He rang his wife about midday."

"What happens if nothing happens?"

"We'll get you in and out of Charlotte Row, like yesterday and hope that something happens on Monday."

"Just as long as you don't expect us to be cooped up there all weekend. Rosemary isn't all that enamoured with Erasmus Street, but that place…"

"No, I think you might put in an occasional appearance, but you're supposed to be in a safe house, not showing yourselves in public. And we have methods of making it appear people are in once the curtains are drawn."

"So what happens if certain phone calls are made?"

"Well, it'll also depend on whether anything goes out from Watling's or Seymour's contacts, presumably in the Cabinet Office."

"Do you know who these are?"

"Obviously, it'll depend who they ring, but Watling is likely to ring Sir Rodney Walmesley, Rupert Lennard, the top Treasury man in the Cabinet Office, or possibly Derek Kirtley, Walmesley's deputy, also from the Foreign Office. Seymour's contacts appear to be Simon Osbaldistone, one of the Principals in the Cabinet Office, who is deputy secretary to your Committee or possibly Richard Lewis, Osbaldistone's boss, who's the main secretary to the Committee. Hopefully one of them will ring someone of a rather more dubious nature."

"But, let's assume that phone call is made."

"Then we're on. Now I know you two said that you wanted to be in this together. And you can be – but not in quite the way I suspect you think. It's pretty clear from that last message that they want to influence you by threatening to kill your wife. I think we can only assume that's what they would have in mind for next time. Whether they've understood the psychology right, beats me. Personally, if someone had just killed my wife, what reason would I have for doing what these people wanted? But they may think that a subsequent message on the lines of 'you next' might persuade you. In your case, I guess it'd have the opposite effect."

"Can you get round to what you are proposing to do, please?"

"WPS Storey has to be the only one of you who enters Charlotte Row. There's nothing to stop you being there. You can come in via Lillieshall Road. But I believe there's a strong risk that they may do nothing if they think there's a possibility they'll kill you both. I may be wrong, but that's how I see it."

"I can't fault your reasoning. But I want to know what you're doing to protect Rosemary."

"A very great deal. I don't believe she'll be in any danger at all. We have men posted in the pub on the corner and upstairs in the house next door. Both have radios and are armed. If anyone in the van looks likely to use a weapon against WPS Storey, a marksman will shoot them on the spot. Of course, if, as I believe, they plan to use a missile again, their preparations will be obvious. And WPS Storey won't be anywhere near Charlotte Row by the time they fire it. She'll be with you in Lillieshall Road. Essentially, she'll just go straight through the house and down into the cellar and away. I hope that satisfies you?"

"Thank you. It seems pretty comprehensive ... So what happens now?"

"I suggest that as no-one is watching you here, we go back to Lillieshall Road and await events there. Presumably you can square your people?"

"The only real problem would be if someone like Watling or Seymour tried to contact me."

"If it's by phone, we can take care of that. If they want you to go and see them, you'll just have to think of a plausible excuse ... Which, from what I've seen, shouldn't pose an insuperable problem for you."

I left a note for my Section, explaining that I'd been suddenly called away for a meeting and encouraging them to depart early and enjoy a good weekend. I hoped I would do the same.

We were in Lillieshall Road by 3 pm. The building was a hive of activity, with a room full of police officers manning phones, others with radios were keeping constant touch with the men in the pub and the house next door to our 'safe house' in Charlotte Row. There was even someone detailed to provide cups of tea and coffee and sandwiches, as required.

Apparently there were two men and a woman in the Commer van. They had singly gone to the pub and had fruit squash and sandwiches. They had walkie-talkies, but evidently some sort of scrambler system was being employed, so Special Branch were unable to learn what they were saying.

I took a cup of tea and sat in the kitchen with the lady who was providing the catering service. I felt rather like a spare wheel.

At about 3.30, Mike Elliott came in.

"Two interesting calls from your end. Seymour rang his oppo Osbaldistone and gave him a pretty full account of your latest report. Apparently it's 'good stuff and heading the right way' but needs an awful lot of 'polishing'."

"No surprise there, then!"

"The second call was from Watling's personal assistant to a number we've suspected of being used by Irish Republican sympathisers. The person at the other end just identified himself as 'Donal', but she gave him a pretty good summary of your report....I must say I never expected the Irish to be involved in this – or why they would want to be. But let's see what develops. We're tracking the location of the number as we speak."

"Tell me, why did you leave Woodruffe out of this?"

"Stan Woodruffe's far too canny to get involved in anything like this. Whoever's running this seems happy to allow a pretty uncontrolled operation to run, possibly because he has to be distanced from it. That's not Stan's style at all ... Besides, he's got everything he wants already."

"I see."

A WPC came in. "Weasel has now phoned."

"That's Watling, I take it?" I asked.

"Yes. Let's see the transcript," said Mike. "Spoken to Kirtley and given him the gist of your latest report. Suggests Kirtley tells Walmesley that it's going the right way. Kept it short."

"He tried to get Walmesley, but Walmesley's secretary said he was busy," added the WPC.

"What have you called Seymour?"

"Stoat ... I know you regarded them as mice, as indeed, they probably are ... but we needed something memorable."

Another PC joined us.

"Otter has gone crazy. He's phoning round all over the place!"

"Bugger!" exclaimed Mike. "Who's he ringing?"

"A R J Brown in the Foreign Office, P F X O'Malley in MinTech, J Spendiff in the Treasury, K M Martin in the Home Office and just now L F Watson in MoD."

"Bugger! Bugger! Bugger!" cried Mike. "He's ringing all his oppos in Whitehall, isn't he? We haven't got tabs on half their exchanges. We might just about get the Foreign Office, but we won't get any of the others."

"So you won't be able to tell if someone contacts the people who give the orders to the people in the van?" I asked.

"Not unless Watling or Seymour, or someone in the Cabinet Office either phones a dubious number directly from the office or goes outside to use a convenient public call box. We're monitoring those in the vicinity."

"Presumably someone from any of those Departments - other than MinTech which is too far away – might do the sensible thing and go out and use a public line. And they're all in the same area."

"Let's hope you're right. The trouble is we won't know who it was."

"But you can back-ullage. If they've left their building, there's likely to be some sort of a record."

Twenty-five minutes later, the WPC returned.

"There's been a call to a number we don't know from a public phone box in the Whitehall area. The message was 'The Britnice thing is tilting badly in the wrong direction. Urgent re-balancing will be required if it isn't to fall over.' Then the caller hung up. It wasn't any of the numbers that we know PIOT use. We're checking it now."

"It'll be a dummy," growled Mike. "Evidently we'll have to follow this Customs process called 'back-ulling' … But I think we can assume tonight will be on."

There was an eerie lack of activity for the next hour or so. The only thing that happened was that the number the Irish girl who was Watling's personal assistant had rung was confirmed to be one used by Irish republicans and a recce of the location had confirmed occupants. Mike Elliott gave the order to bring them – and the Irish girl – in for questioning.

Then one of the black cars, known as 'Rat 2', appeared in Charlotte Row. The back doors of the Commer van were opened and various packages handed in. Then the black car did a three point turn at the end of the little street and sped away.

"WPS Storey should be here in about half an hour," Mike informed me. "The car has gone to pick her up.

215

There's no point playing games at that end. Like you, she's no longer being watched. They're just waiting 'till she gets here."

"I hope she knows what to do."

"I saw her this morning. She knows that she gets out of the car on the pavement side and goes straight into the house. Of course, she'll have to use her key. But we'll be watching their every move. Besides, if I'm any judge, the people outside have just been given their instructions and their equipment. I think we're looking at another missile, so when WPS Storey comes in, I suggest you meet her and take her straight away back over here."

"I suppose there's no possibility that Rosemary and I could actually see these people being arrested, is there?"

"I suppose you've earned the right ... Don't go into the cellar, but into the back garden. There's a gate in the fence to the house next door – the one further up Charlotte Row. Go in the back door there and go upstairs. But until we're actually dealing with them, please keep well away from the windows."

The tension was almost unbearable. If I'd ever liked smoking, I would have lit up now, whether I'd given up or not. The fug of everyone else's cigarettes was beginning to make my throat sore.

"If you don't mind, I'm going to go over to Charlotte Row."

"I don't think there's any danger of you getting there too late."

I made my way through the cold, clammy passageway and up from the cellar into the kitchen. At the table was a bespectacled young man with a large panel, that looked as though it had been made out of Meccano, with about a dozen switches on it.

"This is how we turn lights on an off," he explained, "when there's no-one actually there. I've also got a model of your wife up there. She's not very mobile, but I hope she can do enough to convince the people in the van outside that she's the real thing."

I would like to have gone up and seen this creation, but clearly that was out of the question.

About ten minutes later, Mike Elliott joined me.

"She'll be here in a couple of minutes," he said.

A couple of minutes later, I heard the sound of a car drawing up. A car door was slammed shut and I could hear the key in the lock of the front door. Rosemary stepped inside. I ran to her and held her briefly in my arms, breathing an almighty sigh of relief. Then I grabbed her hand and took her out through the kitchen into the garden.

"Where are we going?" she asked in a whisper..

"I thought you might like to see what happens to these people. We're going next door."

Just as we went through the back door of the house next door, there was a small bang, like a car exhaust followed by a tremendous explosion. We could even see debris flying out through the shattered back window of the 'safe' house. To do that, the missile must have blown the interior wall down. I guessed it was even more powerful than the previous one. I could hear cars racing into Charlotte Row, so Rosemary and I ran upstairs in time to see policemen with guns arresting the three people who had just attempted to kill her in a particularly violent and brutal way. Rosemary shuddered. I could tell what was going through her mind and put my arm round her shoulders.

"The Chief Inspector asks if you want to come down," said one of the police marksmen who we had joined.

"Thank you for keeping me safe," said Rosemary.

217

"Fortunately it didn't come to that."

We went downstairs and out through the front door. The road was completely sealed off with police vehicles. The three people were standing by their van, handcuffed and looking a little bewildered. Remembering the episode with Khrestinsky by the Grand Union canal, I hoped Rosemary wouldn't decide to hit any of them.

"Have you seen any of them before?" Mike asked us.

"Yes," replied Rosemary. "They were all with the 'Peace in our time' people at the demonstration last Sunday."

"They certainly made a big enough hole," I remarked, staring back at the 'safe' house. The front window had been completely blown in and many tiles and bricks had been knocked out or displaced.

"But you missed!" exclaimed Rosemary.

"So what are we charged with," demanded one of the men. "Blowing up an empty house?"

"Murder and attempted murder, for starters," said Mike. "But I suspect that's only the start."

"We demand to contact our lawyers and our Embassy," said the other man.

"No," replied Mike. "You are violent and dangerous killers. You're going somewhere secure where you'll be interrogated for as long as we consider necessary. Your diplomatic status is bogus. When you've told us what we want to know, then you can contact your lawyers and any embassy you choose. But not before then."

"You really are a pathetic bunch of cowards!" declared Rosemary.

"You'll be pleased to know that we've picked up Rat 2," said a PC getting out of his car.

"I think we've got a sufficient link to the PIOT people to pick up all those we know about," replied Mike. "Can you radio Jim Burns and ask him to set it in hand."

A large police van arrived and the three PIOT people were driven away.

"I've been looking at the stuff in their van," said one of the police marksmen. "This isn't home-made stuff. I'd say most of it looks military … Russian, I'd say."

"All this stuff needs to be taken away and analysed. We'll need to see where that stuff came from. The fact that it was made in Russia doesn't necessarily mean that the Russians supplied it," replied Mike.

The police were all busy getting everything in order before it got dark.

"We could get a cab back to Pimlico," I said to Mike. "We realise you probably need everybody here."

"No. We'll get you a car. The question is whether you're prepared to work this weekend after all this excitement?"

"Uh?"

"First thing tomorrow, we're going to arrest everyone who knew about your latest report and do this 'back-ulling' thing you talk about. I think it'd be helpful if you sat in on the interviews and asked any questions you wanted. We're not as clued up as we should be on some of this Whitehall stuff, so your contribution would be very welcome."

"As long as Rosemary can sit in – if she wants to. I'm sure she doesn't want to spend the weekend alone in Erasmus Street."

"I'd like that. But first I want to go home with my husband and have a good dinner. I'm absolutely starving!"

ELEVEN
BACK-ULLAGING

Rather than have to do all the cooking in the safe house, we got the driver to drop us off at an Italian restaurant in Pimlico, before returning. Though Mike Elliott had assured us that we were likely to be pretty safe for the next few days while the 'Peace in our time' organisation was severely disrupted, we decided to remain cautious. After all, we knew little about them. If they were really smart, they might have worked out that evening's events were a set-up and then followed us home to do what they intended to do.

"Oh hell!" I exclaimed. "I got another message today at work. I put it in my briefcase meaning to give it to Mike Elliott. With all that was going on, I completely forgot."

"You can always give it to him tomorrow."

"Do you mind spending your weekend on police business?"

"Not if I'm with you. Anyway, one of these people passed on a message knowing that it would mean those people trying to kill me. I'd like to see him face to face."

We made good use of the large bath that evening and went to bed happy, almost wholly sure that the threat which had been hanging over us had been lifted.

A Special Branch car arrived for us early the following morning. It was a cold, grey, wet day so we had even fewer qualms about spending some time trying to find out whose actions had been aimed at killing Rosemary.

We were driven to Charing Cross police station. There we had to wait for a few minutes until Mike

Elliott appeared. I remembered to hand over the latest message.

"It doesn't really add anything, except to confirm that they felt it was no point sending you any messages when they didn't know where you were living … But I'll take you through to meet my boss, Chief Superintendant Vaughan. He'll be leading the questioning."

Vaughan was six-feet two inches and burly. Although in his early forties, his hair was already grey. He was very much the steel fist in the velvet glove.

"I'm pleased you could come along," he began, with a slight London accent. "We'll probably take your man, Watling, first."

"May I ask whether you've got anything out of the 'Peace in our time' people yet?" I asked. "Obviously, we're not sure how safe we are until we know what's going on with them."

"They've not said much yet," replied Mike. "But it's early days yet."

We went into an interview room, where Commissioner Watling was seated, looking extremely angry.

"What the hell is going on here?" he demanded, as we trooped in. "Oh you!" he exclaimed, staring at me. "I should've known!"

"I am Chief Superintendant Kingsley Vaughan. With me are Chief Inspector Michael Elliott – and Mr Storey you already know. WPS Storey – Mr Storey's wife – is observing. We are enquiring into leaks of confidential information to an organisation which subsequently attempted to kill WPS Storey, using a high-explosive missile. You have been brought here, Mr Watling, because you were one of those - those very few people – who had access to this information."

221

"I don't know what on earth you're talking about. I thought someone tried to kill Mr Storey's wife a couple of weeks ago."

"I'll come on to that later. Let me start from the beginning. Do you deny receiving a copy of Mr Storey's most recent confidential report on the possible use in this country of certain American technology – yesterday lunchtime, to be precise?"

"Of course I don't deny it. Roisin O'Neill handed it to me just after I returned from lunch."

"Opened or unopened?"

"Opened. Roisin opens all my mail unless it's classified 'Secret'."

"So she could have read it?"

"Of course. I expect her to read stuff and use her judgement about what I see immediately and what gets sent to a subordinate for some work or some briefing."

"You may wish to know that she informed people with Irish republican sympathies of its contents yesterday afternoon."

"And they were the ones who tried to kill Mrs Storey?"

"No. I believe that's unlikely."

"But presumably you were aware of Cabinet Office Security instructions regarding the transmission of 'Confidential' material?" I asked. "To put it on record - a record must be kept of all people who have access to confidential material. I left the draft of my report with Miss O'Neill in a double envelope with the required security markings. Is there any record in your office that she had access to this material?"

"These Cabinet Office requirements are frequently a case of over-egging the pudding. I trusted Roisin to handle my incoming papers sensibly and securely ..."

"I wonder what other sensitive papers that have gone through your office has been passed on to the

Irish republicans," cut in Vaughan. "We shall need to carry out a thorough investigation in your office, starting from Monday ... But that is only part of it isn't it? Shortly after you received Mr Storey's report and presumably read it, you tried to speak to Sir Rodney Walmesley in the Cabinet Office and when you failed to get him, you told Mr Derek Kirtley, Sir Rodney's deputy, what was in Mr Storey's report."

"And why not? Whitehall runs on people knowing what they need to know. This was clearly a useful development in the work of Walmesley's Committee and I believed he would wish to know before the weekend."

"Why? It was just a first draft and at least one further visit was lined up for Monday, as Mr Storey told you in a memo attached to the draft. Why did Sir Rodney need to know on a Friday afternoon? What value was it to him?"

"He had asked me to keep him fully updated about anything significant. I suspected that Seymour was doing the same with one or more of the Secretariat. If one of them told the Foreign Office and Walmesley didn't know about it and subsequently was made to appear not up to speed by one of his Foreign Office rivals, he'd do his damndest to ruin my career."

"Surely you're overstating it."

"Look! I want to be Deputy Chairman of Customs & Excise. The post will fall vacant in the next nine months, when Freddie Parr retires. I can't afford to have anyone in Whitehall whispering against me when the Cabinet Secretary and the Permanent Secretary at the Treasury decide who to recommend for the post. So I'd rather do a belt and braces and make sure there's no chance Walmesley could be left in the dark."

"Even to the extent of breaching Cabinet Office security instructions?" I asked. "As I'm sure you're aware, Commissioner Watling, these forbid the discussion of 'confidential' material on an open telephone line."

"The CRESTA phone wasn't working. Normally I'd use that. Sometimes, young man, you'll realise that following instructions isn't everything."

"I'm sure Mr Storey is aware of that," said Vaughan. "But it's a matter of when you do it and whether you get caught – and what the consequences are. In this case, the telephone calls you and Mr Seymour made to the Cabinet Office led in a direct trail to certain people attempting to kill WPS Storey."

"Well, I admit I broke Cabinet Office security instructions when I rang Kirtley. But I had absolutely no knowledge of anything they might do with that knowledge thereafter."

"You were, I believe, at the last meeting of the Committee MISC 38 (67) where Mr Ffoulkes of the Security Service told the Committee about the previous attempt on WPS Storey's life and the link to the production of this report, specifically the direction it was heading?"

"Yes."

"Didn't you ever wonder how the people who did that gained their knowledge of the content of Mr Storey's report? Didn't it occur to you that this knowledge could only have come from someone who attended that Committee or its supporters?"

"I can't say I ever considered the matter. I have a lot of things on my plate – and this was by no means the most pressing or important."

"What that the wife of one of your people had nearly been killed? And someone else had been horribly killed?"

Watling declined to reply.

"So evidently you were so eager to pass this information to the Cabinet Office to further your career that you were prepared to breach Cabinet Office security instructions, without any regard to the consequences – indeed, without ever even reflecting on the possible consequences?"

Watling again declined to reply.

"I believe that's all we require from you – for the present. Special Branch officers will be in your office first thing Monday morning to conduct a thorough investigation into the information which Miss O'Neill may have got from you. They will expect your full co-operation or I will inform the Metropolitan Commissioner. I shall also be contacting the Cabinet Secretary about the need to conduct a full disciplinary investigation into breaches of security instructions by you and others. Good day to you."

Watling rose, his pallid skin clammy, beads of sweat on his forehead. I had half-expected the customary stare of contempt and loathing, but he had been devastated – not, I think, by the interview itself, but by the knowledge that his craved promotion was now out of his grasp. (It also appeared to prevent him from asking what would've been an obvious comment from where I sat – how did the police know all this?)

"We'll get Seymour in next," announced Vaughan.

"I don't expect to learn much more from him," whispered Rosemary to me. "I want to spend a bit of time checking something, if you don't mind"

"No," I replied. "You do what you want."

Seymour looked close to tears. A thin man at the best of times, now he looked as though he wished he could disappear altogether. If Vaughan was able to impose his personality on Commissioner Watling, Seymour was already defeated.

"Why have I been brought here?" asked Seymour hesitantly. "I haven't done anything wrong."

"That remains to be seen. I am Chief Superintendant Vaughan and with me are Chief Inspector Elliott and Mr Storey you already know. We are investigating the train of events that led to a criminal organisation firing a missile into a house where they believed they would kill Mr Storey's wife ..."

"I don't see ..."

"Let's start at the beginning of this chain of events. Yesterday lunchtime, Mr Storey left a document with you, the latest draft of his report in a form that would be sent to a Cabinet Committee MISC 38 (67). Is that true?"

"Yes. I read it once my meeting had finished."

"And what did you do then with it?"

"I locked it away in my combination and left a message with Mr Watling's office that we should discuss it."

"Why? What needed to be discussed?"

"I wished to be sure he was content with what was emerging from Storey's report. Also I assumed he would wish to have a drafting session on it."

"What did you think of the way the report was heading?"

"I'm a Civil Servant. I had no views on whether it was the right direction or not. My impression was that it would be broadly welcome in Whitehall."

"So was that it? Was that all you did in relation to the draft report yesterday afternoon?"

"I ... er ... I phoned someone in the Cabinet Office to give him the gist of the interim report."

"Who?"

"Osbaldistone. He's my opposite number in the Cabinet Office, the deputy secretary to MISC 38."

"Why did you ring him?"

"We agreed at the start of this I'd keep him up to speed. It's normal practice in this sort of thing. Committee secretaries need to know what's going on, to make sure the process is managed smoothly, without unwelcome surprises. In the same way, I'd expect him to tell me if there was something we needed to know."

"So you rang him on an open telephone line, in clear breach of Cabinet Office security instructions?"

"He's in the Cabinet Office. He didn't appear to object."

"That's not the point, is it? You discussed confidential information over an open line. What would you have done if, say Mr Storey here, did something like that?"

"I'd have his guts for garters."

"Precisely. What do you know about this Osbaldistone?"

"Nothing much. I believe he's on secondment from the Foreign Office. He seems a decent enough chap."

"This 'decent enough chap' or someone he passed the information you gave him subsequently telephoned someone else who clearly envisaged an attack on Mr Storey's wife."

"Oh God! ... I assume she's not dead?"

"No. The perpetrators were apprehended immediately after firing their missile."

"So I was part of your trap ... Storey helped to set me up! ... and you've been bugging my phone!"

"Think back for a moment, please, Mr Seymour. I believe any righteous indignation is a little overdone, don't you? When the previous interim report was produced. On what day did you see a first copy?"

"Thursday - a week before the MISC 38 discussion."

"Did you inform Osbaldistone about its contents at that stage?"

"No. I reckoned he'd get a draft when we sent it over the following Tuesday and that'd be soon enough for his purposes?"

"So why did you rush to phone him the moment you got the latest version of the report yesterday?"

"Because he complained. After the last MISC 38 meeting, he told me he needed to know the moment I knew where things were heading – not a few hours before everyone else. He said his boss had been on at him ever since the weekend about where the Customs stuff was heading."

"Did you tell anyone else about the content of that version of the report in advance of the papers going over to Cabinet Office?"

"No. I just discussed the draft with Wilf Watling and Storey."

"Well, I believe that's all for the time being. I should inform you that I shall be recommending to the Cabinet Secretary that a full investigation should be undertaken into breaches of Cabinet Office security instructions."

"Oh God!" Seymour seemed close to tears again, as he realised that such an enquiry was bound to put a large black mark in his record and, at best, delay the upward march of his career, at worst, halt it in its tracks. He almost staggered out of the room.

"Why a man with such an evident lack of backbone aspires to reach the upper levels of the Civil Service beats me," observed Vaughan. "Let's have a short break … I need some coffee!"

While we were drinking coffee, Rosemary reappeared from wherever she had been.

"I've been looking at the log of phone calls from the Cabinet Office. Special Branch have also located the phone which was rung from a call box in Parliament Square yesterday with the message about us. They've got a list of numbers rung from that phone and to it. I think you should have a look at it," she said quietly.

"OK. I should be able to duck out of one of these interviews."

"You'll need to look at them before Chief Superintendant Vaughan interviews anyone from the Cabinet Office, though."

"OK."

"A bit of strategy," said Vaughan. "I'm inclined to the view that our man is in the Cabinet Office - effectively Kirtley, Osbaldistone, Lewis or possibly Walmesley. But before we get to them, I want to cut off their line of retreat, by eliminating, if possible, the various people we believed they informed. So I'm going to have a few words with Mr K M Martin from the Home Office next."

Martin was a plump, owl-like man with a very public school voice.

"I'm extremely displeased about this," he began.

"As an official in the Home Office, you'd be equally displeased if the police failed to follow up thoroughly two missile attacks in London, one of which resulted in a particularly brutal and unpleasant death," retorted Vaughan. Having introduced Mike Elliott and me, he continued. "Were you contacted yesterday afternoon about material relevant to Cabinet Office Committee MISC 38 (67)?"

"Yes. Osbaldistone from the Cabinet Office rang me and told me that Customs initial investigations into the firms that would get this American high-tech stuff were giving them the thumbs up. I thanked him and made a note to brief my man on Monday."

"So you didn't inform him yesterday afternoon?"

"He was already off down to the country, with all he needed for the weekend. As the Committee wasn't

229

meeting 'till the following Friday, there was plenty of time to fill him in."

"And you didn't tell anyone else?"

"Why would I? This isn't a particularly big issue for the Home Office. Generally, Friday afternoon is a time to contemplate the weekend's activities, not to be flying around giving people information they neither need nor want at that time in the week. In fact, to tell you the truth, I was a bit surprised Osbaldistone felt the need to ring me."

"Did you leave the office at all yesterday afternoon?"

"I went to the staff restaurant for a cup of tea ..."

"No, sorry, I meant outside the building."

"No."

"Thank you. I'm sorry to have taken up some of your weekend, but you'll understand that when a major incident occurs we have to make sure there are no loose ends."

Martin left, looking grumpy.

"We're pretty certain he didn't leave the building," observed Mike Elliott after he had departed. "We've been getting our hands on the logs for these various buildings. If he did go out, he must've found some back way."

"But don't these logs identify who it was, without the need to interview all these other people?" I asked.

"I just wonder whether it'd be too obvious. Also, it's not clear from our conversations with the reception desks in some of these Departments whether they actually know who everyone is. So someone could've given a false name, for instance. But the Home Office people knew Martin, mainly because he brings a bicycle to work."

"For the Cabinet Office people, have you checked whether any went through the door into No 10

230

Downing Street?" I asked. "If I was trying to disguise the fact that I was going out of the building, I might use that route."

"We'll need to check that," replied Vaughan. "While you're at it, Mike, check up on whether anyone can gain access to that tunnel that runs under Whitehall. I don't know whether it goes as far as the Cabinet Office, but I recall it certainly runs from No 10. I'd expect access to be carefully controlled and recorded, but it's worth checking. Try the Cabinet Secretary. I've already briefed him about what's going on."

The next person Vaughan chose to see was O'Malley from MinTech. Since I regarded him as a highly unlikely suspect, mainly because there was insufficient time between when he was telephoned by Osbaldistone and the time of the phone call from Parliament Square for him to have got there, I decided to see what Rosemary had discovered.

She was in an empty interview room.

"I've been looking at these lists of phone calls. They're quite illuminating. If you look at the calls from the Cabinet Office, there are none to the PIOT number that was rung from Parliament Square. But there were two phone calls from the Parliament Square phone box to it – one yesterday afternoon and the other the Wednesday morning before the missile was fired into our flat. But if you look at the PIOT numbers, there are three phone calls to a Whitehall number. I rang it and got the operator, of course. She told me it was the number of a John Wordley-Smith. She told me he was a Principal in the Secretariat, whatever that means when it's at home. No-one has mentioned his name at all. I wonder how he fits in?"

"I'll try and bring it up in the course of the interviews. Are there any other interesting PIOT numbers?"

"Inspector Gurney was only prepared to let me ring the one number on the basis that it was a Cabinet Office one and might be relevant to these interviews."

"I think it'd be worth checking whether any of them are for any other Government Departments. Were there any overseas numbers?"

"Yes – four or five to France around the time we were in Paris, so I think we can guess what they were about. Several to Ireland, at various times. I know they're checking whether any of the other numbers are linked to embassies or proxy numbers for embassies, but if they've found something, they aren't telling me … Hello, Mike. Do you need my husband?"

"Yes. We're going to grill Brown from the Foreign Office"

After Brown, there was Watson from MoD and Spendiff from the Treasury. Each told very similar stories. All expressed slight surprise at the need to be phoned at that hour on a Friday afternoon. None looked a likely suspect.

Next up was Kirtley from the Cabinet office, on secondment from the Foreign Office. Vaughan explained why these enquiries were being undertaken and then asked about the phone call from Commissioner Watling.

"I wasn't quite sure why he rang me," explained Kirtley, a dapper, sandy-haired, middling sort of man with a well-trimmed moustache. "I assumed that he'd failed to get Walmesley. I imagine Walmesley told him to keep him updated with all the latest gen, so he was doing his bit and hoping for a pat on the back."

"You were aware that you were discussing confidential material over an open line?"

"He was. I was just listening. Nothing I said could be construed as confidential."

"So what did you say?"

"He asked me to ensure Walmesley was aware of what he'd told me, as a matter of urgency. I told him I would. He rang off. That was it."

"So did you inform Sir Rodney?"

"No. It wasn't so important that it couldn't wait 'till Monday. I wasn't going running off to do the errands of some sycophantic twerp from Customs."

"And if your boss got caught looking out of touch if he met a Foreign Office colleague, for instance, over the weekend?"

"What would they know that he didn't?"

"Well, Osbaldistone was busy phoning round all his Whitehall contacts passing on the glad tidings that very afternoon."

"Was he? What a very eager beaver! I didn't know anything about that."

"Would it've made any difference?"

"Not really. Walmesley is a jumped-up, conceited, ignorant poltroon who needs bringing down a peg or three regularly."

"So did you inform anyone of Commissioner Watling's phone call?"

"No."

"Can you tell me anything about how John Wordley-Smith fits into all of this?" I asked.

"Not at all, as far as I know. Wordley-Smith had a nervous breakdown about three months ago and, as far as I'm aware, is still being contentedly regressed by an army of shrinks."

"So his office would normally be empty?"

"Yes, as far as I know … Why are you so interested in him?"

"His name has come up recently, but I couldn't see how he fitted in."

233

"Essentially he doesn't – for the foreseeable future. His work was parcelled out, most going to Osbaldistone."

After he had gone, Vaughan asked me why I'd asked about Wordley-Smith. I explained about the phone calls from the PIOT telephone number to his number in the Cabinet Office.

"So you think someone else was using that number? Presumably his absence would be well known? This does look more and more as though the Cabinet Office is where we should be looking. But I doubt Kirtley is our man. He's not logged as going out and he appears to have made no calls that afternoon."

"It might be worth checking what calls were made on Wordley-Smith's number," I suggested.

"I'll set that in hand," said Mike Elliott.

"Could you also possibly get Cabinet Office to let you know whether Walmesley, Kirtley, Lewis and Osbaldistone had keys for the door into No 10, please?" I asked.

"Now, I'm inclined to see Lewis next. As far as we're aware, he wasn't informed about any of this. But Osbaldistone may have wandered up the corridor and told him. After all he was busy yapping to everyone else. Why not his boss, too? To my mind, he was putting out a smokescreen…not least because I understand that he was actually logged out of the Cabinet Office and logged back in at times that fit the phone call from Parliament Square very tidily. I'd like to cut off his avenues of retreat before we grill him. So let's do Lewis now and let Osbaldistone stew a bit while we have some lunch."

Richard Lewis was tall, saturnine, in his late thirties, with a quiff of unruly hair and a strong public school accent. He seemed very self-composed. If he was irritated about having his Saturday ruined, he hid it well. Vaughan gave the usual introductions and explanation. I notice that Rosemary had slipped in for this interview.

"Were you aware of the phone calls from Commissioner Watling and Mr Seymour of Customs to Mr Kirtley and Mr Osbaldistone respectively yesterday afternoon, about developments relating to the Committee MISC 38 (67)?"

"No. No-one mentioned the Committee that afternoon. I was finalising briefing for Roddy Walmesley for FD on Monday."

"FD?"

"The Foreign Affairs and Defence Committee of Cabinet."

"I see. And you didn't speak to Kirtley or Osbaldistone?"

"I didn't speak to anyone except my secretary and Walmesley's SPS. When I'd finished the briefing, I breathed a great sigh of relief and shot off home."

"About what time was that?"

"Around five."

We left it at that and Lewis departed to make the best of his interrupted weekend and we relaxed over sandwiches and tea. Inspector Gurney mentioned that all but Osbaldistone had keys into No 10. I rang the Cabinet Office security people, masquerading as a Special Branch Officer – "DS Storey" – and they confirmed that people going through the front door of No 10 weren't logged in or out. Rosemary confirmed that the PIOT telephone appeared not to have called any other Whitehall numbers – or any in Customs, for that matter.

Now it was Osbaldistone's turn. I was pretty sure that Vaughan had him down as the principal suspect. My only reservation was that, for someone who must have known he would be vulnerable in any subsequent investigation, he had been extraordinarily slipshod.

Vaughan made his usual introductions and explanations. Osbaldistone seemed younger and even more like an overgrown public school boy than he usually did.

"Can you confirm please whether you received a telephone call from Mr Seymour of Customs early yesterday afternoon?"

"Yes."

"What was the nature of the call?"

"It was about the latest developments in the work on high-tech American computer components for MISC 38."

"Why did Mr Seymour telephone you?"

"I'd encouraged him to. Roddy Walmesley had impressed on me the need for the Secretariat to be absolutely up to speed on what Customs were up to. He's got some fairly hated rivals over in the FO and he's terrified they'll score points off him."

"Were you aware that your conversation with Mr Seymour breached Cabinet Office security instructions?"

"He did. I'm not sure anything I said could be construed as such."

"So what did you do when you got Mr Seymour's information?"

"I went to see Richard Lewis and told him. I asked him whether I should inform Roddy Walmesley. But he said we could be confident that Watling would do that for us. But then he said, it would be a good thing if I told my oppos in MISC 38 …"

"Did he suggest why?"

"He said it'd give them something positive to end the week on. But I suspect he was hoping they'd brief their seniors and one of them might catch Roddy

236

Walmesley out at some dinner party over the weekend. Richard's star is hitched to Roddy Pilkington, so obviously he's going to take any opportunity to do Walmesley down."

"So you didn't think to inform Sir Rodney direct?"

"Richard Lewis is an extremely tough chap and vindictive if he needs to be. I just try to keep my nose clean."

"So after you'd made these phone calls, what did you do next?"

"Just as I was finishing speaking to Spendiff at the Treasury, Richard came into my room and asked me to drop in immediately I'd finished. So I went to his room and he asked me to do him a favour. He said he'd just completed some Top Secret briefing for FD on Monday, but it was essential that Sir Nigel Spinks in MoD got a copy of the briefing that afternoon. Apparently, he'd just spoken to Spinks's secretary and he was waiting in a car by Admiralty Arch before setting off for some weekend conference near Bath. Because it was so urgent and Top Secret, could I be a decent chap and take it over to Admiralty Arch for him. It was essential that I got a receipt from Spinks. I'd got nothing else to do that afternoon, so I said I'd do it. So I went over to Admiralty Arch and saw a black car parked in the bay just in front of the Arch. The driver took the envelope and passed it to Sir Nigel in the back, who gave me a hand-written receipt a couple of minutes later. I took it back to Richard Lewis who was profuse in his thanks. Then I did a bit of sorting out my papers and filing my committee notes away and went home about 5.30."

"Did you speak to Sir Nigel Spinks?"

"No I could only see the driver, who took the envelope and handed back Sir Nigel's receipt. I couldn't really see Sir Nigel."

"Thank you. I'd be grateful if you could remain for a little longer, please."

After he had left, Vaughan remarked "I don't quite know why I didn't just charge him. There was just something stuck in the back of my mind."

"We can check whether this story about Sir Nigel Spinks has any truth to it," said Mike Elliott.

"If I were you, I'd get Lewis back," I said. "Osbaldistone appears to have done a whole series of things that lead us to point the finger right at him. And if, as I suspect, Sir Nigel Spinks claims no knowledge of what he told us, he's been dropped right in it. But Lewis is completely in the clear. He can deny seeing Osbaldistone or sending him on a errand to take papers to Spinks. Apparently he didn't leave the building, while Osbaldistone did. There's no record, other than Osbaldistone's word, that he even knew anything about the latest version of my report."

"But Osbaldistone was the only one who left the building. He could be just trying to turn the suspicion on to Lewis. But Lewis never left the building."

"I believe he did" I replied. "He has a key to the inter-connecting door to No 10, so he knew he wouldn't be logged going through. Then he could march through No 10 and go out through the front door without being logged out. And he could come back the same way. Now someone might recall him – but people are going in and out of No 10 all the time. If you were involved in this, working for very high stakes with some very ruthless people, would you be as amateurish as Osbaldistone, or would you cover your tracks extremely cleverly like Lewis?"

"But how could he set up the black car being in the right place at the right time to provide a subterfuge while he slipped out?"

"At a guess, he used a radio, like the PIOT people were using at the demonstration the other weekend. While his main contact was out of range, the car may need to be within range in case it was needed urgently."

"So why not pass the message about your report through the people in the car? Why put up this great subterfuge to go and make a separate phone call?"

"I'd suggest two reasons. First, to put someone else's head in the frame. If Osbaldistone has all the evidence stacked against him, Lewis can remain happily in place, free from suspicion. If no culprit was found, he'd be among a number of people under suspicion and would expect to have to operate under close surveillance. Second, I'd guess that whoever he spoke to on the phone is the one who gives the orders. I doubt whether the people in the cars have the authority to go off and fire missiles at people without his say-so. And if you ask why the people in the car didn't contact the boss, I'd say it was because that would provide a direct link between Lewis and the bloke running all this. My feeling is that they're too cautious to do that sort of thing."

"Hmmm, I'm not wholly convinced that hangs together" mused Vaughan. "What you're saying sounds a bit far-fetched – unfortunately, my guts tell me that it feels more likely than this Osbaldistone ..."

"But I wouldn't get Lewis back," said Rosemary.

"Why not?"

"You haven't really got any proof against him. It's just Osbaldistone's word against his. You won't be able to corroborate Osbaldistone's story about taking the envelope to Sir Nigel Spinks. But there may be a way to catch him ... . If you look at the pattern of calls from the PIOT telephone number and into the Cabinet Office, something stands out. A quarter of an hour before the PIOT phone rings Wordley-Smith's number,

239

there's a call from a public telephone box to Lewis's secretary's number. The conversation lasts no more than thirty seconds. My guess is that it's some sort of code to prepare Lewis for a call on Wordley-Smith's phone. What I think we need to do is to get hold of Lewis's secretary and get the code out of her. Then if we replicate it on Monday morning and he answers it, you've got the proof you need."

"But he may well have been busy contacting his PIOT chums from home - or, more likely, a local telephone box," said Mike Elliott.

"If he's as canny as we think, he'd be a fool to do anything of the sort," I said. "All you have to do is pull the logs of his home phone and any nearby public call boxes and you've got him."

"But we clearly need to do that – and tap his phone," said Vaughan. "And I'm also inclined to arrest Osbaldistone. For two reasons – first, because he may actually be the guilty party, and second, because it'll allay Lewis's suspicions … . That was a helpful contribution from you two …"

That was probably as much as we could expect.

While Osbaldistone, his public school composure shattered into howls of tearful protests about his innocence, was taken through the formalities of being arrested, we tried to find out a bit more about what was happening to the PIOT people who had been arrested – and in particular about how safely we could move around.

"They've apparently been saying very little," explained Mike Elliott. "But with people like this, it usually takes a while. They generally feel they have to show us how tough they are. And, of course, there's always a degree of hope that their people will know they've been arrested and will be able to get them out somehow. So it's mainly a question of time. As for the two of you, I think the advice has to be to stay alert and travel warily. If you need a car, give the usual number a ring – and I'd still try to keep your journey to and from the safe house disguised, if I were you."

"That's what I feared," replied Rosemary. "Have you any idea when we might be able to live a normal life again?"

"I don't think it'll be long, but I can't really say when either, I'm afraid."

"What about these Irish republicans and Watling's secretary?" I asked.

"From what we've got out of them, it was entirely an intelligence operation. They don't appear to have any violent connections, just a desire to know what the British Government is up to that might affect the Catholics in Northern Ireland or information that might be used against the British Government. It appears that Miss O'Neill volunteered to provide information when she became engaged to Donal Ryan. They're not very tough these people and we've got half a dozen names elsewhere in Whitehall who've been doing what Miss O'Neill has been doing. Though they've all broken the Official Secrets Act, I guess we may not go through all the cost and publicity of a trial and just ensure they're sacked and are never let anywhere any sensitive information again. That may depend, of course, on the nature of the information they've leaked – but so far it seems pretty low-level stuff. Ryan told our people – and they believed him – he couldn't understand why Miss O'Neill had told him about the American stuff. Of course, it still won't do your Commissioner much good."

With that news, it appeared that the day's operations were starting to wind down. Chief Superintendant Vaughan was already on his way to another destination to supervise the interrogation of the PIOT people and the lesser follow-up work had been delegated to Mike Elliott and his people.

We were just about to depart when a PC mentioned to me that I had received a phone call from a man with a German accent. It just gave me a phone number to call back. So I sat at one of the desks and rang it.

"Yes?" said the voice at the other end. It sounded like the man I had met at the East German Embassy.

"It's Storey here. I believe you wished to speak to me."

"Not on the telephone. Can you meet later this afternoon?"

"Yes. Provided it's in Central London."

"Do you know the café upstairs in the Royal Festival Hall?"

"Of course."

"Be there in an hour. Come alone."

"My wife will come with me. Since I feared she'd been killed, we like to be together when we can."

"Can she speak German?"

"No."

"Then we shall conduct our conversation in German and I will not object to her presence."

"OK."

"I wonder what this is about?" I said to Rosemary, as we left. "But I think we might get a car direct to the Royal Festival Hall, just in case."

TWELVE
A JOINT ENTERPRISE

"Do you think you should've told Mike Elliott about this?" Rosemary suggested.

"Let's see what he has to say first. He might not be prepared to talk if he thought Special Branch were involved."

We got a Special Branch car as far as the south end of Waterloo Bridge and then walked to the Royal Festival Hall from there. The café, I assumed he meant, was on the upper level. There were a few people there, but no-one I recognised. We took a table at one side by the wall and started to drink a cup of tea.

"I can't say I found any of the men I saw being interviewed very pleasant – especially your boss," Rosemary observed. "They all seem obsessed with their careers or putting one over on their rivals. It wasn't really what I'd expected."

"I've begun to see a bit of it in the last few weeks. Most people at lower levels seem to want to do a good job. I don't get the feeling many people are often busting a gut – they like their coffee breaks and tea breaks and going to the canteen or a pub at lunchtime – but I don't think they're constantly spending their time working out what they need to do to get their next promotion."

"Do you think that Watling will have a go at you on Monday?"

"I doubt it. I expect he'll have his hands full with all the Special Branch people checking through his records and having to explain why he's being investigated for breaching the security instructions. I'll be the least of his concerns."

Just before the hour was up, the man from the East German Embassy appeared. Despite the flat cap and light raincoat, there was no disguising his military bearing. He saw us and came over.

"Would you like some tea or coffee?" I asked.

"Auf Deutsch, bitte," he replied. "Aber kein Tee oder Kaffee. Unser Gespraech soll schnell sein."

"OK," I said in German. "Let us be brief. What do you wish to tell me?"

"The organisation who killed Lt Hoefgen is called 'Peace in our time', as you undoubtedly know. We understand several of them have been arrested after firing another missile. You knew about this?"

"Yes. You learnt about it quickly."

"We have been investigating this organisation. The Russians believe they set it up, using an American double-agent who was turned when captured in Cuba. Having an American there distances the organisation from them. Of course, the Americans believe that this man is still working for them and the Russians encourage him to give them less important information and even to do smaller things for them. But from what we have uncovered, he has given them very little. They didn't even know about the American proposal to the British about high-technology computer equipment. Indeed, we believe he asked the Russians to get us to plant listening devices in your apartment, using someone who looked like your wife."

"So he set it up deliberately to kill Lt Hoefgen as a warning to me."

"That's what it looks like to us. Of course, our need to delay your wife played into his hands."

"Are you sure he's really working for the Americans?"

"Not completely. Also we don't think he's got any direct links. He's supposed to have been killed in a road accident in Florida after his return from Cuba. The whole thing was staged by some unofficial organisation which receives its money from secret CIA sources."

"Where did you get all this?"

"Mostly from the Russians. They are beginning to concern themselves that they may have been duped, but they don't like admitting to themselves they might have been wrong – and they have complicated procedures to work through in such circumstances – not least because whoever finally is left responsible for recruiting and supporting this man is liable to be shot."

"So what did the Russians want this man to do?"

"Get British secrets - and American secrets by way of the British. This 'Peace in our time' organisation seemed an excellent cover, as they get lots of valueless information from sympathisers. So it would be easy to pass over useful stuff concealed with it as well."

"And what do you think the Americans get out of it?"

"They know what information the Russians are seeking. They get some contacts. They can use people in an organisation which runs on KGB money to further American ends, while any blame would fall on the Russians if it all came out."

"So who is this man?"

"He's called Jerome D Petterson. Or, at least, that's what he's been calling himself for the last three or four years. Officially he's listed as one of 'Peace in our time's' legal advisors. But we've no doubt he's the one who really runs the organisation."

"And do you have an address for this Petterson?"

"Before I say any more, I need to know what you plan to do next."

"I'm not really sure. I ought to inform Special Branch and probably the Security Service too. I imagine this man is armed and likely to be dangerous?"

"He was a field agent for an arm of the CIA in Cuba and elsewhere in Latin America. He will undoubtedly carry a gun and won't be afraid to use it."

"My natural instinct is to go and have a look at him. Frankly, I'd like nothing more than have my gun against his head while he explained exactly why he thought this stuff was worth killing my wife and Lt Hoefgen for. But I've got into trouble before for going off and doing things which should've been done by the police or others."

"I believe if you decided to inform your Special Branch, by the time they arrived Mr Petterson would either no longer be at home or would be dead. Neither the Russians nor we could allow him to get into the hands of your authorities. The risk that the Americans insist that you hand him back to them is too great. For us, this is mainly about the death of Lt Hoefgen, but for the Russians it is rather more. But we are prepared to give you the opportunity to get information from him before he is no longer available for you."

"I see. What exactly did you have in mind?"

"His residence is, of course, being watched and all avenues of escape are blocked – including the motor-boat which he keeps on the river. We believe that if you confronted him, with a gun in the way that you envisaged, he might talk. Particularly if you said you were there on your own and wanted to avenge the attack on your wife and hadn't told your police you were coming. We believe that in such circumstances he might talk. If you wore a small transmitter, everything he said would be on tape and we would let you have it. We won't need anything like that."

"If I was him, I wouldn't talk. I'd just try to kill me."

"Perhaps going with your wife would be a better idea. Especially if you were both armed. Don't I

246

remember it was you two who subdued two KGB operatives in London two or three years ago and your wife pushed a Counsellor from the Russian Embassy into a canal after poking a gun in his neck? Don't forget, he won't be expecting anything. The people your Special Branch have arrested don't know his real name, only what he looks like. Nor do they know where he lives. We only know because the Russians told us – and they only told us reluctantly because they felt they owed us for the death of Lt Hoefgen."

"I'll need to talk to my wife about this, you understand."

"Please do so. But this thing must be done today. The Russians will almost certainly do whatever they plan to do during the night or in the early hours of tomorrow morning."

So I explained what he had said to Rosemary.

"Oh God!" she exclaimed. "Not again!"

"Well, at least we know who it was who planned to kill you - and we know he's either going to be shot or have an extremely unpleasant time in the hands of the Russians."

"That wasn't really what I meant. It's all the explaining afterwards and the people who look down their noses at you – with some justification – for risking your life and doing things you know you shouldn't've done."

"So you think we should go along with the East Germans?"

"Have we really any other choice?"

"Well – yes, we have. But at least we'll be doing this thing together."

I told the East German what we had decided. He led us to a car parked in one of the roads that run into Upper Ground, where a driver with a thick head and neck and short, bristling ginger hair set off westwards.

We followed the same route as we had travelled to Charlotte Row, but continued along the Wandsworth Road until we struck the South Circular which we continued along until we turned off at Kew. We drove along Forest Road and stopped about two hundred yards from Mortlake Road.

"Pettersen lives a little way round the corner in Bushwood Road," explained the East German, turning round from the front seat, speaking in English. "It is the eleventh house along on the river side. He calls himself Dwight Smith here. Pettersen's neighbours are at home and, as far as we know, are not part of any escape plan he might have. We have a couple of cars in Bushwood Road itself and covering every exit. We also have several people in the allotments behind the house."

"Let's hope they're all keeping their heads down. We don't want his suspicions aroused. How many people will there be with him in the house?" I asked.

"At the moment – none. His wife has taken the car to play a round of golf. If she comes back when you are still in the house, we shall detain her. Have you thought how you will get in?"

"I've no idea whether he'll know who Rosemary and I are. So we may need to use our weapons very smartly. I take it you have got guns for us? We don't tend to walk around London armed."

He opened a case in the front of the car.

"I suggest this one for you – and this lighter one for the lady."

"I think I'll have one the same size. If I have to shoot, I want to make sure he's properly incapacitated, not able to come after us," said Rosemary.

"Do you want silencers too?"

"No," I replied. "If we have to start shooting, we'll be out of there like the clappers and we'll expect you to get us away as fast as you bloody well can! Now what about this transmitter?"

He handed over a metal box thing the size of two packets of cigarettes which I put inside the inside pocket of my jacket. There was also a tiny microphone, which I clipped onto the breast pocket of my shirt. When I buttoned up the jacket, it couldn't be seen.

"Have you any handcuffs or something like that I can restrain him with?"

He handed me a pair of shiny handcuffs. I put them in another pocket of my jacket.

"Ok, well, here we go," I said as Rosemary and I got out. We walked slowly up to the corner of Bushwood Road, kissed, and I switched the transmitter on as instructed and checked that it was working. Then we proceeded along Bushwood Road.

The houses were pleasant brick dwellings with small front gardens, but all seemed well tended. Few people were about, presumably at this hour, they were either having their tea and listening to the football results or possibly working in their back gardens.

We approached Petterson's house. My heart was pounding and my mouth had gone quite dry. I held Rosemary's hand as I took a few deep breaths. Then, with my hand gripping the gun in the right pocket of my jacket, I went up to the door and hit the knocker twice.

A man in his early forties opened the door. He was tall, but without any noticeable features other than a rather bland face and thinning hair. I recognised him instantly as the man with the walkie-talkie who seemed to have been running the demonstration in Trafalgar Square and in Whitehall outside Downing Street.

"Good afternoon," Rosemary began. "We're from St Mary's. My husband and I are planning to swim the Thames from Putney to Mortlake and we're looking for people who'll pay a pound for every mile we swim. It's for a good cause. The proceeds are going to repair the church roof."

"St Mary's …? Where's that? … Uh … Don't I know you from somewhere …?"

He was about to push the door to, but I shoved him and it backwards with my left shoulder. He staggered backwards into hall. We both drew our guns and as he recovered his feet, I pressed the nozzle of my gun right under the left side of his jaw.

"Yes. This is my wife, who you tried to kill yesterday."

"Storey …" He croaked.

"Yes. Now let's go very slowly and smoothly into the back room here. Any jerky movements and this'll go off."

We went slowly into the back room. There were a couple of easy chairs and a settee. Rosemary sat in one of the easy chairs, with her gun pointed on Petterson all the time. I pushed him on to the settee and crossed the room to the other chair.

"Now put your hands above your head."

Very cautiously, I went towards him, always allowing Rosemary a clear shot at him. Then I put the handcuffs on his right hand and then moved to put them on his left. As I did so he jerked away and tried to grab my arm. A shot went off like a small explosion and he leapt forward in the settee clutching at his knee.

"Next time it'll be higher up," said Rosemary calmly. "Now put your hands up and be sensible."

This time he did so without trying to be clever. I sat down in the other easy chair. Petterson was grimacing with pain.

"It's not nice having your kneecap shot is it?" Rosemary remarked. "What do you think it feels like the instant before you realise you're going to be blown to pieces?"

"The neighbours will've heard the shot. You can bet the police will be here in a few minutes."

"Fortunately, British police announce their arrival well in advance with their sirens. You'd better hope they don't come – or by the time they're here, you'll be dead on the floor and we'll be out of the back and well away," I replied.

"So why have you come? For some kind of revenge?"

"Yes. We haven't decided whether to kill you or just incapacitate you – perhaps by shooting your balls off – and then leaving you to the East Germans or the Russians….You need to understand that we're not here officially. We came here because the East Germans found you. The way you got that poor Lt Hoefgen killed, just to give me a warning, seems to have really upset them."

"Who gives a shit about the East Germans! The Russians surely don't!"

"So, you mean, they encouraged you to set Lt Hoefgen up to be horribly killed? That's not what they've been telling the East Germans. They both believe your claim to be a double agent is a lie. You're almost unique – you're a triple agent, according to them."

"And why should you believe those Commies? We're on the same side after all?"

"Sorry. Can you actually remember which side you're actually on?"

"I was turned by Major Camillo Pons Guercia when I was captured in Cuba. My ghost in London is Major Sergey Viktorov, Military Attache at the Russian Embassy. If you can get me out of here, I'll happily tell all I know about the Russians and their East German lackeys to you Security Service."

"But that's not why we're here….You see we want to know why you killed Lt Hoefgens and tried to kill my wife."

"And suppose I don't wish to tell you, what then?"

"I'll shoot you in the groin," replied Rosemary. "I understand it's quite painful."

"You are a fucking…."

"Language, language!" I reproved him. "You see we know quite a bit of it. But I doubt your people who Special Branch arrested yesterday know enough to fill in all the gaps. But I'm a tidy person. I don't like gaps or loose ends. I'm prepared to give you a chance to get away before the East Germans or Russians come after you. It may not be a big chance, but it's the only one you're going to get."

"But I'll happily tell your Security people anything they want to know."

"I doubt that greatly… Besides, that isn't an option. The East Germans will undoubtedly kill you before any British authorities could get here."

"So if either you or they are going to kill me anyway, why should I tell you anything?"

"You haven't been listening. We'll give you a chance – a few minutes at best – to make your escape. The alternative is certainly more final."

"I don't believe you. The East Germans wouldn't tell you how to find me and then allow you to let me escape."

"That's up to you. All we want to know is why you tried to kill my wife. Specifically, who was employing you to prevent my report coming out in favour of American high-tech stuff coming to this country?"

"If I'm going to die anyway, why should I tell you anything?"

252

"This is going nowhere!" exclaimed Rosemary getting to her feet. "I thought you'd probably be tiresome and just play for time as long as you could. Well it won't work!"

She thrust her gun under Petterson's jaw.

"I saw what happened to that poor East German woman and I saw yesterday evening what you had in mind for me! Just as I pull back this trigger, you can imagine what it feels like in those few instants before you're dead!"

She pulled back the trigger, each movement clicked, reverberating like a hammer on a sheet of steel.

"Ok! Ok! I'll tell you! Just give me a chance to live!"

"Get on with it then!"

"I worked for Global Intelligence and Security in Latin America. They get money from the CIA by various backdoor routes, but they're also funded by certain US companies who want their interests protected. When I got picked up in Cuba, it was pretty much deliberate. I was always working for GIS. They came up with this 'Peace in our time' thing, mainly to spot anti-US sympathisers in Britain and elsewhere. The neat bit was that the Russkies really thought they were running the show. They thought it really neat we could organise demonstrations against the Vietnam war and gain recruits for their cause. But they had no idea what we were up to, the suckers! I built up quite a list of Russkie contacts and stooges in Britain and France. As for your high-tech computer parts, it wasn't the old CIA who were bothered about that, it was some of the businesses who are our shareholders, as you might say. They just didn't want the competition. Besides they think you British are as leaky as a sieve. But State were keen to get you in – mainly because they want you in the tent over in Vietnam. So we got our people to do

253

some analysis – and you turned up as the poor sap who would make it or break it. So you were the one we needed to influence."

"With obscure messages that didn't mean anything to me?" I exclaimed.

"We didn't want to make it too obvious. Otherwise, we'd have your Foreign Office going off to State and bleating away. We were trying to find a way to influence you. But your record told us bribery wasn't likely to work and though you've surely been doing things worthy of blackmail, they've all been with your wife. Like when you were in Paris"

"So why didn't you give a clearer warning before killing poor Lt Hoefgen?"

"You got going too quickly. We never expected you British to get moving so fast. We had to do something big – and fast!"

"And the people who told you to do all this?"

"GIS is in the security business. I have no named contact. Just a procedure. We call it triple insulation."

"And who are the people who did the analysis that turned me up as your fall-guy?"

"You mean the British?"

"Yes. We know you were alerted yesterday by someone in the Civil Service."

"… Osbaldistone … that's his name … Osbaldistone."

"Rosemary!" I called out, "He's a liar! Blow his brains out!"

The trigger on Rosemary's gun clicked again. But I knew he wasn't going to risk his own life for one of his stooges.

"OK! OK! It was Lewis. He's been a stooge for the CIA ever since his time in Washington. He's a true believer – a real Cold War warrior. He doesn't believe you British could keep this stuff secret anyway. I'm not his normal contact, but we were put in touch with each other for this particular assignment, you might say."

"That wasn't so hard was it?" said Rosemary, sitting back down in the easy chair.

"What about the 'Peace in our time' organisation? Where are they located? You know we can't have them messing us around when you're no longer there."

"They're based in Compton Street in Clerkenwell. The office is called 'David Jacobson and Associates'. There's a safe there with names and addresses of 'associates', who are my active operatives, and 'members' who are the people we recruit off the streets. I'm sure your people won't need the combination."

"And what will the 'associates' be up to at the moment?"

"I told them to lie low after the arrests yesterday. Sooner or later those people would start to talk. But they don't know my name or where I live….It's all part of the triple insulation process. But, obviously, as they were recruited here …"

"Or in Ireland?"

"or in Ireland, they know each other."

"That tallies …"

"So that's all your gaps and little loose ends? Can I make my getaway now?"

"Not on your life," I replied. "You're staying here until the East Germans come for you, which I guess will be any time now."

"You fucking bastards!"

"Yes – we lied!" said Rosemary, almost sweetly. "But after what you've done, did you really expect us to let you get away with it?"

"There's over a hundred thousand dollars in my safe. It's yours if…"

"No chance," I replied. "I think I hear footsteps at the front door … Rosemary, I suggest you let them in,

255

while I keep an eye on our friend here. We wouldn't want him doing anything rash, would we?"

Though he looked as though he might try something, I was too far away - and he knew it. He sat silently – presumably trying to work out how he might bargain his way out of whatever fate the East Germans had in store for him.

My East German contact came in, with a couple of other men.

"You have what you came for?" he asked in German.

"Yes," I replied. "Did you get it all on tape?"

"Yes. The tape has just been given to your wife … I think your part in this is now ended. If you were to continue along this road and across the bridge, you'll come to a station. It is best, I think, that you spend no more time in our vehicles."

"Or have your guns and transmitter any more either."

"It sounded as though you made good use of them," he remarked, a thin smile appearing round the edge of his mouth for the one and only time in our acquaintance.

As Rosemary and I made our way as unobtrusively as possible towards Kew Bridge and then across it, both of us were silently wondering what was going to happen next to Petterson. Indeed, though we kissed and hugged each other, as much with relief and the release of tension as for any other reason, we barely spoke all the way back to the flat in Pimlico.

It was only when I'd made a cup of tea and Rosemary prepared some cheese and marmite on toast that she suddenly burst into tears.

"How could I do that? I really got so close to blowing that man's brains out!" she sobbed. "How could I get so evil? So much like him!"

"But you didn't," I replied, putting my arm round her. "And I don't believe you could've done. I never thought you would for a second."

"I just hope you're right."

"We both know you better than that. If I'd seen him just after I thought he'd killed you, I'd've shot him without a second's thought. I think you just put so much into persuading him you were serious, you almost persuaded yourself too."

"I'd certainly have shot him in the groin."

"I'd've certainly shot him in several places, if I needed to."

"What do you think the East Germans will do with him?"

"I think it depends whether he's more valuable alive than dead. Though I imagine they'd really like to kill him in revenge for Lt Hoefgen, they're aware he's got a lot more useful information than we got out of him. Besides, they may even want to trade him with the Americans."

"I hope not. He might decide to come back and take his revenge on us."

"I can't think so. Even if he does get handed back to the Americans, he's damaged goods. I can't see how this GIS would want to use him any more. He's too well known now - and he's messed this assignment up. He's talked - to us and probably to the East Germans or the Russians. So who's going to regard him as either competent or reliable?"

"What are we going to do with the tape?"

"I wish we had a tape recorder, so we could check that the East Germans didn't give us a dummy. But we'll have to hand it over to Special Branch..."

"When were you thinking of?"

"Soon...I can't say I'm looking forward to the explosion when they learn – and hear – what we've just done. Even though we had a choice of either getting it this way or not at all, I can't see Special Branch being too pleased that we've gone off and done something like this on our own – again."

"What could they expect? Should we just have let the East Germans kill Petterson or spirit him away? Or should we have taken the opportunity to get this information out of him?"

"So we should tell Mike Elliott now?"

"We might as well get it over and done with."

THIRTEEN
"AND YOUR BIRD CAN SING"

I rang the Special Branch number for Mike Elliott and a voice told me that he had finished for the day. I realised it was almost 6 pm and he'd probably been working much of the previous night too.

"If it's important, I can get a message to him."

"Though I'm reluctant to drag him away from his well-deserved rest, I think we've got something for him that will tie up a lot of the loose ends of the case he's been working on."

"Will you come to Charing Cross? We'll send a car."

The car duly took us to Charing Cross Police Station. We hung around twiddling our thumbs for about half an hour, fortified by a mug of frighteningly strong tea. When Mike Elliott arrived, he looked in a particularly foul mood.

"This had better be good!" he growled, as we sat down in an empty office. "I've had practically no sleep for thirty hours and my family are beginning to forget what I look like."

"We are very sorry to drag you away from your rest and your family," I began. "But I think you'll find what we've got for you is worth it. Basically, this tape contains all the information on who was behind the attempt to stop the Americans sending these high tech components to this country."

"Oh God! What have you been up to now?"

"Unfortunately, I fear you'll like what we've got, but not how we came by it."

"Tell me all," he said wearily. "The tape can wait 'till later."

"You know I went to the East German Embassy after I thought Rosemary had been killed…"

"How could I forget it! It took quite a lot of persuasion and the goodwill you had over there to keep the Security boys from getting you in and giving you a good going over."

"Oh! Well, the East German chap I met when I went there …"

"Captain Guenther Droehn."

"Oh! I've never known his name … Anyway, he telephoned this morning while we were interviewing and suggested a meeting …"

"Which you couldn't refuse to attend, of course! And which you felt unable to tell anyone about!"

"I wanted to hear what he had to say. Besides he's already made it absolutely plain that if I involved any of the British authorities, he'd have nothing to do with me."

"So you met him …"

"He said they'd been investigating who had caused the death of Lt Hoefgen, the young woman who was killed at our flat. They'd managed to get stuff out of the Russians about 'Peace in our time'. This was partly because they and the Russians began to realise that the 'Peace in our time' people had deliberately set them up to get Lt Hoefgen killed as a warning to me. He told me that 'Peace in our time' was funded by the KGB, indirectly, of course, because it was a useful way of acquiring and disguising information about Western technology and weapons and organising demonstrations against the Vietnam war. The mastermind was an American agent who, they'd been told, had been turned when captured in Cuba and was now working for the Russians, while pretending to his American people he was still working for them. What the East Germans reckoned they'd discovered was that he was actually duping the Russians and that the attempts to get me to make my report go against sending the American stuff here were masterminded by him."

"So who is this mastermind they identified?"

"An American called Petterson ... I forget his Christian name ..."

"Jerome D," added Rosemary.

"So, knowing that, what did Captain Droehn expect you to do?"

"To tell you or the Security Service. But he said if I did that, we'd never find Pettersen. Either he'd be dead or they'd've spirited him away."

"Did you believe him?"

"Yes. It seemed to me they had a strong motive for revenge, which would only be tempered by what Petterson might disclose or be worth to the Americans."

"Evidently he offered you a deal."

"Yes. He'd give us the opportunity to get information we wanted out of Petterson before they dealt with him. So either we got something, but not Petterson, or we got nothing, but not Petterson either. I thought it was a deal worth having."

"So you just popped over to Petterson's place ..."

"Yes. He lived in Kew, close to the river. The East Germans reckoned he had a motor-boat parked nearby. Anyway, they fitted me up with a transmitter and microphone, so our conversation could be recorded and we went in ..."

"Both of you?"

"Yes. Apart from being less suspicious at the critical moment when he first opened the front door, he was the sort of bloke you wanted two people to have their eyes on at all times."

"When you say 'eyes', you mean ..."

"Guns. Yes – both of us have been in possession of East German guns this afternoon."

"I should also confess to firing one," added Rosemary. "He tried to make a move, so I shot him in the knee."

"Illegal weapons … causing grievous bodily harm … the list mounts up."

"But you've only our word for it – and if you find anyone with a shot kneecap, he'll be past worrying about GBH," remarked Rosemary.

"Or so you hope….Go on."

"We managed to get inside and got him into handcuffs. He wasn't very co-operative at first, but, as you'll hear on the tape, Rosemary was quite persuasive and eventually he began to talk….."

"I'm not sure I even want to think about that."

"He told us that the work he was doing with 'Peace in our time' was essentially cover for working for the Americans. It was a good way of identifying Russian stooges, but the Russians liked all the demonstrations, etc. His employers, if you can put it that way, were a group calling themselves 'Global Information and Security' and are funded by both CIA unofficial money and certain US business interests. It was the business people who wanted to stop the computer components coming here."

"Could he name names?"

"Unfortunately not. He claimed not to know even his contact in Global Information and Security. He said things were arranged through procedures, which he described as triple insulation."

"That doesn't surprise me. But presumably he did know the name of his Whitehall informant?"

"Yes – Lewis. He was very reluctant to give the name, as you'll hear on the tape. I suspect because Lewis is actually a regular informant of the Americans, recruited when he was in Washington. Blowing a CIA stooge isn't likely to endear him to his American colleagues."

"And the 'Peace in our time' organisation?"

"Based in Compton Street in Clerkenwell. The office front was ..."

"David Jacobson and Associates," added Rosemary. "Apparently there's a safe there with loads of names and addresses, including the people who've been going round doing the surveillance and firing off missiles."

"And this Petersen's address?"

"21 Bushwood Road, Kew ... But I'd be amazed if he's there ... unless he's dead, of course."

"And that's it?"

"Yes. I'm sorry we couldn't deliver him to you – but that was never on the cards," I replied. "I hope the information will be useful."

"Of course, the tape can't be used in evidence - even if we did lay our hands on this Petterson. Indeed, as you evidently acquired it under duress – probably extreme duress, knowing you – it couldn't be used to catch Lewis either. At best, we could use it to get him moved and we could keep a close watch on him ..."

"But there is still Rosemary's plan to catch him using that phone."

"Always assuming he doesn't twig something's up over the weekend. What if he tries to contact Petersen?"

"The plan fails, I suppose. But at least you know who the stooge is and can deal with it."

"You do realise that you could be in deep trouble as a result of this, don't you?"

"We expected it. But there didn't seem to be much choice. Would you rather we left the East Germans and the Russians to deal with Petterson without us being able to get anything out of him?"

"But you have no real proof he was what you think he was. You could've been led up the garden path by the East Germans. Had you thought of that?"

"It crossed my mind. But sometimes you have to go with what your guts are telling you, rather than your head."

"I'm afraid I'm a rather conventional copper. I prefer to use my head and stick to the rules. I've no doubt the Chief Super will be pleased by all this. But he's another one for going on what his guts tell him. Even so, you've been consorting with our Cold War enemies, and probably gave them some information contrary to the Official Secrets Act. You've forced entry into premises without a warrant and on dubious grounds. You've held and threatened a man at gunpoint. Indeed an officer of the Metropolitan Police shot him, with an illegally-acquired weapon. I suspect that your tape, which I accept can't be used as evidence in a court of law, would prove grounds for a serious investigation. At best, I imagine it'd end your promising career as a policewoman, WPS Storey. And heaven knows what it would do to yours, Storey. So I'm going to compound your felonies, by sending this tape off for destruction as confidential waste in the incinerator … Was there no opportunity when you could've contacted us? After you met Captain Droehn? When you were in the house with Petterson? Presumably he had a phone?

"There was no opportunity from the moment we met Captain Droehn until we were in the house. Yes – we probably could've phoned you, though I bet the East Germans had the phone tapped. But if Petterson had believed you were on your way, I believe beyond a shadow of a doubt that he would've told us nothing. And you'd've got nothing out of him either. He'd've pulled as hard as he could on his links to the CIA and offered all sorts of information about the Russians and 'Peace in our time' and would've denied anything to do with stopping this American high-tech stuff coming to this country. In view of what and who he knows – notably Lewis – don't you think the Americans would have bent heaven and earth to get him out of our hands?"

"The fact that you may well be right, doesn't really justify what you did, you know? If you believe that the ends justify the means, you're not really very different from them."

"I'm not sure that's really how it was. We took advantage of an opportunity that would otherwise have disappeared for good. Despite what it might've appeared to Petterson, neither of us would ever kill anyone - and certainly not plan to kill an innocent person purely to send a warning message to someone else … Though actually, if I'd seen Petterson that evening when I thought Rosemary was dead and I knew he'd planned it, I probably would've killed him."

"That's different. Though if you had done that, you'd now be behind bars. As it is, you can leave here without a stain on your characters – except with a warning from me that next time you might well not be so lucky, either with the people you take on or with the Metropolitan Police. As it is – and with this tape safely destroyed – I can offer you the Metropolitan Police's thanks for providing some very useful information."

"We're grateful for your tolerance, Sir," said Rosemary.

"Now, I'd better get in touch with colleagues who can make use of all this information. Then I can get back to my family. I suggest you two go straight home and keep out of everybody's way until you're asked for."

"Fine by us," I replied, "and thanks. I hope you get away soon."

Magnanimously, Mike even got a car to take us back to Erasmus Street. Once there, we were too tired to do anything other than boil up a packet soup and eat a couple of slices of toast with it. Unlike our usual Saturday night, we flopped into bed and fell asleep the moment our heads hit the pillows.

"That was novel," remarked Rosemary, as I brought her a mug of tea in bed the following morning. "I didn't realise I was so tired."

"Threatening to kill people must be more exhausting than you realise … perhaps we're just getting too old for all this excitement!"

"I hope you don't feel too old for all forms of excitement!"

"I thought that was what Sunday mornings were made for."

We were just having a mug of coffee and a couple of ginger biscuits when the telephone rang. It was Inspector Gurney informing us that a car would be coming round to pick us up in half and hour. Chief Superintendant Vaughan wished to see us.

I think we both feared that somehow the tape had failed to make its way to the incinerator and Chief Superintendant Vaughan was on the warpath.

We were driven to New Scotland Yard and taken up to the eighth floor.

"I take it you two are Mike Elliott's informants about this man Petterson and his connections to 'Peace in our time' and the case involving you two?" he demanded, not unpleasantly. It was just his size and bearing that made you feel as though you were being interrogated.

"Yes. I expect he explained the circumstances."

"I believe he very wisely did no such thing. All he told me was that the trail of information which you'd given him couldn't be used in evidence, though it was sufficient for us to use search warrants, etc.....And before you speak, I really don't want to know."

"Mike Elliott is a good bloke," I said.

"A good bloke, yes. A good copper – yes and no. But we have to play the ball where it lies, don't we!"

"Yes, Sir," said Rosemary, whose knowledge of golf was on a par with mine – practically zero.

"You should know that your information has proved very useful. Lots of valuable stuff at that place in Clerkenwell. Nothing in Kew, however. The house had been thoroughly ransacked and Mrs Petterson was having kittens - not least because her husband was missing and there was a fair amount of blood around the place. Apparently they've been married nearly twenty years, so I can't believe she didn't know what sort of game he was in. But she just claimed she thought he was a security consultant and had been hired by 'Peace in our time' to prevent them being infiltrated by people who might damage their aims. We picked up almost all of the so-called 'associates' of 'Peace in our time'. Some of them may be about to sing because we discovered about an hour ago that a body fished out of the Thames first thing this morning was that of Jerome D Petterson or, as he was known in Kew, Dwight Smith. He'd been shot in the knee and given a thorough going-over, electrically and surgically, so the pathologist informed us. But he was actually killed by suffocation. The pathologist thinks through the use of a plastic bag. I imagine your East German friends made sure his last few hours on this earth were far from pleasant. And from what he appears to have told you, I can't say I blame them."

"Do the Americans know?" I asked.

"Not yet. That is a pleasure in store for someone other than me, I fear. I expect Jacob Ffoulkes will wish to extract the maximum he can out of his CIA contacts in return for maintaining anonymity for Petterson and his activities in this country. The Commissioner will inform the Permanent Secretary at the Home Office later today and no doubt he'll tell the Home Secretary."

"What about Lewis? ... and Osbaldistone?

"The information will be given on a 'top secret' basis. As far as we are aware, Lewis is unaware of what has been going on. He hasn't attempted to contact Petterson, which isn't really surprising. Interestingly, two 'associates' of 'Peace in our time' have spent much of their time sitting in their car about three streets away from where he lives – in Purley – presumably in case he needs to send a message or perhaps make a quick getaway. Obviously, we won't pick them up until he's safely on his way to work tomorrow morning."

"What's going to happen then?"

"I've been in touch with the Cabinet Secretary. Well – actually he got in touch with me. Complaints about senior officials being dragged off to Charing Cross Police Station during their weekend. Rumours that a Cabinet Office official had been arrested and charged with spying. He's been given some of the story – what he needs to know. He also understands that we need to trap the real culprit or there'll be no chance of getting any information out of him. But he doesn't want a massive police presence in the Cabinet Office tomorrow morning. That wasn't my idea either. Mike Elliott has earned the right to be there and he'll have a couple of plain clothes officers with him. We also agreed that it'd be sensible to have you there, Storey, as you seem to know the layout of the place – and you can be explicably over there to brief the Cabinet Secretary in greater detail. If WPS Storey wishes to be there as well, I'm sure we can arrange that."

"I'd like to be there, Sir."

"Then you'd better report to Mike Elliott here first thing on Monday. Plain clothes, of course ... But wear something appropriate please. From what I hear your plain clothes tend to be ... er ... a little short."

"I'm sure I can find something suitable, Sir."

"If anyone has earned the right to see the final chapter, it's you two ... But I don't know whether you wish to see the next bit. I've got all the 'Peace in our time' bigwigs together downstairs for what I called a 'confidential briefing'. I propose to explain to them how their self-righteous organisation has been manipulated for purposes contrary to their aims by people who don't share their opinions and act completely counter to the beliefs they espouse so publicly. They may be naïve, but in future they don't need to be so blind or so immeasurably stupid."

"I think we might pass on that," I said. "Thank you."

"I assume we don't need to be in a safe house any more, Sir?" asked Rosemary.

"Certainly not after Monday ... But though you won't get transport, don't feel you've got to move out instantly ..."

"Our insurance company told us they would find a flat for us as close to home as they could while ours was being repaired, Sir. So I hope it'd only be a week at most," replied Rosemary, undoubtedly delighted to leave a place she detested.

"Was there more you wanted from us?" I asked.

"No. I think that's all. I think you'd better go direct to the Cabinet Office on Monday and I'll arrange for the Cabinet Secretary's Private Secretary to get you to the right place. We're aiming to tee Lewis up at around 10.30."

"Then if you don't mind, we'll get off back home."

"Of course. And thank you for what you've done … But in future, if you come across anything strange or suspicious, phone us – and then take a long holiday, as far away as possible, please!"

"How much do you think he knows?" whispered Rosemary as we left the building.

"Just about the lot, I suspect," I replied. "But they've got better things to do than go after us. Besides – how much of this do you think'll end up in court?"

"Precious little."

"Quite so. Even if we catch Lewis red-handed on Monday, I doubt they'll want to put him on trial under the Official Secrets Act for leaking stuff to the Americans. I guess his punishment will be dismissal from the Foreign Office and the end of a glittering career."

"It doesn't seem quite fair, does it? I know Petterson has got his just deserts. But Lewis fed him information knowing that it'd result in innocent people being killed … I'm still upset about the fact that they killed that poor East German woman purely to send a warning! It's just so horribly cold-blooded and evil!"

"On the other hand, what can we do? I don't think I'd want to leak his name to the East Germans to let them wreak their revenge on him. That'd make us just like Lewis and Petterson … But I guess they got that out of him anyway."

"It still doesn't seem right!"

As it was a pleasant, sunny April day, we walked past Parliament and sat on one of the seats in Victoria Tower Gardens.

"How nice to feel we're not being watched!" exclaimed Rosemary.

270

"Or that there's no longer anyone out there who wants one or both of us dead," I added.

"It's easy to forget just how nice an ordinary life is … I hope we can get back to that as soon as possible."

"I can't see why my report shouldn't be finished in the next fortnight – and then I'll start looking for another post."

"I hope it won't be too long before we can go home properly. I really love our little flat. We were really happy there."

"And we'll be happy there again."

"Are you sure? After what you saw that evening?"

"I don't think sights like that ever leave you. But I don't associate it with you being killed any more. And it didn't really seem like our flat. Now it seems more like a nightmare. I don't see why I shouldn't be as happy in our flat as I was before. Just as long as you are."

"I just saw it shattered and burnt and lots of things smashed…but it didn't feel like home then."

"Once we've got some new furniture in and got used to it, I don't see why it shouldn't be just like before."

"Let's just walk for a bit. I want to enjoy feeling I'm free again … Put your arm round me….I'm complicated … I want to feel free, but I want to feel protected too … You're always so calm and so strong …"

"I'm not sure that's always what's going on inside."

For an hour we wandered all round those old streets around Smith Square, Vincent Square, Rochester Row, behind Westminster Cathedral, the ecclesiastical area round Dean's Yard and the quiet streets around John Islip Street. There were few people about and we enjoyed looking at the ancient buildings, just the two of us.

By the time we realised what the time was, it was too late to get lunch anywhere, except from a café on Victoria Station. Then we made our way back to Erasmus Street. Remembering that we wouldn't be living there much longer lightened Rosemary's spirits and we frolicked in the huge bath and the small bedroom for much of the evening.

The following morning, I arrived at the Cabinet Office at nine o'clock. Evidently, the Cabinet Secretary's business didn't commence for another half an hour, as I had to wait in the lobby until 9.30 before a tall, lean, supercilious man of about my age appeared and announced himself as Sir Philip's Private Secretary.

"For the time being, I propose you remain in Sir Philip's waiting room. I doubt he'll wish to speak to you. You can expect further instructions later."

"I assume this will involve Special Branch?"

"They are expected in due course."

It struck me that this peculiar brand of self-satisfied arrogance added to driving personal ambition, lack of any moral foundation and limited experience of life outside their own small milieu of public schools, Oxbridge, Whitehall and the Reform Club had contributed in no small way to this mess. It seemed to me that these so-called 'Mandarins', whether of the junior or senior variety, had no concept that they were Civil Servants, paid by taxpayers and supposedly providing good government and services like schools, hospitals, even tax collection in return. That world of routine, of drudgery, of danger even – that 'Outfield' – was alien to them. Worse, its existence barely, if ever, crossed their minds. Yet Ministers, representatives of those millions of electors, dealt almost exclusively with people like the Private Secretary. How could Ministers achieve anything real for those people who had voted for them and expected things to change, to improve, in such circumstances?

After a quarter of an hour, a messenger arrived and offered me a cup of coffee. It was execrable. Ten minutes later the Cabinet Secretary's Private Secretary reappeared.

"Will you come with me," he stated.

We went into a small meeting room.

"Sir Philip is at FD," he began. "I must ask you some questions. First, why was it necessary to summon senior Cabinet Office and other officials to a police station in the middle of their weekends?"

"I understood that the reasons for that have already been explained to the Cabinet Secretary by the Metropolitan Police. In any case, the decision was a matter for them."

"I believe I was seeking your perspective on the matter."

"Why? Isn't the Met's briefing of the Cabinet Secretary sufficient?"

"This is for my information."

"I'm sorry, but I have nothing to add to what the Met said to the Cabinet Secretary."

"Surely you can understand that as his Private Secretary, I need to know."

"It seems to me that's his decision. In any case, from what I've seen of this place I would have grave doubts about the security of any information I divulged to anyone."

"That's extremely unhelpful and unwarranted."

"From the mouths of your own people and others, it's plain to me that security of information is secondary to self-interest in this office. People appear prepared to break or connive at breaches of your own Security Instructions."

"The briefing on you indicated you were insubordinate and a trouble-maker. I can see why. I'm senior to you in grade and I expect you to do as I ask."

"You aren't my line manager, so I don't believe I have any duty to do what you tell me. Furthermore, if my line manager asked me to do something which I considered to be wrong, I'd refuse to do it. I'm sure that's seen as being insubordinate – and probably a trouble-maker, too. But I do what I believe in, not what I think will assist my career."

"So you're not going to tell me anything?"

"Not unless the Cabinet Secretary tells me to. And if he does, I would advise him not to – at least, not until this morning's work has been completed."

"Why? Do you think I'm somehow implicated in whatever's going on?"

"I don't know – and that's why it'd be unwise to take any risk."

He gave me an evil stare and stalked away. I was virtually certain that it was sheer curiosity that had prompted his demands, but I had no idea whether his star was hitched to Lewis's coat-tails. Besides, if the Cabinet Secretary had decided not to tell him, there might well be a good reason for it.

Five minutes later, a young lad – probably the office clerk – appeared and asked if I would mind returning to the waiting room. I followed him without demur. I wondered how the visit to Qomputix was going. I had left a message saying that I was required in Whitehall during the morning, so Ken, Morry and Bernard should go without me. I suggested they should encourage Mr Jones to take the lead, assuming he turned up. I wondered whether they would learn anything new. It would be ironic if they found huge flaws in Qomputix's security, which would begin to cast doubt on the sort of guarantee we could give the Americans. In any case, with our knowledge of Petterson's activities and those who paid him, perhaps our bargaining hand with the Americans had been strengthened?

I read the 'Guardian' and the 'Financial Times' while I waited for something to happen. Shortly before 10.45, Mike Elliott, Inspector Gurney and a very soberly-dressed Rosemary appeared in the waiting room. Within seconds, the Private Secretary appeared and led us into the Cabinet Secretary's room. I noticed that he was not permitted to remain.

"Well," asked the Cabinet Secretary, a medium sized, bespectacled man with greying hair and a face which reminded me of a large tabby cat. "Are you set to go?"

"Yes, Sir," replied Mike Elliott. "The telephone call which we believe is the signal will be made in six minutes time. His secretary told us there have been two different messages. We believe that the one we're using this morning encourages him to telephone the external number. Of course, doing that is much more incriminating than merely receiving an external call."

"And then what?"

"Mr Storey and I will wait in Room 35/3, which I understand will have been vacated by its occupant, Mr Peregrine Bell."

"Yes. He's assistant secretary to MISC 26 (67), so he'll be out of the office from 10.30 until noon at least."

"The door will be slightly ajar, so that we can detect our suspect going past. Neither of us will be visible from the corridor. Once he has gone into Mr Wordley-Smith's room, we'll give him a couple of minutes until we get the signal that he's phoned out. Then we'll go in and detain him."

"Where will you take him?"

"There is apparently a room available on the second floor. I was told it is quite private. Inspector Gurney and WPS Storey will join us there."

"And you will then interview him? How long is that likely to take?"

"It's always difficult to predict how long interviews like this might last. But I'd be surprised if it went on for more than an hour."

"What will you do then?"

"That depends on the outcome of the interview. It's likely that we would at least wish to detain him, probably to arrest him."

"And charge him?"

"That goes with an arrest. An arrest has to be for a specific offence."

"I see. And what happens then?"

"He'd be offered a chance to speak to his lawyer. In normal circumstances, we'd take him to a police station, charge him and then place him in the cells. He'd then normally go before a magistrate who'd decide on bail."

"That would be in public?"

"Yes. There are occasions when such hearings are held in camera, but they are rare and I doubt whether this case would be seen as qualifying."

"Not even if national security was involved?"

"If it was, we might be able to persuade a magistrate to hold the hearing in camera. But I don't see that it is."

"There are some important wider issues here than purely this case, Chief Inspector. There are our relations with the Americans, for example. If it came out that we identified this man as the result of information supplied by and covert co-operation with East German security people, Ministers might well be greatly displeased. While we wish to see justice done and those who have broken the law dealt with, the public aspect of this needs careful and mature consideration."

"I'm not clear what you are saying, Sir?"

"Before this man is formally charged with anything – always assuming that you have sufficient evidence to do that – I would wish that we convene here again. There may be other eventualities."

"If that is what you wish, Sir."

I led Mike up to the third floor and the room occupied by Peregrine Bell.

"He's going to let him wriggle out of it, isn't he?" whispered Mike.

"It looks like it. It'd be all too embarrassing all round if this was to get out. I wonder how much Ministers really know about it, though. I suspect this is more about the mandarins closing rank," I replied.

We waited in silence while the minutes ticked by. Then we heard footsteps going along the corridor, but, squinting through the crack between the door and the door-frame, I could see it was a messenger. Presumably Lewis would need to wait until the corridor was clear. More footsteps – and Lewis came past.

Mike pointed to his watch and indicated 'two' with his fingers. The seconds seemed to tick by ever more slowly, but eventually we were up and round to Wordley-Smith's room. There was Lewis, sitting on the desk with the telephone at his ear. Of course, he turned as we came in and slammed it down.

"Don't worry, Mr Lewis," said Mike, "Your call has been logged and in a few moments I'll get confirmation that it was the number we expected you to have dialled. In any case, the person you were ringing is no longer there. But he did confirm you as his contact here in the Cabinet Office before he left."

I don't know what on earth you're talking about!" declared Lewis brazenly. "Who the hell are you? And what are you doing here, anyway? And Storey?"

"Then perhaps we should explain. But not here. Will you please come with us to a room which awaits us downstairs?"

"And if I refuse?"

"I'll be obliged to arrest you and this will necessarily become a lot more public than it need be."

"Very well. But I must make it clear that my co-operation shouldn't be taken as any sign that I admit to any improper or illegal act."

As we made our way to the second floor, I wished it had been possible to stick a gun under the chin of this smooth, smug, supercilious, duplicitous and despicable man. I wondered how his public-school sang-froid would stand up to that. Even the hardened and experienced Petterson hadn't done very well.

We arrived in the room set aside for the interview..

"For the record, I am Chief Inspector Michael Elliott of Special Branch. With me are Inspector Gurney, also of Special Branch, Mr Storey of HM Customs and Excise and WPS Storey of the Metropolitan Police. Would you please identify yourself for the record?"

"I'm Richard Lofthouse Lewis, Assistant Secretary in the Secretariat of the Cabinet Office, on secondment from the Foreign Office."

"Your address?"

"56 Valley Road, Purley, Surrey."

"When we entered Mr Wordley-Smith's room, you had a telephone at your ear. May I ask who you were telephoning?"

"I deny I had a telephone at my ear."

"I believe that both Mr Storey and I would state that you had – in a court of law if necessary. Is that right, Mr Storey?"

"Yes," I confirmed.

"So, what if I did. I was just going past the room and heard the phone ring, so I aimed to be helpful and pick it up and tell the caller that Mr Wordley-Smith wasn't there."

"Now surely you don't expect us to believe that, do you, Mr Lewis? You know as well as I do that statement can be checked. As we were in a nearby room and heard no telephone ring, can we perhaps take it that you'd like to withdraw that last statement? I can always ring your switchboard and ask them to check."

"Very well."

"So you didn't pick the telephone up because you heard it ringing as you went past?"

"No. Damn you."

"On the same basis, do you wish to continue to deny that you rang this number and were awaiting a response when Mr Storey and I entered the room. For the record, I am showing Mr Lewis a card with a telephone number written on it, witnessed by Inspector Gurney, Mr Storey and WPS Storey."

"May I ask why she is here? And Storey, for that matter?"

"No, you may not. Answer the question I put to you please, Mr Lewis."

"Yes."

"Who did you expect to speak to on that number?"

"I don't know. My secretary got a message to ring it."

"Indeed, so why did you not telephone from your office?"

"I thought my secretary might listen in on my call."

"But you said just now you didn't know the number, so why would it be a problem if your secretary listened in?"

"Occasionally I play away from home, you might say. I thought it might be a call of a personal nature, if you get my drift. This place is a network of gossip and I wouldn't want any private peccadilloes getting to the ears of my seniors."

"Of course not. But the telephone call to your secretary didn't give you a number to telephone. You see, the telephone call to your secretary was made by a member of Special Branch who will testify to that as necessary, as will your secretary who took your call. She will testify that no telephone number was mentioned in the call made to her and that she passed no telephone number to you to call. So perhaps you'd like to explain why you telephoned that particular number and who you expected to speak to?"

"I wish to speak to a lawyer."

"Under the offences we are investigating, that privilege is not immediately available to you."

"Then I wish to speak to the Cabinet Secretary."

"All in good time, Mr Lewis. The Cabinet Secretary is aware of our presence and what is happening this morning. He will certainly not wish to speak to you unless we advise him to do so. Now will you answer my question, please?"

"Then I refuse to answer any of your questions."

"Very well. We have sufficient evidence to charge you with several serious offences, any one of which will merit several years in prison. If you refuse to co-operate, we will convey you from here and arrest and charge you in a nearby police station. You will then be taken before a magistrate's court, where I will apply for your continuing detention on the basis that you are likely to flee the country. In view of the nature of your offences, especially the involvement with foreign agents in murder and attempted murder, I believe a magistrate will agree to remand you in custody. I imagine it is likely that news of these proceedings will become public and the press and TV will quickly drag you from your present obscurity to being a national celebrity."

"You utter and complete fucking bastard! That's blackmail!"

"I believe I was merely informing you what would occur if you refused to answer my questions. Do I understand that you will co-operate?"

Lewis nodded. He was beginning to sweat. He was beginning to realise that his only hope was to tell all - or at least as much as he had to – and rely on the desire of the Cabinet Office to keep this sort of thing out of the public eye.

"I repeat my question, why did you go to Mr Wordley-Smith's room to use his telephone? And who did you telephone?"

"My secretary received a coded call – which evidently you had worked out. It informed me that I should ring a man named Jerome D Petterson."

"What was your relationship with Mr Petterson?"

"He was an occasional contact. He supplied me with information about the activities of an organisation called 'Peace in our time', which is a front for the Soviets."

"And what did you do with the information he supplied you?"

"I passed it on to the Foreign Office and to the Security Service."

"Please be specific, Mr Lewis. Who did you give this information to?"

"I can't recall."

"Please, Mr Lewis. I don't want to remind you every time you refuse to co-operate what I shall do next. Shall we just save ourselves the trouble and just all go to Charing Cross Police Station now?"

"Reggie Henshawe in the FO and David Robertson in the Security Service."

"Mr Lewis, why are you telling me lies that you know I'll check and discover you've lied? Shall we just stop this now?"

"Very well, you bastard! I supplied him with information, largely relating to British relations with the US and to a lesser extent with the Soviet block. But my area is really the US and the Americas. But it was pretty low-grade stuff."

"Why did you give him this information?"

"When I was stationed in Washington, the CIA caught me in a little peccadillo. In return for my career, I've been co-operating with them ever since. But I don't really see very much of importance."

"Don't you attend FD among other committees?" I asked.

"Yes."

"I suspect what Mr Storey is saying that you might as well be hung for a sheep as for a lamb, Mr Lewis," Mike continued. "Or, to put it more bluntly. None of us believe you … Now we have evidence that the number which you telephoned this morning was also telephoned last Friday afternoon from a public call box in Parliament Square. Did you make that call?"

"No. I was in my office all afternoon, as I told you on Saturday….But Osbaldistone did go out at some point. I tried to find him …"

"Yes. You did a nice job to try and point the finger at Mr Osbaldistone, including ensuring he would be logged in and logged out neatly around the time of that telephone call. But after you came into the office and before we did, we detained the people who were in the car that was stationed a few streets from your house all last weekend and which appeared within radio range of your office shortly before you got to work. Mr Osbaldistone has identified the driver of that vehicle as the driver ostensibly of Sir Nigel Spinks, who you sent him to take an envelope to. Your associates aren't quite as good as you at avoiding loose ends, I fear. An envelope addressed to Sir Nigel Spinks in what I guess is your handwriting, with several sheets of blank paper inside, was discovered during a search of the boot of the car. That does give Mr Osbaldistone's story considerably more credibility."

"But I didn't leave my office."

"I wonder if we asked the man sitting by the door to No 10 whether you went through and came back at about the same time Mr Osbaldistone was logged out and in to the Cabinet Office? Or the constable by the front door in No 10? Or the constables at the Whitehall end of No 10? In any case, the only person we know of in this building who knew this number is you, Mr Lewis."

"I believe you'll have some difficulty proving it. They may have seen me, but could they truthfully swear to time in a court of law?"

"Since Mr Petterson has confirmed that you made the telephone call to him, that point appears to be irrelevant, doesn't it, Mr Lewis?"

"Then why did you go there?"

"I wanted to see how far your co-operation stretches. Evidently not very far. Now I'm not going to say this again, either you co-operate and tell the truth or we will leave for Charing Cross Police Station. Do I make myself clear?"

"Yes. Damn you!"

"Then I ask again, did you make the telephone call to Mr Petterson from the public call box in Parliament Square?"

"Yes."

"And did you deliberately try to make it appear as though Mr Osbaldistone had done so?"

"Yes."

"Was this a spur of the moment thing?"

"No. I always had a plan if I needed to contact Petterson."

"Why didn't you use your radio and call the car? That would've avoided there being any record of your contact with Petterson."

"I reckoned there'd be a witch-hunt after Storey's wife was killed, so I needed someone to take the blame. Osbaldistone was the obvious candidate – but I needed a smoking gun, you might say. Besides, using radios and cars would be too slow. They'd have to drive somewhere nearer Petterson to pass my message on to him."

"So you knew that your message would set in train events that were aimed at killing Mrs Storey – WPS Storey?"

"I suppose I assumed that would be the case. The decision was down to Petterson. But Storey had been warned. It was his fault that he didn't heed the warnings. They were certainly clear enough by that stage."

"Yes – we'll come on to the previous warning in a moment. I just want to be absolutely clear – you did expect WPS Storey to be killed as a result of your message?"

"Yes. It was nothing personal. That's why I have the car close to hand – just in case anything went wrong."

"Why were you in such a hurry?"

"We needed to get Storey to revise the latest version of his report before it became an official MISC 38 paper. Then it'd be too late. If his wife was killed, Petterson believed he'd either change his mind or be so distraught – like he'd been when he thought she'd been killed – that someone else could take over and we could influence them more easily. As I said, it was nothing personal. Petterson's US backers were adamant that this stuff wasn't to come to the UK and they weren't going to allow State to pussyfoot around the Foreign Office in return for something on the Vietnam War."

"That broadly confirms what Petterson said. Now the previous occasion, I take it you contacted Petterson about Mr Storey's draft when you saw it?"

"Yes. Unfortunately by the time I got to see it, it had been sent over from Customs as an official MISC 38 paper, so all we could do was give Storey a warning he wouldn't forget in a hurry. But killing that East German woman was entirely Petterson's idea. When I heard, I was quite upset. But Petterson pointed out that Storey wasn't the sort of person to be put off by a 'near miss' hit and run or something like that. It needed to be something big to grab his attention. And getting an East German killed in the act of bugging his flat was quite neat, too – as he saw it."

"So that time, you had no idea that your information would lead to someone being killed?"

"No. I swear it."

"That ties up with what Petterson said, if I recall correctly. Did you have anything to do with this 'Peace in our time' organisation?"

"Other than the fact that they supplied me with some surveillance, a radio link and a possible escape route, no."

"Right. I think that completes my questions for now. I imagine others will have questions about your relationship with the Americans since you were in Washington, but my concern is entirely with the murder of Lt Hoefgen, the East German who died at the Storeys' flat, and the attempted murder of WPS Storey. At this point, I need to report to the Cabinet Secretary. You will remain here, Mr Lewis. I fear that I don't trust you sufficiently to believe that you won't try to escape, so Inspector Gurney will handcuff you to this table and will continue to guard you in our absence. I don't expect we'll be long."

Just as we were going out, Lewis cried "You set me up! Storey, you fucking bastard, you set me up!"

"No, Mr Lewis" I replied. "I just gave Seymour and Watling in Customs a first version of my draft paper for MISC 38. I'm afraid you and they did the rest. We expected something to happen – and you played your part. I'm sorry you didn't get to see the body of the poor East German woman, then you might've had an idea what you were planning for my wife."

"Perhaps while you spend those long years behind bars," added Rosemary, "you might contemplate how you'd feel if you came into your house and found the body of your wife blown to pieces! You are truly one of the most despicable men I've ever met!"

As we went downstairs to the Cabinet Secretary's office, Mike whispered, "Of course, even with that confession, the chances of making a prosecution stick are poor. Once he learns Petterson is dead, he'll know that his confession is the main evidence against him, as the best we would have from Petterson is what he told us. A good lawyer would make it difficult to use Petterson's evidence to you and he'd probably argue that we'd tricked Lewis into confessing – and threatened him as well. With the right judge, he'd probably get off. So I'm pretty clear we don't want to sit on too much of a high horse with the Cabinet Secretary."

"So that despicable man gets away with it!" growled Rosemary.

"Let's see what the Cabinet Secretary proposes," I suggested.

We were admitted almost instantly and the Private Secretary told to withdraw.

"Well?" demanded the Cabinet Secretary.

"He confessed. It took a while, but he eventually confessed," replied Mike.

"To what?"

"Supplying the Americans with information ever since he was stationed in Washington. Supplying Jerome D Petterson with information which led to the death of Lt Hoefgens of the East German Embassy and to the attempted murder of WPS Storey last Friday. To be fair, he claimed he didn't know the information he supplied before the death of Lt Hoefgen would lead to her death – and I believe him. But he admitted to knowing that the information he supplied to Petterson last Friday would cause WPS Storey's death."

"I see. He clearly admitted that, in front of witnesses?"

"Yes, the four of us."

"Knowing that Petterson is dead and that there was an East German link in the chain that led to his evidence, how strong do you think the case would be against him, assuming he gets a decent lawyer?"

"Pretty strong – but not overwhelming."

"So he might get off?"

"That's always a possibility, Sir."

"Right ... Well, I've been speaking with the Metropolitan Commissioner while you were interviewing Lewis. I assumed you'd get him to confess, you understand. But Douglas and I are agreed that the best course in this matter is to hand Lewis over to the Security Service. You can close your files with Petterson, which is a decent enough result. Of course, the Americans will be aware that Lewis is no further use to them now, so you can be sure he's got no value for us. So he'll undoubtedly be dismissed the Service without pension, etc, and will spend an uncomfortable time while the Security Service sweat out of him all that he's revealed to the Americans. But Ministers are agreed that relations with the Americans are too delicate for us to put a senior official publicly on trial for supplying them with information. They wouldn't take too kindly to evidence appearing in public about an American citizen with CIA links operating some kind of death squad here in Britain. Don't ever forget that in our relationship with the USA, we are the supplicants, they are the masters. They're deeply unhappy about the PM's stance on the Vietnam War and we can't afford to make it any worse. So Lewis will disappear into deep and unloved obscurity. After all, he never actually did anything..."

"Actually he deliberately passed on information he knew would get me killed!" exclaimed Rosemary. "In my book – and in anyone's morality but yours – that's conspiracy to murder! With all your cavilling and high flown words, you just want to protect one of your own! What you really don't want is for people to know exactly what went on in the heart of Government! For you, words mean more than people's lives! You're actually no better than he is! You're despicable!"

"I agree," I added, my voice sounding strangely loud. "There has been evil at work here, but you're prepared to sweep it under the carpet. You know as well as I do that the Americans can easily deny any link to Petterson and the fact that Lewis was leaking stuff to the CIA wouldn't be relevant to any court case, unless you chose to charge him under the Official Secrets Act. I agree with Rosemary. This is all about saving the Cabinet Office's face....But let me tell you, if I ever discover that Lewis has been reinstated, or given some post – however humble – in any of the many organisations linked to the Civil Service, I'll tip the East Germans off that it was him who fingered Lt Hoefgen. And if that doesn't work, I'll give a nice juicy story to the press. And if any of that costs me my job, so be it! I'd rather be able to look myself in the eye when I'm in front of a mirror than build a career on your sort of morality."

"I give you my word that Lewis will never darken anyone's doors in or around the Civil Service. But if you do what you're threatening, you'll get yourself into a lot of trouble, young man! We do have the Official Secrets Act and D Notices, you know!"

"I'd like to see you charge me. What do you think the first question my barrister would ask me in court? 'Why did you pass that material to the press?' And then not even D notices will stop it getting out."

"The Service takes a dim view of blackmail."

"I take a dim view of a Service that fails to punish appropriately someone who deliberately and knowingly conspired to kill my wife! Your world is so convoluted and refined, I can only assume you've forgotten what it's like for those of us who actually risk our lives. I wish you'd had to see the body of that poor East German woman, blown into pieces in my flat. Perhaps even you might see things differently."

"I'm going to overlook your insubordination because of what you've been through, Storey. But I've warned you – and I hope that's enough. Have you anything to add to this conversation, Chief Inspector?"

"Only that I entirely agree with Nick and Rosemary. The stench in this place is such that I can't wait to get out!"

"Thank you for that. Now there should be people from the Security Service in the waiting room. Perhaps you will do me the kindness of handing Lewis over to them, please?"

With that we were dismissed.

"I don't know what sort of career you'll have in the Civil Service after that," remarked Mike. "But it was well said by both of you. If you ever want a job in the Met …"

"Once the dust has settled, I'm only an obscure junior official in an obscure Department far from Whitehall. I think I'll be quickly forgotten."

Rosemary just gave me the most enormous hug and kiss.

I didn't recognise any of the Security Service officers who were waiting to take custody of Lewis. I agreed to take them to him. When we got to the room, I asked whether I could just see him for a few moments alone. Inspector Gurney unlocked the handcuffs and left him with me. For a moment it looked as though Lewis thought I was going to do him an injury.

"Don't worry," I said quietly. "I'm not going to hurt you. At least, not now. You're going to escape the justice that the East Germans served on Petterson. But I can bide my time. One day, when I've worked out how to do it without any possibility of being caught, you or someone you love will find out what I felt like when I thought my wife had been killed. Just bear that in mind."

Then I left. I didn't know how seriously he'd take it. I certainly had no intention of carrying it through. I'd better things to do with my life. Rosemary and I would be looking forward, not backwards. But even if it clawed at his nerves from time to time in those dark, quiet hours in the dead of night, that would be some of the punishment he deserved, but wasn't going to get.

"So much for avoiding the high horse!" remarked Mike as we met up in the lobby by the front door of the Cabinet Office. We all laughed heartily, but it was a laughter which was as much a release of pent-up anger and tension as good spirits.

"The last time I was here," I said, "I had to plan how to get out and escape people who were shadowing me. It's nice just to walk out without having to worry about things like that."

"I think we all deserve a beer!" said Mike suddenly. "Shall we mark the end of this in a local hostelry?"

"Definitely," replied Rosemary and I together.

FOURTEEN
THE SUMMER OF LOVE

"We knew something like that was going to happen," I began, sipping at a pint of beer. "So why did we get so annoyed by it?"

"For my part, it was because that man had already phoned my boss without even showing the courtesy of allowing me to complete the interview and report to him" replied Mike. "He'd already decided what was going to happen, pretty well irrespective of what we did this morning … and getting that little weasel to confess wasn't easy at all."

"I absolutely detested his complacency – the complacency of the powerful," added Rosemary. "It was as though justice and morality were just another lot of words, factors which he had to weigh against much more important considerations, not least how to ensure that his Office didn't come out of it looking bad in public."

"I fear it was ever thus," remarked Mike.

"Still, he had to put up with hearing a few things he didn't like," I said. "Though I expect he's heard worse and survived it comfortably enough."

"I hope he won't take it out on you," said Rosemary.

"As I said, I think I'm too junior for him to worry about. Besides, he could never be sure how I might react. If anything, I guess it may go the other way – make sure my career goes smoothly, so I feel content and let all this fade back into old memories."

"And will you?" asked Mike.

"Well, other than keeping an eye out in case Lewis emerges somewhere with his nose wiped clean, yes. I can't get rid of the bad memories, but I know they'll fade in time. But Rosemary and I have our lives ahead of us and we want to get back into our flat…"

"… and start a family," added Rosemary.

"You'll have to …" said Mike.

"I know – but I want a family with Nick."

"Well, if you ever want to come back, get in touch with me, if I'm still around. The Met needs officers like you – in spite of the unorthodox things you get up to with your husband … Now what are you two laughing at?"

Of course, we had to return to work. I arrived in Custom House to find only Paul Barton-Jones, all the rest of my team being on the visit to Qomputix. Paul was just completing his revision of the annex containing all the relevant legislation. I realised that I didn't have much to do, so I began to look through recent OWOs to see what post I might contact Estabs about. Within half an hour or so, the phone rang and a youthful sounding man's voice asked me if I would go and see Mr Parr, Deputy Chairman as soon as convenient. I took this to be an urgent request and made my way over to the Board's corridor in King's Beam House. I went into the Deputy Chairman's Private Office. Even from there, the labours of a Special Branch team investigating what Roisin O'Neill had passed on to her Irish republican friends could be heard.

"It was good of you to come over so quickly," said the Private Secretary, a very youthful-looking man, which doubtless explained his decision to grow a beard. "I'll just see whether Freddie is ready to see you."

I was ushered in a couple of minutes later. Frederick Parr was shortish, with light hair turning grey, a bird-like face with quite a prominent, pointed nose. All I had ever heard about him was that he liked a good quarrel, but almost in the manner of a game. His bark was said to be worse than his bite. He could, in Customs parlance, be a bastard, but never a shit.

"Ah Storey. Do come in and take a seat." I sat in a chair indicated, in front of his massive dark mahogany desk. "As your name seems to be on everyone's lips, I thought I'd better see you ... ex-Outfield?"

"Yes."

"I thought so. You know a bit about what's been going on here, I take it?"

"If you mean Miss O'Neill, Commissioner Watling's secretary, yes."

"And a Cabinet Office security investigation into Watling and Seymour?"

"That too."

"Both of them have indicated that you deliberately set them up, as the saying goes. Is that true?"

"Could I perhaps explain the context? Shortly after I started doing this job – looking at export procedures to see whether we could guarantee that certain US high-tech components wouldn't be leaked to the Russians – I received some rather opaque messages, which I passed on to the IB. Then, after my first interim report was sent to MISC 38, someone fired a missile into my flat and at first I thought they'd killed my wife. It turned out to be someone else. Then I got a subsequent anonymous message which made clear that the killing was a warning to me to get my report saying what these people wanted, or I or more likely my wife would be killed. But when we started ..."

"We? Who do you mean by 'we'?"

"Special Branch and me ... We did some back-ullaging and it seemed that in order for the people who fired the missile to know what my interim report was saying, someone had to have leaked it to them. And the timing meant that only people here in Customs or the Cabinet Office could've done it. My wife and I were also under continual surveillance by these people. But after they destroyed our flat, they didn't know where we were living, as Special Branch had put us in a safe house. So we hit on a plan to lead them to a fake safe house, where we could set a trap. Then I sent Mr Seymour and Commissioner Watling a copy of the first draft of my latest interim report – essentially what I'd done on the previous occasion. I must say I expected them to pass on its contents to their contacts in the Cabinet Office. I didn't think either of them were in cahoots with the people who fired the missile."

"And you expected them to breach Cabinet Office Security Instructions?"

"No. I'd no idea how they would contact them – or even if they would. The fact that they did break the instructions was their decision."

"Do you know why they were so keen to pass this information on?"

"I think both of them had been encouraged to do so by their oppos in the Cabinet Office."

"And keeping them sweet would do their careers no harm, either, of course."

"When they were interviewed by Special Branch, they implied something to that effect."

"You attended the Special Branch interviews with them?"

"I was asked to because of my knowledge of Civil Service processes – and the fact that I could corroborate what various people said – or not. For instance, Special Branch would have no knowledge what 'MISC 38 (67)' meant or how it worked."

"You evidently have a close relationship with Special Branch."

"With one officer mainly. He knew my wife and me from a previous matter and when he heard that it was our flat that had been attacked by the missile, inevitably had a strong interest. You should perhaps know that for the whole of one evening until the next morning, I believed my wife had been blown to bits by the missile. If they hadn't given me a sedative, I'd undoubtedly have killed myself."

"Evidently it wasn't her ... And I take it that the people who fired these missiles and the person who passed information to them have been caught?"

"Yes. But I don't know what is happening to them. That's a matter for Special Branch and possibly the Security Service."

"I see. So what happens now?"

"I intend to complete my report and presumably MISC 38 will take a decision based on it. My Section are visiting a firm today. In the light of what they come up with, we'll revise the draft Committee paper I sent to Mr Seymour and Commissioner Watling last Friday and I assume it'll be discussed at the MISC 38 meeting on Friday. Assuming they are content with the general direction, we have one more visit to undertake, then I can complete my report. I'd expect it to be ready for a final discussion at MISC 38 a fortnight on Friday."

"It'll be me representing the Department at MISC 38 for the time being. The Chairman has decided to ask Wilf Watling to take some gardening leave while these investigations are going on. I'm proposing to leave Seymour where he is for the time being, but in view of what's happened, I'm proposing that you should send your drafts directly to me in future. He won't be attending further meetings of MISC 38 ... Did you suspect this Miss O'Neill at all?"

"No. Picking up what she was doing was a sheer accident. We knew she had access to Commissioner Watling's papers and phone conversations, so she was seen as a potential – but unlikely – suspect and her phone was monitored. For a brief moment I think

296

Special Branch thought there might be an Irish organisation doing all this, but it became clear pretty early on that wasn't the case."

"Well, I think you should know that the Cabinet Office – I can't say who – advise me that you are not a typical Civil Servant at all, and a watchful eye should be kept on your progress ... Not that it'll be me, of course. I'm going in nine months ... and that care should be taken to ensure you are in the right post, most suited to your undoubted abilities. Have you any idea what that means?"

"Not really. I find that words in the hands of people like the Cabinet Office frequently have several layers of meaning."

"I can see why they might find you uncomfortable. I take it you'd never want to work there?"

"A little bit of me says I'd like to, just to make it more difficult for them to do the things I don't like about them. But the realist tells me that one junior member of staff would just get swallowed up. So - no."

"Fascinating ... I'll look forward to seeing your next draft paper for MISC 38. When do you expect to get it to me?"

"By tomorrow evening."

I returned to Custom House and spent an hour or so going over what Ken and Morry had done to flesh out the latest pieces of information and analysis in the main report. I realised that I would have to go over it all before it was finalised, to give it a unified written style. But what was there seemed good. I locked it all away and went back to Erasmus Street.

Rosemary was already there, in shorts and a tracksuit top.

"I've found somewhere where we can play squash – there's a Civil Service sports club in Chadwick Street.

It's really close – and you're a Civil Servant still, aren't you?"

"Yes. I thought our racquets got smashed in the explosion?"

"I rang them up – apparently we can hire them there."

"OK … How many points start do you want?"

"Cheeky man!"

The following day, Ken and Morry told me about the visit to Qomputix, who appeared to be a very scientific organisation, almost as worried about whether they would have to give up their own technological secrets to the Americans as whether the American stuff would be of value to them. Nevertheless, their procedures were at least as tight as in the other two firms. So while I made relatively minor amendments to my paper for MISC 38, they added a more detailed section to the main report. Deputy Chairman Parr evidently did not regard drafting as the be-all and end-all of his job and sent my draft on to Cabinet Office virtually untouched.

The meeting of the Committee MISC 38 (67) on the Friday felt strange. Apart from the difference in the Customs line-up, Lewis was noticeable by his absence and Osbaldistone had a permanent scowl on his face. Next to him, as the new main Secretary to the Committee, was a woman in her early forties, with curly, prematurely greying hair and a broad, plump, intelligent face. Of course, no explanations were given about the changes in attendees.

Indeed, the meeting ran through quickly and smoothly. For some reason Walmesley and Pilkington eschewed their usual combat and the meeting concluded in less than an hour.

Osbaldistone almost grabbed me on my way out.

"What the hell have you been playing at!" he exclaimed in a hoarse whisper. "That was the worst weekend of my life!"

"Do you think this is the right place to be having this discussion?" I replied.

"Very well. We'll use this office. It's empty."

Ironically, he had chosen Wordley-Smith's office for this tete-a-tete.

"Well? What were you up to?" he demanded.

"Hasn't anyone told you anything?"

"No. After I pointed out Sir Nigel Spinks's driver, the police told me I was free to go. No-one here has said anything. Only evidently Lewis has gone and this woman from BoT has taken his place."

"Perhaps you should be asking people here rather than me?"

"But you're evidently as thick as thieves with those police who arrested me and locked me up all weekend. You know what's been going on."

"I'm really not sure I can say much. You really will have to speak to someone here. All I can say is that evidence of a link to a serious incident appeared heavily against you after the interviews on Saturday. Between Saturday lunchtime and Monday morning more information came to light which altered the nature of the evidence against you."

"That's really not good enough! If you know more, you should tell me?"

"Why? Instead of finding someone to shout at, why don't you think about what you told the police, what was disclosed by Jacob Ffoulkes at the previous MISC 38 meeting , and what has happened in the Cabinet Office over the last week or so? I can appreciate your anger. Nobody likes to be locked up for something they didn't do. But there are worse things in life, believe me!"

299

"I demand that you tell me!"

"You can demand away, but I'm not saying any more … Actually, I will say one thing – if it wasn't for my wife and me, you might well still be sitting in a cell today. If you're not happy, go and speak to the Cabinet Secretary. And if you want my advice, you'll think carefully about what sort of organisation it is you're working in and what sort of person you have to be to flourish in such an organisation – and whether you want to be that sort of person!"

With that I left.

The following Monday, Rosemary and I moved into a flat in Bromley close to the top of a long hill, overlooking the Ravensbourne valley. It was quite small, with only one bedroom, but it had a balcony large enough for a table and a couple of chairs. The insurance company told us we'd probably be there for about six weeks. It was pleasant enough, though we knew it would never feel like home. But it did give us time to recall the mixed joys of commuting.

The final stages of my report followed smoothly. The final firm we visited clearly wanted to make use of the American stuff and had put in place procedures that were up to scratch. So, with Ken and Morry's help, I completed both a long and detailed report and a much shorter final report for MISC 38 (67). The discussion at the Committee in early May was brief. I supposed that nothing significant had changed since my previous report. However, the subsequent discussion was more illuminating. Sir Roderick Pilkington from the Foreign Office announced that the Americans were pulling out of the deal. At a late stage, they had made it conditional on an active British involvement in the Vietnam War, something which the Government wasn't prepared to countenance.

"A victory for Defense and the US computer companies over State," observed Pilkington in his urbane way. "And probably predictable from the off."

"So why did the Foreign Office not advise the Committee of this at the start?" demanded Walmesley. "An immense amount of valuable time has been wasted, in practice, for nothing."

"I suspect we've learnt more than we realise," observed Jacob Ffoulkes opaquely. "It's possible we've obtained benefits in other ways."

"Like what?" demanded Walmesley, plainly irritated that there appeared to be things that had been going on without his knowledge.

"Customs have the information to strengthen their export procedures. The firms that they visited have all tightened up their security significantly. In any case, I suspect we'll get this stuff much faster than the four years the Americans have been talking about."

Though I would never get the chance to ask, it wouldn't have surprised me if he hadn't done some sort of deal with the CIA.

"And Customs may well have identified a way of keeping their costs down through clearing more goods inland," added the man from the Treasury.

Osbaldistone continued to scowl throughout. No doubt he was thinking that if this Committee had never been established, he wouldn't have had to spend a couple of nights in a police cell, permanently wounding his self-esteem.

For myself, I couldn't help feeling a surge of anger. Though I suspected it couldn't really have been played any other way – and, as Ffoulkes had obliquely indicated, a violent organisation and a traitor had been uncovered and removed from the scene – but an innocent woman had died, Rosemary's and my lives had been put at risk, and we'd had our flat destroyed

301

and our lives turned upside down – essentially for nothing.

Anyway, the Committee concluded shortly afterwards, with Walmesley thanking all concerned, with special mention of Customs, who had done most of the work. Deputy Chairman Parr was decent enough to put on record that the work had been led by me. However I doubted whether that scored quite as much weight within the Cabinet Office as my involvement in matters they wished to keep secret.

"It was much less of a waste of time than you might think," remarked Ffoulkes as I came past him out of the Committee room. "I met a certain Kapitan a few days ago. He sends his regards."

By the end of June, Rosemary were back in our flat and starting to furnish it again. I had a new job, on permanent promotion to SEO, working in a special project team that was examining alternatives to Purchase Tax. The front runner – because it seemed to be where the EEC was heading – was a value-added tax. My job – because of the great knowledge of computers I was supposed to have acquired in preparing my report for MISC 38 (67) – was to help devise processes that would enable the new tax to be run by computer. A challenge, indeed! But a welcome one – and one which as far as I could tell would keep me well away from any of the sort of people who had been plaguing my life for the last few months. Even my new boss was congenial – Mr Jim Round, newly appointed as CEO, with even less knowledge of computers than me, but with a proven ability to get things done.

In August, Rosemary and I took an overnight train to Rijeka in Yugoslavia and a coach on to a quiet resort a little further south. There we achieved our ambition not just of swimming naked in the sea, but making love on a deserted beach at midnight, on several occasions.

On our journey back, Rosemary announced that she thought she was pregnant and she bore a little daughter the following March. Ours had not been the 'Summer of Love' plastered all over the newspapers and on TV, but it had been a summer of love, nevertheless. And, as I held little Emily Jane in my arms for almost the first time, a momentary shudder reminded me that we might not have had a summer at all. But that was the past. My future was with Rosemary, lying tired but happy in the bed beside me, and this little pink creature smiling contentedly in my arms.

GLOSSARY

AC	Assistant Collector (regional manager in Customs & Excise) Also Assistant Commissioner (in the Metropolitan Police)
Assistant Principal	Most junior grade of the Administrative Class of Civil Servants, a training grade
Assistant Secretary	Head of a Division, Administrative Class Civil Servant
BoT	Board of Trade
Box 500	Civil Service reference to the Security Service
CA	Clerical Assistant (Clerical Class of the Civil Service)
CEO	Chief Executive Officer (Executive Class of the Civil Service)
CIA	US Central Intelligence Agency
CI's Office	Chief Inspector's Office
CIO	Chief Investigation Officer (the "Chief")
CO	Clerical Officer
Commissioner	Member of the Board of HM Customs & Excise Metropolitan Police Commissioner
DCA	Departmental Clerical Assistant
DCIO	Deputy Chief Investigation Officer
DCO	Departmental Clerical Officer

DEA	Department of Economic Affairs
Defense	US Department of Defence
Division	Group that develops policy, consisting of staff at Principal/CEO level and above, sometimes with an Assistant Principal
EO	Executive Officer
Estabs	Establishments - broadly equivalent to Personnel, HR
FD	Foreign Affairs & Defence Ministerial Committee
FO	Foreign Office
GIS	Global Information & Security
HEO	Higher Executive Officer
IB	Investigation Branch
IGW	Inspector General of the Waterguard
LAP	London Airports
Min of Ag	Ministry of Agriculture, Food and Farming (also MAFF)
MinTech	Ministry of Technology
MISC	Title given to Cabinet Committees normally of a temporary nature (Miscellaneous)
OCX	Officer of Customs & Excise
OGD	Other Government Departments
'oppo'	'opposite number' – official of equivalent rank in another Department
Outfield	Customs & Excise regional organisation

OWO	Omnibus Weekly Order (containing information & instructions)
P&Rs	Prohibitions and Restrictions
PIOT	"Peace in our time"
PO	Preventive Officer
Principal }	Member of the Administrative Class of Civil Servants, equivalent
Prin }	to CEO
PT	Purchase Tax
Regs	Regulations, Statutory Instruments
Secretaries Office } Secs Office }	Customs & Excise HQ
Section	group who carry out instructions of Division, consisting of staff from the Executive & Clerical classes up to SEO
SEO	Senior Executive Officer
SIO	Senior Investigation Officer
SPS	Senior Personal Secretary
State	US State Department
TI	Temporary Importation
TPR	Temporary Processing Relief
T/SEO	Temporary SEO
UO	Unattached Officer

HM Customs & Excise – Organisation Chart 1967

THE BOARD
CHAIRMAN
DEPUTY CHAIRMAN
COMMISSIONERS (5)

SECRETARIES OFFICE
Assistant Secretary/PEO
Senior Principal/SCEO
Principal/CEO
SEO
HEO
EO
CO
CA
Revenue Constable
Messenger

CHIEF INSPECTOR'S OFFICE
Chief Inspector

INVESTIGATION BRANCH
CIO
DCIO
ACIO
SIO
HIO
IO

SOLICITOR'S OFFICE

ACCOUNTANT & COMPTROLLER-GENERAL

VALUATION BRANCH

STATISTICAL OFFICE

OUTFIELD
Collector
Deputy Collector
Assistant Collector
Surveyor
OCX
DCO
DCA

OFFICE OF THE INSPECTOR-GENERAL OF THE WATERGUARD
Inspector General
Waterguard Superintendant
Assistant Waterguard Superintendant
CPO
PO
APO